Far from the Truth

Also, by Ronald A. Feldman

little secrets BIG LIES - book 1 of the TRUTH thriller series

If Truth Be Told - book 2 of the TRUTH thriller series

The Crossover Mystery

Red Hook, Brooklyn

Ronald A. Feldman

Ronald A Feldman

Far from the Truth

Gemini Print and eBook Publishers

Boca Raton, Florida, USA

Published in the United States by Gemini Print and eBook Publishers

The book cover is designed by Renee Luke of Cover Me Book Covers

ISBN-13: 978-0-9978433-4-7

Ronald A Feldman

Chapter
1

Air bubbles burst from the snorkeler's lungs toward the surface near Cruz Bay, St. John, U.S. Virgin Islands. He gasps repeatedly for air but only receives large quantities of seawater. The snorkel, once clenched tightly between his jaws, drifts to the bottom of the water. He kicks his legs in vain trying to free them from the grip that holds him down under water. His arms flail bloodied from the knife wounds that slashed at hands and forearms when he tried to reach down and free himself. He turns and faces the man in a diving suit who holds the snorkeler's life in his gloved hands; with eyes bulging he mouths, "Why?"

But the steely eyes give no clue why the diver is pulling Andrew Riccardi to the bottom of the bay on the second day of his honeymoon with Collette Corrigan Riccardi. When the darkness surrounds Andrew a calm overcomes his being. His transition begins and there will be no retreat. Once the transition is complete, the diver releases the body. Andrew sinks slowly near the diver who peers into his opened eyes confirming the quarry is dead. With powerful strokes, the diver swims away around the tip of the inlet that leads into Cruz Bay. The diver goes ashore at an uninhabited tiny slip of beach where his rental Jeep is parked. Once removed, the wetsuit and gear are tossed in the Jeep. A quick look around for witnesses and he drives off never seeing the two sets of eyes that saw him come ashore and rumble away through the wooded area to the road above.

"Do you think he saw us?" sixteen-year-old naked Bevey asks from nearby secluded bushes.

"Nah, he was too quick to get out of here." Anthony laughs and continues to grope Bevey's young breasts as his manhood rises once more.

"You so fresh Anthony," she scolds him but does not stop the boy's hands from their exploration.

"Karl, I don't get it. You're good at your job. Hell, maybe the best we have."

New York Police Department Homicide Captain James Grover, newly assigned to replace Captain Whitehead who left soon after his wife lost her battle with cancer, rose from his office chair to his full height of six feet five inches. He stretched and moved around the desk, palming a basketball he kept nearby and sat on the desk facing Detective Karl Dieter. He flipped the ball back and forth as he sat waiting for the right words to come.

"Ah, shit Karl. Now's a terrible time to leave me. I'm the new guy here from another precinct, hell another division."

"Narcotics," Karl answered.

"Yeah, yeah narcotics. I still got plenty to learn you know. You're the right guy to have around."

Karl rose to his lesser height of six feet and looked at the Captain.

"I appreciate your confidence in me. But you have good detectives here. Some very seasoned and some really smart young guys."

"McClure?"

"Yes, he's very smart and a good detective."

"I know he's smart. When I interviewed each guy after I came on, he did impress me. Smart, young and maybe a little innocent." Captain Grover chuckled mockingly, and Dieter joined him.

"Yes, but that will change."

"It will, but until it does, he needs a mentor and I need someone to have my back." Grover's eyes searched Dieter's for a weak spot that he could manipulate to his advantage.

"Captain, I will always have your back while I'm here. I'd expect the same."

"You know that already."

Dieter knew that the Captain had his back especially if it helped the Captain. Dieter's last case brought him outside the purview of his department several times. Captain Grover had been alerted to watch Dieter's move from now on and keep him in check. A new mayor and a new list of priorities filtered down to all departments especially since a police shooting of an unarmed young African American man brought the press and civil rights groups back to life. Grover explained all this to Dieter soon after his arrival.

"Listen, Captain, you know that I'm not a political guy. I don't have the taste for it, nor the necessity. I've put in my time."

"Yes, you have."

"And I'm ready for something new." There it was, that little blink in Dieter's eyes that said, *"I have no idea what's next."*

"Something new?" Grover asked.

Dieter chuckled. "I have no idea."

"Then where are you going if you have no destination? Karl don't be that guy who leaves because he feels burned out and finds that he can't do anything else and ends doing odd jobs or tending bar."

"Not fair Captain. Lots of guys retire and are okay."

"Yes, but is being okay enough for you?"

The Captain's desk phone rang. He moved around to pick it up but waited. "Karl, take your time, think this through and let's talk about it again. I have to take this call."

Dieter turned to leave the office as the Captain spoke to the caller, "Hey Ben, good morning. What can I do for you?"

Ben Ferguson, the second assistant to the Deputy Mayor, is the son of Grover's college friend Patrick Ferguson. Grover had put a word into the Mayor's office helping young Ben get his job. Patrick Ferguson had become a Vice President at Gleason Capital, one of New York's leading investment firms. The men stayed friends since college days enjoying a growing symbiotic relationship.

Andrew's body returned to the surface of the waters offshore Cruz Bay more than a half mile from his departure from life. His bloated body rose and bobbled face down in the calm nighttime waters. Moonlight directed a path of light at him, but he couldn't notice the shimmering waters dancing around him. Local schools of small fish had feasted on the flesh of his fingers attracted by the bloodied wounds. Only bones protruded. The lacerations on his arms from the diver's knife were no longer visible. Large chunks of his arms were eaten away along with bites and chunks taken from his legs and buttocks. The new wedding band that Collette agonized over in the jewelry store had slipped to the sea bottom, but the expensive waterproof watch hung loosely from his wrist and kept perfect time.

Collette called Andrew's cell phone for the eighth time with the same result. "It's Andrew, leave a message and I'll get back to you. Yeah, I know everyone says that, but I will." Followed by laughter and a beep.

When Andrew failed to return from his day of snorkeling while she shopped in the local resort town not far from Cruz Bay, she called him immediately. It wasn't until after eight P.M. that she called the US Virgin Islands Police Station in St. John.

Sergeant David Griffon answered and was very polite but asked her to wait awhile.

"He went snorkeling on a little blow up-boat."

"A motor dinghy," he corrected automatically.

"Okay, yes, whatever but he hasn't returned."

"Where did he rent the boat?"

"Where? I don't know. Nearby I guess."

"Where are you staying?"

"We rented a house overlooking the Bay. We just got married." A flood of tears followed.

Sergeant Griffon told the commanding officer about the call from Collette Riccardi. They easily tracked the rental to the most popular boat rental shop in town.

"Yes, this man, Andrew Riccardi, rented a dinghy today. Here's the credit card receipt." The very tired fellow manning the shop had said. "I been waiting for him to return."

One hour later a police skiff found a dinghy afloat far outside the Bay. A shirt, shorts, running shoes, and socks were neatly folded on the seat. The driver's license identified Andrew Riccardi from New York City. Two hundred dollars in cash along with two credit cards from the small Tumi wallet clipped to his back pocket did not indicate robbery the Sergeant postulated. No signs of a struggle. The shorts held a cell phone with many calls from Collette Riccardi and one early in the day to Lindsay Riccardi. Collette's calls were unanswered but Andrew's call to Lindsay Riccardi lasted six minutes.

Sergeant Griffon decided to call Lindsay Riccardi since she was the last person with whom he spoke and since she has the same last name. Perhaps a family member. The New York City 212 area code was very familiar to Griffon having spent a year living in Astoria, Queens as a young man with his mother and her new boyfriend before returning to St. John.

Lindsay's office phone rang but she considered rejecting the call with the unusual area code and number. She had received many intrusive phone calls after her name was printed in the newspapers regarding the murder of one of her patients more than a year earlier.

"Hello, who is this?"

"Is this Lindsay Riccardi?"

"Yes, who is this?"

"I am Sergeant David Griffon of the St. John, US Virgin Islands Police."

Lindsay struggled to stay calm.

"What is it, Sergeant?" She rose from her desk and began a circular path around her office.

"Do you know a person named Andrew Riccardi?"

"Yes, yes, I do. Why? Is he all right?"

"Is he related to you?"

"Yes, ah, no. He is my former husband."

"I see," was the laconic reply.

"Sergeant, please tell me, is he all right?"

"He is missing. It may mean nothing, but his wife has declared him missing."

"Missing?"

Chapter
2

Dieter looked sharply at the desk's ringing phone and picked it up.

A man's voice asked, "Detective Karl Dieter?"

"Yes, who's calling?"

"My name is Spencer Arnold, I'm Valerie Hudson's attorney."

"What can I do for you?" Dieter's cell phone buzzed on his desk.

"Nothing thank you, but I can do much for you. Can you come to my office and bring...ah, here it is, can you bring Doctor Lindsay Riccardi with you tomorrow around ten?"

"What is it?"

"I am the executor of Valerie Hudson's estate – her considerable estate."

"What does this have to do me and Doctor Riccardi?"

"Please come in tomorrow and I will explain fully."

Dieter's cell phone buzzed again showing Lindsay's picture and consuming his attention.

"Okay, sure at ten."

Dieter clicked off the office phone and picked up his cell.

"Lindz hi, what is..."

"Andrew is missing."

"Your Andrew?"

"Andrew, my former husband, not my Andrew. I don't own him."

"Lindsay, take it easy. How do you know?"

"A police officer called from St. John."

"St. John? You got a call from a cop in St. John, Virgin Islands?"

"Yes, I did."

"Okay, Lindsay, do you have a contact phone number for this officer?"

"Well, yes, I have it but…"

"Give it to me. I'll call and make sure it's legit."

Silence from Lindsay while she gathered her thoughts.

"Lindz, are you still there?"

"Yes, yes I am. But I don't understand."

"Just being cautious. Phone calls from other countries about such things sometimes are a scam."

"It's *U.S.* Virgin Islands."

"Let me check it, please." Dieter could hear the tension and stress in Lindsay's voice.

"Give me the phone number and the officer's name. Now tell me everything he said. Take your time."

Lindsay reported the conversation, the officer's name, and number to Dieter who wrote down the information on his pad.

"I'll call you later." Before disconnecting, "Are you okay?"

"Not really."

"St. John Virgin Island Police," a man's voice answered.

"This is Detective Karl Dieter, New York Police Department. I'd like to speak with officer David Griffon."

"This is *Sergeant* Griffon Detective. How can I help you?"

He exists Karl thought. However, he typed in the St. John police site on his computer and began to scroll looking for the name of the officers. Sergeant David Griffon with his photo was the second listing.

"Did you call Doctor Lindsay Riccardi in New York today?"

"Yes, I did. And how are you connected to this case Detective?"

"This case?"

"Yes Detective, this case."

"Sergeant, I'm validating the call you made to Doctor Riccardi. Didn't mean to offend you."

"Good. Now let's start from scratch. I called her because we have a report from Andrew Riccardi's new wife…"

"New wife?"

"Yes, they are here on a honeymoon. Collette Corrigan Riccardi called my office last night reporting Andrew missing. We investigated, found the inflatable dinghy he used to go snorkeling."

"By himself? Isn't that dangerous?"

"Yes, by himself, and it surely may have been for Mr. Riccardi."

"How do you know it was his?"

"We found the dinghy rental company and then the dinghy with his identification and other belongings on board."

"He's missing," Dieter declared.

"Seems that way Detective."

"And today?"

"Nothing so far. We have our boats out looking. Sergeant, may I ask how you are connected to this case?"

"I'm connected to Doctor Riccardi."

"I see. I guess you want to be kept up to speed on this case."

"I do Sergeant."

"Please call me David, Detective."

"I'm Karl, Sergeant."

Each man's appreciative smile went unnoticed by the other. The two men exchanged contact cell numbers.

"Hey Karl," JB McClure stood unnoticed near Dieter's desk.

Without looking up, "Hey."

But JB was bursting to talk to his partner.

"How are you doing partner?"

Dieter looked up at JB and saw the boyish look that shouted the need to tell something.

"What is it JB?"

"I met the next Mrs. McClure last night."

JB had ended a relationship and was 'between girlfriends,' a poor joke at any measure. Dieter noted JB's excitement and pushed back on his desk chair.

"How'd you meet her?"

"Where else?"

"A bar," Dieter quipped.

"A sports bar, she's a sports nut like me. She's smart, funny and very pretty. Played volleyball in college."

"She's tall then."

"Five nine...just right."

Dieter's forced attention to JB's excited jabbering was waning. His eyes went to his computer screen. He read Sergeant Griffon's background. Born in St. John, lived a short time in New York, returned to his birthplace and became a cop. He's for real.

"Karl, so what do you think?"

Dieter wasn't thinking at all about JB's last comments which went unheard.

"Yeah, sounds good. Go for her," a shade south of dismissive.

"Yeah, yeah, I will, thanks."

While JB ambled away, Dieter dialed Lindsay.

Lindsay's excited voice answered before the second ring, "Karl. What did you learn?"

"He's for real. Spoke with him and he will keep me up to date. Maybe this means nothing."

"Nothing!"

"I mean, maybe he's not missing. You know cold feet and all."

Long pause, "Karl, I spoke with him yesterday morning."

"You did?"

"Yes, he called me. He wanted to apologize – no, make amends – for our split."

"Cold feet as I said."

"No, he said he really loves this woman. He asked for my forgiveness for the affair and our breakup."

"He said those things?"

"Yes, so he didn't run off. He was very happy."

Dieter knew this was not a good omen. If he didn't run away from the marriage, he must be in trouble or worse.

Gentle waves slowly pushed Andrew's body closer to shore southeast of Cruz Bay towards Chocolate Hole Inlet. It slid into a buoy stationed beyond the Inlet's mouth in the Caribbean Sea where it got hung up and waited to be found.

Chapter
3

Lindsay ate her Mediterranean Salad at trendy Healthy Bites absentmindedly. Her hand held the fork which speared bits of the chopped red, yellow and green vegetables topped with Humus then the hand lifted it to her opened mouth. The jaws operated causing the teeth to chew but there was little consciousness of the action or the savory taste.

A busboy carrying a heavy tray of plates, glasses, and utensils lost control of the top two plates which slid and toppled noisily to the floor. Diner's heads turned momentarily, glancing at the busboy who scurried to the kitchen while another began the cleanup of broken glass and food.

The brief commotion returned Lindsay to the moment. She placed her fork on the table, reached for the iced Green tea and enjoyed a luxuriously long drink.

She opened her purse, found the cell phone and clicked it to see if there were any new messages. Notifications would have been on the screen but she, like so many, engaged in magical thinking, checked for a message anyway. She was wrong.

"Are you finished?" asked the waitress.

Lindsay looked down at her plate which was indeed almost empty.

"Yes, thanks." She pushed the plate forward to prove her point.

"Did you like the salad? It's our most popular." The waitress asked while collecting the plates and utensils. The now harried busboy arrived and took the tray from the waitress. "Would you like anything else? Fresh fruit for dessert?"

"Nothing thank you."

"Then I'll bring your check. No rush."

Lindsay looked around the trendy new health-related restaurant. Thirty-somethings sat in office groups talking excitedly. Her mind reverted to the day she met Andrew. Confidence and an easy swagger from years of competitive swimming kept him fit and self-assured.

"I'm training for an Iron Man event."

"What's that?"

He explained the rigors of the three events and his confidence in the swimming portion.

No way he drowned swimming. What happened? Shark attack? Warm waters down there I think.

Lindsay Googled *shark attacks in the Virgin Islands.*

Sharks Shark attacks are extremely rare in the Virgin Islands.
Prevention: Avoid waters being fished or where fish are being cleaned. Do not swim at night or at dusk and dawn. Remove shiny jewelry and do not enter the water if you are bleeding. Move out of the area or exit the water if a shark approaches too close, makes sudden movements or appears agitated.
Remedy: Seek medical care immediately if bitten.

Did he cut himself on some coral? He loved snorkeling and exploring coral beds. Blood could trigger an attack.

"Here's the check. Have a good day." A perky smile lingered hoping to get a good tip from the lady who seemed distracted.

Lindsay paid the check with cash and left a generous tip for the young waitress. She looked at her watch and quickened her steps to return in time for the next patient.

Nadia reached her eighteenth birthday long after she began working for the realtors who rented the villa where Andrew and Collette shared the beautiful views of Cruz Bay and the Caribbean Sea. She liked these two happy honeymooners. Like the others, they sought privacy for intimate moments which could arise at any time of the day. This left Nadia free time to study for university exams.

"Did you see my husband when you cleaned this afternoon?" Collette had asked the day earlier once she returned from shopping.

"No, I did not. Nobody was here. I just did my work. Yes, that's all."

"Okay, okay. Thanks, but can you tell me where there's a nearby coral reef?"

"It's all around, nearby and some a little out there where the water is still not too deep."

"Where's the best place?"

"Oh, I'm sorry I never go looking at coral."

"Why not?"

Nadia shrugged "Never liked swimming with all those fishes coming 'round me and stuff. Yuck."

When Nadia arrived to clean the next day, she noticed that the beds were not slept in. She was taught to make the beds with tight corners, so it looks very neat and fluff pillows the right way. It was exactly as she left the large king-sized bed the day before when Collette. Riccardi questioned her about the coral reefs.

Strange.

Shopping bags sat unopened on the bedroom sofa. Nadia fought the urge to look through the bags. She was curious about the empty pocketbook which lay under the sofa.

"Mrs. Riccardi. Are you here?"

Nadia looked inside the large master bathroom where she found everything in place. She moved through each room becoming more concerned because everything seemed untouched since yesterday.

She agonized over what to do next. Eventually, she called the head of the rental service.

"Gladys, this is Nadia over at the Cruz Bay house. Yeah, yeah, that one."

Nadia explained what she saw at the house and what happened the day before with questions about Mr. Riccardi from his new wife. Gladys listened but didn't share Nadia's concern.

"Maybe they had a night on the beach. Full moon last night. My man and I do it all the time under the full moon."

"What should I do?"

"Do your job, that's it."

"Okay."

The doorbell rang, and Nadia went to answer with the phone in hand. A St. John police officer greeted her. He didn't eyeball her as the other men do. Other men looked at her tall slender body highlighted by full breasts and a gleaming white smile under big brown eyes. He was serious.

"What's your name?"

"Nadia, I work here."

"Where is the lady who stays here?"

Nadia shuffled from one foot to the other arranging her thoughts.

"She's gone."

"Gone?"

"I don't know where she is. It looks like nobody's been here all night. Bed's the same as when I…"

The officer walked in. "Stay right here."

He drew his weapon and walked the rooms carefully inspecting each one. When he returned to the front door, he was on his phone.

"The lady is not here. The place hasn't been slept in all night. Okay. Yes, I'll stay here."

He returned the phone to its clip and noticed Nadia's nervous state.

"Are you all right?"

Nadia shrugged.

"Tell me what happened here."

"What happened? Nothing happened. I came to work today and nobody's here. Talk to my boss."

She handed her cell phone to the officer.

"Who's this?" he asks.

Gladys gave him all she knew from Nadia's conversation and added her thoughts about a lover's night on the beach.

"Okay, Gladys."

The officer handed the phone back to Nadia.

Nadia asked, "What now?"

"We wait for my Sergeant to arrive."

Chapter
4

The twenty-six-foot Prowler Catamaran raced along the blue coastal waters southeast of Cruz Bay. John Desmond had the helm as he did on all the family trips on waterways. He learned boating skills at his father's side on Lake Michigan where his Dad also taught him fishing skills and the importance of patience.

He had waited one whole week to skipper the Catamaran around the coast of St. John. Little John, fourteen-years-old and twelve-year-old Pammie enjoyed the adventures that the Desmond family shared. Betty Desmond loved the sun and the warm sea breezes which were a welcome change from the cold winters in Bad Axe, Michigan.

"Dad! Dad! What's that?" Pammie stood holding onto the railing and leaning out over the side.

"Where?" Little John joined his sister looking at the waters.

"Be careful you two," Mom cautioned.

"Holy shit!"

"Little John, you watch your mouth."

"Dad look starboard at the buoy!" Little John exclaimed.

John Desmond adjusted his sunglasses and shielded his eyes from the sun's glare off the waters. Recognition crossed his face.

"Holy shit!"

"John! You too?" Betty Desmond yelled.

But John never heard his wife's remonstration. He quickly maneuvered the Catamaran starboard toward the buoy which held Andrew Riccardi.

"Look, Mom, a guy's over there," Pammie shouted over the din of the splashing waves.

Betty joined her two children at the railing as the Catamaran raced toward the buoy.

She muttered, "Holy shit!"

"Is he alive?" Pammie asked.

"Hey, Mister! Are you okay?" Little John yelled into the wind from twenty-five yards away.

Andrew didn't answer. He kept bobbing.

The Catamaran stopped, "LJ, take the wheel."

John Desmond dove into the water. He swam the twenty yards and was at Andrew's side in splashing, hurried strokes. He saw the bloated face and knew immediately that this trip to St. John with his family would be remembered for a long time.

"Is he alive John?" Betty wanted to know.

John gave a thumb down.

"Holy shit!" from Little John caused Pammie to push her brother aside to see. She leaned over and craned her neck out to see. When she saw the floating dead body, her morning breakfast of waffles and fruit was immediately regurgitated into the water.

Detective Dieter's desk phone rang allowing a respite from paperwork.

"Detective Dieter."

"Karl, this is David Griffon from ..."

"Yes, David, I remember. Any news?"

"I'm afraid so."

"Go on."

"We found Andrew Riccardi's body."

"I'm listening."

"His body was found floating up against a buoy at the mouth of a local inlet."

"Cause of death?"

"Not yet, but it looks like he drowned."

"Drowned? Doubtful."

"Why Karl?"

"He was a competitive swimmer."

"So, you know him?"

"No. Doctor Riccardi, Lindsay, told me."

"I see. Well, let's see what the autopsy reveals."

"Did you see the body, David?"

"Not yet."

"So, no obvious cause of death, like a gunshot wound, strangulation marks around the neck."

"I'll check but nothing like that reported. The officers who found his body at the buoy said his hands and forearms were eaten pretty badly by fish indicating he may have been bleeding."

"Bleeding? Is that unusual?"

"Not really. You can get pretty cut up on the coral if you're not careful."

"He was snorkeling, then?"

"Yes. Karl, I have another problem."

"What?"

"Well, we think the wife may be missing now. She hasn't returned to the rental house overnight."

"And you're thinking?"

"Something's not right."

"Maybe she took off after killing her new husband."

"Don't think so. She seemed genuinely scared for him when she called to report him missing. Also, nothing missing from the house they rented."

"Sounds like you have your work cut out for you."

"What do you know about this guy?"

"Not much really."

"Can you find out for me? Ask Doctor Riccardi? Background on him and his new wife would be helpful."

Dieter waited a few seconds before responding. "David, I'll get as much as I can but she'll be upset by this news."

"I see. They were close after their divorce."

"No, not at all. I'll find out all I can."

"Timing is essential, but you know that. Right, Karl?"

"Yeah, I do David."

Dieter knew the timing was vital to any investigation. Information gets foggy or lost altogether. He also knew that Andrew's death would cause pain to Lindsay. He had hoped to shield her from any further pain. Sure, she was a strong woman but enough was enough.

"Hey JB I got a favor to ask."

"Yeah? What kind of favor? I don't get paid for another two weeks."

"No, money is not the favor wise guy. Need some background checks is all."

JB McClure enjoyed researching backgrounds of perps or possible perps.

"Okay. What do you need?"

Dieter explained the death of Andrew Riccardi and the possible missing wife.

"Get me everything you can on each."

"ASAP."

"No, I need it yesterday."

"Now, who is the wise guy?" JB quipped.

Dieter ignored the jibe and sent a text message to Lindsay's cell phone asking for a quiet dinner at her place later.

The swarthy stranger entered Collette Corrigan Riccardi's modest apartment on the upper west side of Manhattan. He wasn't interested in the photos of her and Andrew that sat atop the bedroom nightstand adjoining her twin bed. Nor did he have interest in the jewelry that Andrew gave her during their courtship. His focus was on the desktop computer which was on a simple writing table facing the small bedroom's window. Quickly and with extreme efficiency, he unlocked the casing from the hard drive and dismounted it from the computer. Next, he rummaged through the desk for papers and additional digital data storage devices. Lastly, he opened Collette's briefcase and placed the hard drive into it. Another look around and he was satisfied that the mission was accomplished. He exited the apartment and walked down the four flights to the street below where he entered the waiting Land Rover with the engine running. The driver drove away as soon as the door closed.

Paulette Ramsey, blind since birth, in the apartment beneath Collette's, wondered if the chatty neighbor above had returned from her honeymoon. The footsteps Paulette heard above and then trodding down the stairs seemed heavier than the ones she was accustomed to from Collette. *Strange.*

Alvin Klausner, a long time patient, sat facing his therapist. His hands folded, then unfolded as though seeking a purpose. After several years in therapy with Lindsay sticking to a rigid schedule, Alvin was fired from his job. His schedule was no longer in place, nor was his angry demeanor since he agreed to take the medication that Lindsay and his internist agreed was necessary.

"I don't like this. Any of it. It's not fair. Not right." He sat shaking his head.

"Your job?"

"Yes, my job. I was good at my job. I was always on time. I was efficient. I was a good company employee."

"Do you understand why they let you go?"

Alvin switched crossed legs and looked away from Lindsay.

"I really didn't mean any harm to her. Not really. Sure, I was angry that she got my promotion."

"Your promotion?"

"Yes, mine. I was there longer than she was."

"Was that everything that triggered your response to her promotion."

Reluctantly, "No."

"What else?"

"You know. I don't want to say it again."

"It hurts to say it."

"Yes."

"Okay, but we both agree that when she rejected your invitation for a date, that added to your frustration."

Alvin begrudgingly nodded.

"And resulted in your response to her in front of the office staff."

Another nod.

"Which led to the charges of harassment against you in the workplace."

No response from Alvin.

"And now?"

"Now. I have nothing. No job. No future. Nothing."

"Alvin, look at me please."

He turned his gaze at Lindsay.

"You are more than your job. We are, all of us, more than our employment. You have a good college education. You are a trained researcher. There's much you can do. However, the important thing to consider is what you think of yourself."

"Unemployed."

"Yes, for now. But you will always be Alvin and you must make peace with him."

"Whoever he is."

"Yes. Let's start there next time. I'd like you to think about that question. Make a list describing yourself."

"It'll be a short list."

Rising, "We will start from your short list."

Alvin rose slowly and turned toward the door, as he did for the last several years, a quick exit was his pattern. However, this time he stopped and turned toward Lindsay. "Thank you for listening."

"Always, Alvin. Have a good week."

Lindsay was pleased with Alvin's breakthrough in civility and perhaps inroads to personal awareness.

Chapter
5

"Good evening Detective," Yang Zi said from behind the counter of her father's Chinese take-out restaurant.

"Good evening. Is Dad off tonight?"

"Card night with the boys," she giggled when she said, boys. She scanned the waiting bundles of Chinese food. "Tonight, I am the boss." Another giggle, "Here is yours," she handed the bag to Dieter and waved off his money.

"No charge for you."

Dieter handed her money, "You sure Detective? My father said never to take money from you."

Dieter smiled at the game the family has been playing with him for a long time. They refuse payment. He refuses their generosity and he pays which they accept.

"Next time Detective. No money."

"Give my regards to your father."

"I will."

Dieter wanted to bring comfort food to Lindsay since his mission was to tell her of Andrew's death. He had delivered condolences to many victims when asked about a loved one. Too many. This might be very different.

A more than perfunctory kiss at Lindsay's door surprised and pleased Dieter. He entered with the food and passed the bag under Lindsay's nose playfully. "Smell good?"

"Yes, it smells very good."

She led him to the kitchen and began to open the containers. A pot of hot water whistled its readiness to pour. The small kitchen table was set for the food and drink. Dieter surveyed the table.

"You've been busy."

"Yes, and hungry too. Let's eat." She placed the containers of food on a large serving plate centering the table. Utensils to serve and two matching placemats with plates and small teacups and saucers were at the ready.

Dieter went around to Lindsay's chair and pulled it out for her.

She looked up at Dieter and smiled. "Is this a date?"

"Yes," he sat and reached for the chopsticks as she served food to their plates.

Just before she picked up the chopsticks she sat back and folded her hands on the table.

"Tell me, please." She sat stoically pushing tension from her forehead.

"The Sergeant called me earlier."

"When?" She sat forward.

Dieter ignored her and continued. "He said that a family on vacation was out on a boat…"

Lindsay interrupted, "Is he alive?"

"No."

Her face paled as the blood rushed away.

"How?"

"They said he drowned."

"No way! He was a champion swimmer. I've been with him when we were on beaches where the waves were roaring in and he could swim beyond them to calmer spots and swim parallel to the shore. No way he drowned."

Her chest rose and dropped attempting to remain calm.

31

"I told him what you said."

"And?"

"The Sergeant said he may have cut himself on the coral surrounding the bays."

"So?"

"The forensics people are doing an autopsy. He'll call me with the results."

Lindsay rose from the table and went to the sink. She soaped her hands and washed them.

"It doesn't make sense."

Dieter rose and came to her, "Not yet. They'll have an answer soon and so will we."

No tears came to Lindsay's eyes. Her gaze was fixed on a spot in the past. She and Andrew, on their honeymoon, swam laps in the resort pool each morning. She was impressed with how easily Andrew had moved through the water mirroring her strokes. After their joint laps, he would do his performance laps, varying strokes, and speed. He was a natural in the water.

"He didn't drown. He was murdered."

Her gaze, now penetrating and resolute was aimed at Dieter.

"Because?

"He would never drown, not possible."

"Lindz, you seem very certain."

"I am. He was murdered."

Dieter walked back to the kitchen table where he rested his hands on the back of his chair.

"What is it? Is there more? Please don't hide anything from me," she pleaded.

"There is more but not about him. The police have come to believe that his wife is missing."

"Come to believe?"

He explained the discussions he had with Detective Griffon and his belief that she was not involved in Andrew's death.

Lindsay said, "He sounded very happy when he called, almost silly, which he never was. No, Andrew was always very serious. She filled a void that I never did. We were a successful couple meeting the standards that the world had set for us; not the needs that each of us longed for. We had, for some reason, many things to prove; but, obviously not to each other. She met his needs. I guess I felt he had no needs. I was clueless in my own marriage."

"Lindsay, listen to me. I'm not a therapist, but I am a man. Andrew made decisions that fit his needs. Understand? His needs, his decisions and not yours. We are responsible for our actions. You are not culpable."

Lindsay stepped back, smiled, then laughed. "Who are you and what have you done with my Karl?"

Dieter moved in and encircled his arms around Lindsay's shoulders enclosing her arms against her body.

"Your Karl?"

"Yes, Karl, you are mine and I'm not letting go."

"I'm *not* letting go." He pulled her very close and kissed her waiting lips.

Lindsay's lips quivered as her eyes watered releasing tears. Dieter pulled her closer. Her body trembled followed by full-blown sobbing.

Chapter
6

The black Land Rover sat with its engine running near Andrew Riccardi's apartment. Cigarette smoke trailed out of the partially opened window. The driver's eyes rapidly scanned the rearview mirror, side mirrors, the front of Andrew's building and people walking on both sides of the busy Manhattan street.

It only took the swarthy man four minutes to enter the building, get by the security desk and elevator to Andrew's fifteenth-floor apartment. Entering was easy, picked with skilled hands and tools. Once inside, he slipped the small laptop into a briefcase, searched and found several zip drives and scooped up Andrew's briefcase and exited.

In another few moments, the Land Rover joined the traffic and disappeared.

Detective McClure, ever vigilant and follow-through obsessed, spent the two hours investigating Collette Corrigan Riccardi. He returned to Dieter's desk and plopped down the printouts of the digital files he found. He looked toward the Captain's office and saw Dieter standing and talking to their giant-sized boss. The Captain listened eagerly. Both men, finished with their discussion, nodded satisfaction. Dieter turned to leave, and Captain Grover picked up his desk phone and dialed a number.

"What's all this?" Dieter asked looking at the folders McClure had put on his desk.

"The life and times of Georgina Corrigan, aka Collette Corrigan Riccardi."

"That's a lot of work. Thanks. Now give me the Reader's Digest version."

"Georgina Corrigan, born thirty-five years ago in New Rochelle, worked at Riccardi's accounting house." McClure checked to see if Dieter got the joke about the accounting firm.

Dieter responded with a perfunctory smile of acknowledgment then waved his fingers in a circle indicating it was time to move on.

"Okay, after graduating from high school she left home to escape an abusive step-father named George," he cocked his head to one side as if to show the obvious.

"Is that when she took her middle name, Collette?"

"No, I mean, yes and no. It wasn't her middle name. The name Collette came from grandma Collette Ryerson who helped raise her during daddy's bouts of abuse after mom's passing. Her legal name is still Georgina on her driver's license and passport."

"How did she meet Riccardi?"

"She worked for the company after graduating from Westchester County Junior College majoring in accounting. Smart kid, good grades and particularly diligent."

"She rose through the ranks?"

"Well, yeah she did, but she rose in the eyes of her boss Riccardi."

"Attractive?"

McClure searched through several folders finally pulling out a photo. He handed it to Dieter.

"Yeah, she's attractive."

He thought about Lindsay briefly. Was she the reason he left Lindsay? Pretty but younger than Lindsay. *Midlife crisis?*

"So, she became his assistant, heading up research and reports on client's accounts to help with the financials."

"Why is she missing?"

"Here's the thing. Her passport, Georgina Corrigan, was recorded leaving St. Thomas, US, Virgin Islands yesterday."

"Destination?"

"Right here," pointing to the floor.

"Airport?"

"JFK."

"And now?"

"No idea."

"She's on the run. Why?"

"She must be involved in her husband's death."

Dieter mulled this over again. The spouse often commits spousal murders. Sergeant Griffon didn't believe it. He said she seemed genuinely worried on the phone. Maybe she's a very good actress, Dieter thought.

"Maybe. Check her apartment. I'll speak with the Captain about a warrant."

McClure took the steps to Collette's floor two at a time testing his quadriceps. Four late nights at the gym were working. The keys given him by the elderly building superintendent who was aching from a recent fall unlocked the door's tumblers efficiently. McClure looked around and saw nothing unusual. He turned on the computer to a lighted empty screen. After several attempts to boot it, he assumed it was broken.

"Hey Karl," he called Dieter from his cell phone, "there's nothing here. Seems untouched for a while. If she came here she didn't stay."

"Maybe she's out."

"Okay, I'll check the neighbors."

McClure knocked on five other doors on the floor. One old lady answered feebly behind the door. Nothing.

He moved down one floor and was met by Paulette Ramsay, a tall, angular woman who moved with slow deliberate grace.

"Can I help you officer?" she surprised McClure, after hearing his through-the-door conversation with the woman upstairs.

He took out his badge, but before he showed it, he realized she was blind. Paulette's unfocused eyes merely looked in his direction.

"I'm looking for Collette Corrigan, one flight above you."

"She's on her honeymoon, I think."

"You think?"

"Well, I've been hearing footsteps up there recently."

"Do you think it was her?"

"The second one was I think."

"The second?"

"There was one set of footsteps of a man."

McClure was puzzled. How could a blind woman know this?

"I spend a lot of time alone. This old building has lots of sounds. Water running, toilets flushing, deliveries. But mostly folks entering and leaving. I listen."

"What did you hear?"

"He came into the apartment. Walked around a little. All wood floors up there you know."

"Yes."

"Then he left. I did hear noises up there. Like drawers opening and such."

"When did you hear her footsteps?"

"Last night, but only briefly. She left right away."

"And you're sure it was her footsteps?"

"Oh yes, been hearing her pattern of walking a few years now."

McClure wrote down what she said, thanked her and left. He almost handed her his contact card.

Lindsay's new patient entered at her prescribed time.

"Please sit-down Karen," Lindsay said after opening her office door to an attractive, but obviously anxious woman in her thirties.

"Thank you."

The woman looked Lindsay up and down with more than a drop of sympathy. Lindsay noticed but shrugged it off.

"Karen, you said on the phone that your relationship has ended, and it hurts very much. You also said something I didn't understand. You said you were scared. What are you afraid of?"

Karen's face showed signs of an inner fight for control. Her hands tightened on the chair like someone afraid to fly. Lindsay noticed rising anxiety.

"Take your time."

Karen's eyes flashed at Lindsay as though she realized she was with the therapist for the first time.

Karen's screamed, "Someone killed him. I think they want to kill me too."

The outburst startled Lindsay. Karen had entered an anxious, scared woman and now was filled with anger. Animalistic anger that needed retribution. Karen sat up straight, took a deep breath and steeled herself.

"My name is not Karen. I am Collette Corrigan Riccardi. Someone killed Andrew."

Lindsay felt the blood rush from her head. Slight dizziness intruded momentarily. Collette's body slumped forward, elbows on her knees. She sat rocking back and forth. Patient and therapist were wandering the same dark landscape. Visions of Andrew's body floating in dark waters filled Lindsay's mind, curdled her stomach and finally shut down her mind. They sat in their private reveries for several moments.

"They're trying to get to me now." Collette looked beseechingly at Lindsay from her bent position.

Years of being a therapist kicked in turning away her personal grief momentarily.

"Who is?"

"I don't know, I don't know."

"How do you know?"

"They came to our villa in the dark looking for me."

"Go on."

"I was home alone in the dark, crying when I heard a car drive up. No lights, so I knew it wasn't the police. I looked up at the driveway which sloped down to the villa and saw two men coming toward me. They couldn't see me, but I could see them. They split up. One came directly toward the back of the house. The other was gone. I panicked and hid in the large box near the pool which held the cushions."

"You must have been terrified."

Collette's eyes glazed. "I was, I am. I heard them talking about how they needed to *take out* the woman too." Collette rocked catatonically. "I knew they were talking about Andrew. I just knew he was dead. Why? Why him? Why me?"

Lindsay sat seeking all the control she could muster. Her hands trembled and her heart beat rapidly. Is death stalking me?

"I lay there for an hour, I think. Finally, I cracked the box lid up a tiny bit and listened. After several minutes of silence, just wind and water sounds, I looked out and went to the side of the villa. The driveway was empty. I packed a few things, money, passport, and some clothes and took a boat taxi to the Saint Thomas Airport and left on the next flight out."

"What about the police? Why didn't you call the police?"

"I just wanted to get away from that place. I couldn't let myself be there another second."

"Why did you come here?"

"I need your help and your detective boyfriend."

"What?"

"Andrew talked about you and him. He told me that you were happy and so was Andrew." Collette said.

"I never told Karl that Andrew would call occasionally."

"Why not?"

"Not sure."

"I didn't know that either."

Lindsay looked at Collette whose misty eyes were locked on her.

"He said you were a very good person, better than him he once said."

"Because he cheated on me?"

"Yes, because he cheated…with me."

The two women looked long and hard at each other seeking a semblance of sanity at the moment. None came for each.

Lindsay's cell phone chirped, and the moment was broken.

"It's Karl," Lindsay's eyes diverted from Collette's.

She answered the call.

"Karl. Yes, yes, I know she left the Virgin Islands. How do I know? She's sitting in my office."

Chapter
7

Simon Winton was eager for the swarthy man to arrive with the personal computers that he stole from Andrew and Collette Riccardi. The office space that Bertram Alan Thompson had built on the lower of three floors of his New York City's tallest residential building left Simon with the other half as living quarters. Forty-five hundred square feet overlooking the City and surrounding areas. Staten Island and New Jersey are visible on a clear day as are the boroughs of Queens and Brooklyn to the south of Queens sure beat the tiny apartment he shared with his mother and two sisters as a child. Simon had always enjoyed the perks that money could buy. The problem, earlier in his life, was that he had no money, no possibilities, and no formal education. His education was gained on the streets of Upper Manhattan where he lived as a child. His fondness for money and the finer things in life were fed by early jobs as a bicycle courier riding the busy streets of Manhattan delivering very important documents to equally important people. The posh offices and the reverence that was shown to them targeted the world that he wanted to occupy. Later he worked in an art gallery where the sycophants came to indulge themselves and spend enormous amounts of money on art. "Your work is so expressive, so rich with color," and many other foolish comments from the rich fawning over a celebrated artist.

One day, while supervising the packing of a sculpture from a distant land that he had never heard of – Montenegro – he decided he needed to meet the buyer.

"I'll deliver this one myself," he had said with thoughts of something more. Although his formal education was meager, his street savvy and a growing intuition had begun to pay dividends. This day he felt a need to go and meet Bertram Alan Thompson.

Ten years later he was sitting high in the sky with a bank account full of more money than he ever dreamed. When he met Bertram, often called BAT which pleased the billionaire who had obsessed on Batman as a child, he knew he had to connect with this man. This would be his ticket to the much more that he had begun to see.

Two months later BAT hired Simon as his assistant in all matters personal.

"I want you to keep the world away from me. Resolve all urgent and difficult issues. Protect me from harm and you will be very well paid. I have CEOs who run my companies but what I want from you is someone to oversee my life. Do this and you will never regret it."

Simon's desk intercom came to life.

"Mr. Winton, there is a man here with a delivery for you. Shall I send him up?"

"Yes, Oscar, right away."

The high-speed elevator to his office announced its arrival with three short musical notes from a classical piece of music.

Simon didn't rise to meet the swarthy man. He had seen how very important people sat as their underlings came to fall at their feet when bearing gifts; he liked that – a lot.

The swarthy man with no name exited the elevator carrying two attaché cases and marched right up to Simon's desk. He stood several feet before the overly large glass and steel desk which only housed a phone, and a computer screen with a keyboard and mouse. He waited for instructions.

"Is everything there?" Simon asked, in the way of the mighty flavored with the accusatory tone he acquired.

"Yes," the swarthy man said and continued to wait.

"You can put them down."

The swarthy man placed the cases near the front of the desk, nodded, turned and left. Simon waited for the man and the elevator to leave the floor before he rose and walked around to the two attaché cases which could have ended his way of life.

He picked them up, walked back to his desk, placed them beneath it where he sat looking at them through the glass top for several moments.

Collette didn't look as attractive as she did in the photo that McClure showed Dieter. However, he held judgment on her complicity in Andrew's death. The bags that encircled her lower eyelids declared the horror she had been through.

When Dieter had arrived, he met Lindsay at her door.

"Karl, this is crazy. I don't know what to do."

She held him until he pushed away.

"Where is she?"

Lindsay walked into the living room where Collette sat with her head resting on the couch. Her eyes were closed. The snug-fit jeans, sneakers and V-neck pullover blouse displayed a youthful physique. Long black hair was pulled into a ponytail and flopped across her right shoulder. No makeup.

Dieter's mind went into cop mode. He evaluated the subject with no empathy. He surmised that she was resourceful – she got here. But, how? How did she know where Lindsay was? Why did she come to Lindsay? Most importantly, what does she want? Why the hell didn't she go to the St. John police? He'd have to call Griffon.

Lindsay looked at him shaking her head.

"Poor woman."

Dieter reacted, "Too soon. Let's find out more first."

Collette stirred. She sat up, adjusted her blouse and blinked away the confusion. When she rose, on unsteady feet, she had to regain balance.

"Hello," she said to Dieter.

"My name is Detective Karl Dieter," he showed his shield. "You got here fast."

Lindsay flashed a puzzled look at him.

"I had to."

"Why? Why did you leave the site of a murder?"

Another flashing look from Lindsay.

Collette looked pleadingly at Lindsay who held her emotions in check siding with Dieter.

Rapid fire speech poured from Collette explaining the events of the last night at their honeymoon villa. She explained about the two men, her hiding place and the extraordinary fear for her own life.

"The local police should have gotten this information before the men had time to leave the island."

"Leave the island? What do you mean?" Collette asked.

"It's possible they were not locals."

"I don't understand." A pained look crossed Collette's face.

"They sound like professionals. I doubt that they were homegrown professionals. If that's the case, then why would anyone want to harm your husband and you?"

"I have no idea."

"Did Andrew have any enemies?"

"Enemies?" Lindsay asked as Collette flashed her a quizzical look.

"No, I don't think so. I don't know." Collette said.

Dieter waited a moment for the next question. He often found it enlightening to let the perp stew waiting for the next question and configuring a lie. That's when he would ask the question.

"How about you? Do you have any enemies? People, who are jealous of your sudden rise in the company?"

"Karl!"

He dismissed Lindsay's remark.

Collette straightened and met Dieter's hard look with her own.

"My rise wasn't sudden. I worked my ass off to get where I am. I earned it far and above the others who were, yeah, jealous. There was talk about me at first. I knew it and maybe Andrew did too. But, as time went on and people saw how hard I worked...."

"They accepted you," Lindsay interjected.

Dieter frowned.

"Yes, they accepted me."

"Did they also accept your new status as his wife to be?"

"Detective, am I being interrogated? Because it really feels like that. I just lost my husband. I had men sneak into our villa in the dead of night and scare the crap out of me. And now..." tears misted and ran down her cheeks.

Lindsay moved to Collette and took her hand. Standing side by side Dieter saw two women who loved the same man. He saw an earlier version of Lindsay, not so much in looks as in persona; strong, intelligent and independent thinking.

Lindsay looked at her Karl, "Now what Karl?"

Collette looked at Dieter for support with pleading eyes.

"Now, we look for the bad guys."

Lindsay let a prideful smile slide to the right side of her lips. She looked up at Karl and saw his resolve knowing that things would be explained one way or another.

Chapter
8

Sergeant David Griffon watched the young Medical Examiner as he eagerly explained the cause of death.

"The lungs are filled with salt water indicating drowning. Fish ate his skin where blood was found. However, there are bruises on both ankles that were probably caused by someone or something holding him under water."

"Like a rope, or seaweeds?"

"Not likely. The bruises were probably caused by a hand."

"Are you saying that someone was holding him underwater?"

"Probably. Certainly, this is a case of at least misadventure, meaning something unnatural occurred. It's likely he was held under water until he blacked out. The lungs filled with water. Oxygen flow ended to his brain and organs. His larynx was wide open indicating the lungs were filled with sea water. No more water could enter, he couldn't breathe, he lost consciousness and he died."

"Any signs of drugs?"

"I will have a report from Toxicology but that takes time."

"Yes, time is an issue. And there are no other signs of foul play on his body?"

"Not externally. When I finish the full autopsy. I will know more."

"More time."

"Yes Sergeant." The young ME shrugged and returned to his work.

Griffon left the morgue and went into the morning sun. Cool breezes ameliorated the rising heat but the heat from Andrew Riccardi's death would be far hotter. The tourist industry doesn't like its patrons being killed on their idyllic shores.

He climbed into his new GMC four-wheeler and headed back to the Leander Jurgen Command "Zone D" Cruz Bay USVI station house only blocks away from the Pedestrian Ferry Dock. As he was turning onto Route 201 he spotted new officer Geraldine Green atop her Segway. The tall, slender and far too young newbie caught his eye the first day she walked into the station. As he drove near, he called out, "Good day Officer Green."

She smiled demurely as he moved on because she had noticed him also. Young men were not on her radar. Serious, purposeful men were.

Once back in his office, he called Detective Dieter.

"Hello, Karl."

"David. I have news for you."

"So, do I. You first."

"Collette is here in New York. I spoke to her last night."

"Really? You spoke to her? Where?"

"At Lindsay's apartment."

"What was she doing at her apartment?"

"She's very scared, wanted help and a safe place to hide."

"Why Lindsay of all people? The ex-wife? Is she staying there?"

"For now. Listen, I'm going to speak with my Captain about this case. He was a New York City resident and so is Collette."

"I know all that. Listen I spoke with our ME and the cause of death is indeed drowning. He thinks someone held him under until he blacked out and died."

"You're calling it a murder."

"Pretty close just need some more ..."

"Time, yeah I get it. One more thing. Her apartment may have been broken into."

"May have? What does that mean?"

"I'm sending a CSI team to her place. Andrew Riccardi's too."

"What do you think is going on here Karl?"

"Not sure. Maybe our search of their apartments will bring new information."

"Okay. Thanks for the letting me know where she is? Also, there's no trace of the guys who broke into their villa. No one saw anything that night. The villa is set apart from other rentals. Honeymooners want privacy."

The two men ended their conversation as JB McClure walked over to Dieter's desk.

"I'm going out with the CSI team. You coming?"

Dieter rose, put his cell phone in his pocket, grabbed his notebook and followed JB exiting the squad room and the building.

Paulette Ramsey heard the rumble of footsteps as the NYC CSI teams ascended the stairs to Collette's apartment. She heard the footsteps inside the apartment indicating several people of different sizes. Then she heard two more men enter the building and climb the stairs.

Dieter entered Collette's apartment followed by JB.

Alison Stone, head of this unit greeted him.

"Hey Karl, JB."

Alison Stone is a petite, very attractive blonde married to a former NFL wannabe who never made it. He became head coach of a New Jersey high school football team where he received the accolades and enjoyment of the game he loved. She, a strong independent woman, needed to be correct. It was this attitude that got her the moniker "No Stone Unturned Alison."

"What have you got?" Dieter asked while scanning the small neatly appointed apartment.

"Just arrived a few minutes before you."

Her team was busy dusting for fingerprints, taking photographs of the room. One tech was seated at Collette's computer. He sat busily punching keys that did nothing to the screen. Dieter noticed and walked over to the tech.

"What's wrong?"

The tech turned to Dieter, "Nothing, but there is no startup, nothing."

"What does that mean?"

The tech turned back to the computer and punched several keys.

"Let me check the hard drive."

Dieter stepped aside and joined JB who was in the small kitchen with a newbie tech.

"Healthy food here only," the tech said.

"Ali, come here please," the tech at the computer called out.

Alison, followed by Dieter, approached the tech who had dismantled the computer.

"No hard drive. It's missing from the tower. Every computer comes with a hard drive attached. This one was replaced or just taken; probably taken out."

"Why?" Dieter asked.

"Can't say, but if it was sent to a repair shop it would have, most likely, gone as an entire unit. Few people would bother to take it apart."

"Or know how to do it?" Alison added.

The tech nodded his approval.

49

Dieter didn't like the possibilities that arose in his head. One was that Collette was involved in criminal activity. Another was that she knew something that got Andrew killed and sent two men to find her that late night. This is much more than the murder of a tourist. But what more?

"JB let's get over to Andrew Riccardi's apartment. I'll call the Captain for another warrant."

"What for?"

"Riccardi's office. He's a Vice President of an accounting firm."

"You think money is at the bottom of this?"

"Most often."

Dieter called Lindsay.

"Hi, Karl." She answered on the second ring.

"Lindz, sorry to bother you but…"

"No, bother, patient, canceled…"

"Is Collette still there?"

"Yes, you told her to stay put, remember."

"I did but that has not been how she is behaving. Can you ask her something?"

"Would you like to speak with her directly?"

"Better. Yes."

Lindsay left her home office and found Collette reading the newspaper in the living room. Collette, still filled with anxiety, rose when Lindsay entered.

"Karl, Detective Dieter wants to talk with you."

Lindsay handed her cell to Collette.

"Hello Detective," Collette began with an intense look on her face.

"Mrs. Riccardi," he began while Collette felt the sharp pain of her new legal name. "Did you bring your computer's hard drive to a repair shop?"

The question confused Collette.

"No, why do you ask?"

"It's not on your computer. The hard drive is missing from the tower. Do you have any idea why it was taken?"

"No, I don't understand. There's nothing there but..." Collette's mind raced through the uploaded files but her confused mind couldn't process the possibilities.

"What is it?" Dieter pressed.

"Sometimes I would take home files that I'd copied from work to finish or put them in some order for a staff meeting in the morning."

"Files? What kind of files?"

"Reviews of client's expenditures to organize them for analysis and reporting back to the client. Routine stuff."

Her brows furrowed attempting to determine if any of the files or companies could be involved. She shook her head attempting to clear away the fog.

Lindsay noticed, "What are you thinking?"

Collette's answer was to stare at Lindsay with unfocused eyes.

"We don't work with companies that conduct illegal business. Never!" she shouted.

"Andrew would never work for such a company," Lindsay added to the room.

Collette and Lindsay were on the same page regarding Andrew. He was honest in all transactions for companies that were midsized to portions of giant-sized companies with worldwide reach and reputation.

Lindsay remembered how quickly Andrew had moved up the ladder in his company from an accountant to account executive to vice president. His work was exemplary, and his efforts were unchallenged by coworkers. Focus on his work and focus on hers were at the bottom of their marriage's demise.

Collette didn't understand the series of events unfolding around her nor could she believe that Andrew was gone. Denial and magical thinking lived side by side housed on a foundation of total confusion. The shattering unreality of the events in St. John brought forth dark places long buried since she left home escaping her abusive step-father.

"Please put Lindsay back on the phone," Dieter said with a softening tone to Collette.

Lindsay took the phone from Collette and walked several paces away.

"Karl, it's me. What happened? She looks very upset." Lindsay turned to see Collette still standing in the middle of the living room.

"I'll tell you later."

"Now, please."

"Okay, I am at her apartment with CSI. Her computer hard drive was taken."

"Why?"

"Lindz, I got to go. I'll call you later." He ended the call.

JB approached Dieter.

"What did you find?"

"She didn't bring it to a repair shop."

"It was taken," JB observed.

"Yes."

Dieter walked the rooms until he found Alison going through Collette's clothes closet.

"Nothing expensive here. Nice, business attire but not high-end stuff."

"Listen, Alison, can you call over to the other team at Andrew Riccardi's apartment? See if the computer there was compromised."

Several minutes later Alison told Dieter that there was no computer found at his apartment. No digital devices at all.

Dieter called Lindsay again.

"Ask Collette if her husband had a computer."

Lindsay left her desk once again now thinking of the phrase 'her husband' attached to Lindsay's former husband; to the man who had shared her bed, her life and much more.

She returned to the office to speak privately with Karl, "He had a high-end laptop used for work at home and some duplicate files from work on it, both computers, hers and his, were connected to the company's mainframe via a password."

Dieter knew that this was getting bigger. What he didn't know was where it was going.

"Thanks, I really got to go now. Later."

He waved to JB and they left the apartment.

"You drive," he said to JB

Moments later Dieter was on the phone with Captain Grover.

"Captain, I'm going to need another warrant."

Chapter
9

Simon Winton sat at his desk in his office in the luxury apartment two floors away from the whim of the billionaire's momentary, often fleeting desires.

The hard drive from Collette Riccardi's computer needed to be read. Its contents sat on his desk challenging him. He could not defeat the challenge himself; someone with the right set of skills was needed to install and read its contents. Simon never had the skills and was incapable of gaining them. A meager education coupled with an inability to focus on details that demanded continuous moments of focus eluded him.

As a youth, it made him angry and a poor student. As an adult, he knew he could resolve this issue with the right person. Money and power could buy anything he learned from his billionaire benefactor Bertram Alan Thompson. Simon desperately needed to know what was on the hard drive and how to break into the locked computer from Andrew's apartment.

Marco would provide the answers; more importantly, Marco could be trusted. If that trust changed or diminished Marco could be deleted like a bad keystroke.

Simon pressed number five on his speed dialing phone. After too many rings for Simon's growing impatience, Marco answered.

"What took you so long to answer? You with somebody?" Simon barked.

Silence followed.

"Well, are you?"

"I was in the toilet if you must know. How are you, my dear Simon?"

Simon softened a drop, "I need your help?"

"Really? My help for what?"

"I need a computer expert...like you."

"Okay. What do you need to know?"

"I need you to meet me."

"The usual place?"

"No, not like that. It's serious stuff."

"It's been a while since we met at our special place."

"Listen, I have a great need for your computer skills right now. That's all. It's very important to me."

"Okay. I hear you. Where and when?"

"You know where my mother's old apartment is?"

"Yes."

"Good. In an hour."

"An hour?"

"Yes, and be on time for once." Simon hung up the phone.

Simon returned the hard drive to the briefcase, packed with Andrew's laptop along with the other digital devices that he could not navigate. The few papers he had been given were of no use and far above his ability to understand.

He walked to his bathroom, combed his hair, brushed his teeth and sprayed cologne on his chest. Perhaps, he could kill two birds with one stone.

Moments later he left the building in his fully loaded Gran Turismo Convertible and drove to East Harlem where his life began. Thirty minutes later, he parked the car at a private garage that he often used. He tipped the middle-aged man in charge fifty dollars with the usual command, "Take care of her."

As he strolled to his mother's meager apartment along streets lined with the stores he inhabited as a kid, he felt nothing for the people or places that he now considered beneath him. He had risen in status, power and wealth; a position he'd fight to protect by any means.

An elderly African American woman shared the elevator staring at him.

"Is that you little Simon?" she asked much too close to inspect his face.

"No." he scowled.

"You sure?" she insisted, "You look just like little Simon who lived up on the fifth floor. He was a funny little boy."

No answer from Simon. He stared her down until she shrugged, waved her hand dismissively at him and exited on the fourth floor.

If the streets leading up to this building didn't bring memories roaring back the tiny, meager apartment did exactly that. The memories were not good ones, however. His time in this place had created a level of insecurity and unease that he fought to shred for many years. It was gone now replaced by the boorish new Simon who liked to win and never lose.

His mother had been gone for five years but he kept the apartment after his sisters moved away; at first for special rendezvous with other men of his ilk.

Three rapid knocks at the door signaled Marco's arrival. Simon opened the door to a smiling young man half his age; tall, slender and fit with an engaging smile. Marco entered and turned toward Simon. He leaned in for a kiss which came begrudgingly.

"Not today," he declared. "Come let's get started."

"What are you looking for?" asked Alex Francisco, the office manager standing next to the head of IT at Crawford and Bigelow Incorporated.

JB McClure rolled his eyes, "Honestly, not sure."

"Then why are you here?" asked Francisco.

JB explained the break-in at Andrew's apartment, at Collette's apartment and the theft of their computers leaving out Andrew's death and Collette's whereabouts.

Francisco looked sharply at Phillip Gross the Internet Technology guy. Gross put his hands in the air indicating he had no clue.

Francisco turned to JB, "You realize we have proprietary information on those computers, links to our mainframe and clients' financials."

"That's why I have this warrant," he waved it again as he did when he first entered asking to see someone in charge.

"Okay, but the named partners are not here. Hell, Riccardi is on his honeymoon with Collette. Did you call them?"

JB chose not to answer. "I need to look at any files that they were involved in."

"As I said the named partners are not here. Crawford is in the hospital..."

"Hospice," Gross corrected.

"I see," JB remarked. "And Bigelow?"

"Deep sea fishing for sailfish off the East Coast of South Africa," with a sheepish grin.

Four NYC forensics police entered the meeting room. Chris Foster came to JB and asked, "Are we all set to start Detective?"

JB turned his attention and the query back to Francisco, once again waving the warrant.

"Sure, okay. Phillip will take you to the servers."

Chapter
10

Bertram's hand fondled the ancient coins that he cherished more than anything in his life. No marriage and no children left him free to grow his real estate holdings in New York, Miami, Los Angeles, and South America. Recent world events allowed him to buy cheaply in countries with struggling economies and corrupt government officials. Investments in new technologies added to his growing wealth. New and medium-sized tech companies became a specialty. The tech companies offered access to other worlds of interest. As a result, he began to collect a variety of small to medium companies. He turned his attention to collections of objets d'art to enhance his cultural standing among fellow super-rich.

The upheaval in the Middle East proved advantageous to his newest passion for collecting antiquities. Bertram met a wealthy man while scouting business in Turkey who was a collector of the one-of-a-kind antiquities discovered during the wars in Syria and Iraq.

Palmyra is an ancient Semitic city in present-day Syria. Archaeological finds date back to the Neolithic period. The city was first documented in the early second millennium BC. Palmyra changed hands on many occasions between different empires before becoming a subject of the Roman Empire in the first century AD. Ancient Palmyra became under the control of the Islamic State of Iraq and the Levant (ISIL) from 2015 until retaken by the Syrian Army in March 2016. Under its control, ISIL destroyed and looted ancient sites. Black and grey markets fed off the stolen antiquities. The money from the sales to mostly naïve buyers, in turn, fed ISIL and its terrorist activities.

Bertram's interest was immediately peaked as was his competitive nature. If others could buy these *special* antiquities, then he wanted to get his share and much more.

His fingertips traced the edges of the Roman coins made centuries ago by hands from ancient worlds; worlds that created a new religion with more than two billion followers. Moments in time that historians traced, researched and gave their lives to know all they could know. Bertram held parts of those early worlds in hands that didn't tremble nor equivocate on the value of their treasures.

The high-powered German-made magnifier that he purchased from an expensive catalog company selling to the super wealthy displayed a coin that showed a face he did not yet recognize from his many hours of research. A man's bearded, regal face, with a prominent nose, gazed back at him. Was he a king? A warrior? A wealthy patron? Certainly, a man of power and wealth like Bertram. He would spend hours learning about this face, its significance and the reason why it was chosen to appear on the coin. Fleetingly, he wondered what it would be like to have his face on a coin that would represent his era in the world's history. Bertram smiled and felt a moment of giddiness rise.

He rose and walked to a large gilded mirror hanging on a nearby wall. Bertram looked at his countenance in the mirror. The face on the coin, not clear after two thousand years but reasonably visible, offered a possibility. He faced the mirror, turned to his left then his right as his eyes tried to catch a glimmer of his side view.

Head up in an aristocratic pose. Chin out in a belligerent despot pose.

The buzzer sounded signaling Simon's request to enter the office.

Begrudgingly, Bertram sighed and pushed the button to let Simon enter.

A wave of obsequiousness preceded Simon's entrance. Rapid steps clicked across the marble floors. Bertram sighed again and waved Simon to his desk to which he leisurely returned and sat feigning disinterest.

"Mr. Thompson, sir, excuse me for interrupting your collections time."

"What is it, Simon? I was busy."

"Yes, yes, I can see that," pointing to the ancient coin on Bertram's desk alongside the magnifier. "However, I thought you might like to hear my news."

"News? What news?" He sat up and leaned forward with elbows and hands in a steeple pose.

Simon's eyes went to the chair near Bertram's desk.

Another sigh from Bertram ignoring the chair, "What is the news?"

"I may have another collectible for you." Simon stood taller and puffed out his chest and shifted his weight right to left and back again anxiously.

Bertram leaned forward with eyes locked onto Simon's, "May have?"

"Have, I have another collectible from a solid source in Turkey."

Bertram shot upright, "I told you I don't want to know about your sources."

Simon nervously licked his lips and placed his shaking hands in his pants pocket.

"Yes, yes, of course, I was just going to say…"

"Say it damn it! What do you have?"

"Two more coins…"

"Give them to me," hand stretched out toward Simon.

Simon stepped back, "They're in transit and will be here soon."

"Soon?"

"The journey is complicated, but they will come soon, very soon…I promise."

"Have you paid for them?"

"No, payment only on delivery as you request sir."

Bertram conceded agreement with a slight nod. His demeanor relaxed allowing an ersatz smile to begin but not evolve fully.

"Thank you, Simon. I do appreciate your efforts on these matters."

Simon smiled broadly. If he had a tail it would have been wagging vigorously. His hands withdrew from the pants pockets and were involuntarily wiped against his thighs.

"My great pleasure."

Bertram indicated with a parting wave that the meeting was over.

Simon turned and walked to the elevator and entered after what seemed like a lifetime of jitteriness provoked by angst. The doors closed, Simon pressed the button to return to his sanctuary. On the ride down, he scowled at his face in the mirrored elevator. He balled his fist and shook it wildly at the face he now detested.

"Damn fool!" he yelled. "I hate you!"

Chapter
11

The two Riccardi women stood facing each other in Lindsay's kitchen, coffee mugs held in their hands.

Anger replaced the fear that had roamed the hills and valleys of Collette's mind. The joy she felt being with her husband on their honeymoon had long since evaporated into the St. John air.

"I have to go to the office," she said to Lindsay.

Lindsay frowned, "Karl and that policeman in St. John agreed you should stay here. Not to get involved."

"Involved! I am involved, you are involved. He was your husband too."

Lindsay felt a moment of shame. "I meant, not to get involved in the case, the investigation."

Collette softened. "Sorry Lindsay, I just feel so helpless."

"I know the feeling believe me but there is nothing you can do except be safe."

Collette put her mug into the sink. "Not true. I can find out what they were looking for on my computer. I was doing work for Andrew. Gathering data for reports to clients. Updates on new data reported to us. I am - we were - the link to whatever those men..."

Collette stopped and faced Lindsay. "I am responsible for Andrew's death. I must have uncovered something that, whoever it is, wants hidden, something important enough to kill Andrew and then hunt for me. Our dreams of the future erased forever. Gone before they could be..."

Lindsay had seen the bubbling up of guilt in her patients as it arose on many occasions, often leading to debilitating states of depression. But, now Collette was wallowing in rage.

"I got to find out who did this to me, to us," looking at Lindsay.

Lindsay's feelings had been all a-jumble at the news of Andrew's death. Collette's sudden appearance in her office had hijacked Lindsay's feelings away from Andrew and placed them at Collette's side.

"I'll call Karl."

"I'll call my office."

Prudy Dillon, Alex Francisco's long-time secretary called into him on his private telephone line.

"Prudy, what is it? I'm kind of busy here."

"It's Miss Corrigan, er, Mrs. Riccardi on the phone for you."

Alex Francisco wanted to talk to Collette but not in front of the police. He stood and with the desk phone in hand. A long look at Detective McClure earned his attention. Alex held the phone up to McClure.

"Personal call," he managed a sheepish smile and a shrug.

Reluctantly, McClure rose. "I'll go check on the IT guy and my people. Be right Back."

"Sure, sure, just a quick answer is all."

Once McClure was clear of the office and with the door closed Alex Francisco answered, "Collette, what's going on?"

"The cops are there now? Right?"

"Yes, yes, but why? Where's Andrew?"

Collette shuddered, the phone's weight suddenly increased. She took a deep breath and fought off tears and panic.

"Alex, he's dead. He was murdered in St. John."

"What!?" Alex's eyes flashed to the door seeking the police who were now scouring his offices. He sat. "Collette, I'm so sorry. Shit! What happened?"

"I can't talk about it now. I need to come into the office to check my files."

"Why?" another flash to the office.

Collette slowed to gain her senses. "There may be something there that... "tears filled her eyes, her throat clogged with air, "Andrew..." was all she could say.

"The police are here looking at our servers."

"I know."

"You know? How do you know? Collette, what the hell is going on here? Damn it, tell me if you know!"

"I don't know. Only that something in the files of one of our clients may be the cause of Andrew's death." Her hand trembled causing her to hold the phone steady with both hands. "I must find out."

"How?"

"I think we need to make a list of Andrew's clients for almost the last ...," she paused, "ten years."

"Okay, but then what?"

"I'm coming in to look through all the information. I will need help."

"Michael Manfredi is a new intern, sharp kid."

"Okay, free him up. I'll be there within the hour."

Dieter sat with Chris Handwirth, the NYPD IT young man newly arrived from McKees Rocks, Pennsylvania. A graduate of the University of Pittsburgh with obsessive-compulsive qualities, he had pored over videos of people entering Collette and Andrew's buildings within the previous forty-eight hours.

"Detective, to the best of my abilities, this is the only person who entered both buildings of your two people, actually within an hour."

Chris handed Dieter several photos of a swarthy man dressed in business attire; dark suit, thick upper body. While Dieter looked over the photos Chris explained, "Each time he entered empty-handed and each time he left carrying a briefcase."

Dieter did not recognize the man in his early forties.

"Let me see the videos."

Chris dutifully pulled up the first video at Collette's apartment building. It showed the swarthy man coming into view near the front door and then several minutes later exiting with the briefcase as Chris had said. He moved out of view and was gone.

"Can you take that walk one frame at a time?"

"Sure."

The frames showed the man walking one step at a time, his left side facing the camera. A slight wind mussed his dark curly hair and pressed his jacket to his body.

"Again. Stop it when I say."

Chris obliged. Each frame showed the man walking deliberately, his head scanned left then right.

Dieter's eyes were on the man's jacket as Chris backed up the video. "Stop."

"There, see that bulge? Get me a picture of that and blow it up."

More finger strokes preceded the paper leaving the printer. Dieter scooped up the photo. He nodded to himself.

"What do you see Detective?"

"A gun. He's carrying a concealed gun. Did he walk away?" Dieter asked.

"No," and he pulled up the second video.

This time the video was more complete showing the front side of a Land Rover, then the swarthy man appeared out of the passenger's side door. When he returned, the car moved forward into view just as a pedestrian walked by, stopped and blocked the view of the license plate as it moved away into traffic.

"Shit!"

"No problem Detective. I could reconnect with the Land Rover at the next intersection camera. Same car, same profile of the passenger. See?"

Dieter saw the man's profile clearly. As the car moved forward the rear license plate came into view.

"Can't read it," Dieter said.

Chris handed him a slip of paper with the plate number allowing a smile to begin then fade.

"Jersey plates. Let's get entrance into New York from the bridges and tunnels. See if they came and returned to New Jersey. Can you check all other possible camera routes to and from Jersey?"

"Sure, but remember I've been here less than a year Detective."

"Yes, but there's a limited number of tunnels and bridges. Let me know what you find ASAP." Dieter walked away, stopped and turned to the young man, "Good work."

Chris Handwirth smiled again this time to the monitors as his fingers clicked along the keypad.

Dieter stopped short as he was about to ascend the stairs to his squad room. He turned and double-timed it back to Chris.

"Chris, I have a question. What if they made another stop or two for that matter? Can we track the Land Rover? I assumed he was heading back to Jersey, but he could have stayed in the City, gone to Brooklyn or Queens or dumped the car."

"The car is a rental from Jersey. If he dumped it, as you said, I can find its location easily. I'll get a BOLO out asap. Okay?"

"Yes. See if you can do anything with the profile photo of the guy leaving the building. I want an ID. Get the sketch artist here to help with a full-face view."

Chris looked and saw a pensive Dieter locked in thought. He waited.

Finally, he could wait no longer. "Detective. There is computer software that can approximate a front view from a profile view. It's been around a while. If he is in our database I can probably find him."

Chris swiveled around to face the monitor and clicked away for several seconds, screens poured into view with changing images of the profile photo of the swarthy man. After a short time, an image appeared of a man whose face was set in a cold rigid expression, deep set wide eyes, a full nose that spread slightly more on his right side. The dark hair was wavy, tightly cropped on the sides but longer on top. Ears were small with the left ear sticking out from the skull more than the other. Lips were thin and tightly drawn against the face. There were no visible scars against a clean-shaven face. Skin color was olive.

"Ethnicity?" Dieter mused.

"Middle Eastern?"

Dieter processed the information and agreed that he could be of Middle Eastern descent. New York City certainly was a melting pot of people from all over the globe. On any given day, there were more different ethnicities in New York than almost anywhere else in the world.

This time, before leaving Chris, Dieter gave him an attaboy tap on the back, causing Chris to smile broadly and tap his right foot involuntarily.

"BOLO," Dieter called out over his shoulder and left.

Chris immediately sent out a *be on the look-out* for the Land Rover as promised to Dieter.

Chapter
12

Collette took the elevator to the offices that she had enjoyed coming to each morning for several years. This was the place where she was accepted for who she was and for how she performed. It gave her a sense of value that increased with Andrew's growing attention. However, this morning as she left the elevator and moved towards Alex Francisco's office that joy was gone. Her mind was focused on the one overriding question. *Why?* She walked quickly and with purpose past Virginia Salsbury whose expression was confusion.

"Collette?" Virginia watched her walk toward Francisco's office, the unspoken question hung in the air heavily. *Aren't you supposed to be on your honeymoon?*

Collette approached Francisco's opened door, knocked and entered. Francisco rose from his desk, hurried toward Collette with opened arms, hugged her rigid countenance, stepped back and looked at her swollen eyes and face sans makeup.

"Collette, I'm very sorry. I didn't know. What the hell happened?"

"He's dead, murdered."

"I don't understand. The police are here going through your client's files, his too. What are they looking for? What's going on?"

"I don't know. I wish I knew, it's driving me crazy."

Collette stood facing Francisco, eyes directed to the heavens. Although her chin quivered she was presenting a level of anger that Francisco never saw in Collette. He reached down to hold her hands. She pulled back, stiffened.

"I'm okay," she lied," Where are they?"

"The detective and some other cops went with Gross to Internet Technology. They're going over clients' files."

"Can they do that?"

"I really don't know. The detective had a warrant so I...."

Guilt rose in Collette's mind. *Did I find something that caused Andrew to be killed? Was Andrew involved in illegal activities? Hell, no. Why did they come looking for me?*

Collette turned to leave.

"Where are you going?" Francisco asked.

"IT, my computer was stolen and so was Andrew's. I got to find out what they were looking for."

"I know, but...wait for me."

Francisco had a difficult time keeping up with Collette's pace. Staffers noticed the scramble toward IT and exchanged open-mouthed, quizzical looks.

Gross's office was simple, none of the usual personal items lined the walls or shelves. No family pictures of kids playing on the lawn. Just business. Several large screen high-speed computers flickered surrounding an oval desk. No paper just technology here.

Detective McClure stood over Gross while his NYPD techs straddled the other computers punching the keys.

One NYPD tech turned to McClure, frustration oozing.

"Detective, it'd be easier if we knew what we were looking for."

Collette and Francisco entered.

"Who are you, ma'am?"

"Collette Riccardi."

"Who are you?" she demanded.

McClure pointed to his badge, "Detective JB McClure, NYPD. What are you doing here?"

"That's my question, Detective?"

McClure had dealt with this demeanor before. Defuse the situation and get information. No ego here.

"Let's find somewhere to talk Mrs. Riccardi." He looked at Francisco.

"Sure, follow me," and she marched off.

They walked to an unused conference room. Francisco started to enter after Collette, McClure stopped him, "Thanks, I'll take it from here."

Francisco looked at Collette who nodded approval. McClure pointed to a chair. Collette sat, he did not.

Let's start at the beginning he thought.

"Ma'am first let me say that I am very sorry for your loss. It must be awful for you and on your honeymoon. Right? You were in St. John?"

A small sigh left Collette before she spoke.

"Yes, my honeymoon." Darkness crept over her. "Now my nightmare."

McClure remained silent, waiting.

"We had planned the honeymoon together. A comfortable, very nice house overlooking the bay. He wanted something fancier than I'd been used to. He wanted to please me he said. I would have been happy in a pup tent as long as we were together. Andrew was the vice president of the company when I was assigned to work with him some time ago. We got swept up in each other." She frowned. "That ended his marriage."

"Mrs. Riccardi, we know that Mr. Riccardi went snorkeling. We also know, now, that he was an accomplished swimmer. I'm wondering why you didn't go with him that day? It's always safer to go in pairs when snorkeling."

Collette shot McClure a nasty look. "He was murdered. He didn't drown in a swimming accident."

"I know. We have a report from the St. John Police. Why, would anyone want to hurt you both? They came after you too."

70

"No idea." She stood to face him defiantly. "More importantly, why were our private computers stolen? And what do you know about that?"

"We have our forensics people working with Gross and his staff, trying to connect both computers and common clients, perhaps common motives."

An NYPD forensics technician called from the doorway of the conference room, "Detective, here's a list of common clients from both computers taken off the company sever."

McClure held out his hand to accept the printed list. "Thanks."

"No problem Detective."

McClure handed the list to Collette. She held it and scanned the names of the eleven companies. Frustrated, she put the list on the conference table.

"What?" McClure asked.

"Someone from one of these companies killed Andrew."

"Maybe, but we need your help…"

"I'm definitely going to help." She sat up, grabbed the list and bent over it as though it held some dark secret.

While she was reviewing the printout, McClure said, "I'm going to need a list of all the contact people you dealt with at each company."

"Sure, okay, I'll do that."

Her mind skipped forward and back from the few idyllic moments in St. John to the fear and trembling moments as she hid in the container near the pool of the rented honeymoon house.

Collette had learned much about the need to be strong from her days of childhood abuse. She knew she had to force all the disturbing thoughts to the rear and focus on the present. She took a pad and pencil from the conference table and began writing the names. She hesitated when she remembered Simon Winton's face from the one meeting they had. He seemed to be nothing more than a lackey to his billionaire boss. His measured disdain for staffers belied an undercurrent of insecurity that she had seen in other men. He seemed harmless, nevertheless, she wrote his name on the growing list of contacts.

Chapter
13

Simon Winton was anxious to get the results of Marco's work on the Riccardi hard drives. Marco had been working on unlocking the information far too long for Simon's impatience and fear of what might be found. Would his fears be verified? The Turkish Broker, in a phone call, warned that his participation in the sales might be compromised.

"How do you know this?" Simon had asked.

A long silence fronted the cryptic answer, "I have a long reach."

Since that day, Simon has been trying to unravel the meaning of the message. The Turkish Broker said, "You should cover your tracks to me."

When a deadly, cold voice called and told him to expect a package he knew it was a message from the Turkish Broker. He didn't know what it would be until the swarthy man arrived with the computers and hard drives. More importantly, he didn't know what it meant.

What could be on these devices that could harm me? Or my boss?

Collette completed her list of clients common to her and to Andrew and their mutual contact persons.

"Now what?" she asked JB.

"We take over. We'll contact each, get them in for a sit-down."

"Why should they come?"

"Those who don't … we go to their offices."

Collette frowned, JB saw it, "Exactly, people would rather come in than have us come to their offices."

"Intimidation works."

JB shrugged, "When it's necessary."

Marco unlocked Collette's computer hard drive. Since he wasn't sure what Simon was looking for he made no sense of the reports until he noticed an internal memo that Collette wrote to herself.

Ask Andrew about certain unusual payments to a company in Turkey connected to an employee of Thompson Industries. After our honeymoon, the note read, followed by an emoji heart.

He had no idea of any business that Simon did on behalf of his boss anywhere in the world, let alone Turkey; but, he decided to find out. The Turkish company name brought no hits to his Internet research. Marco wondered if the company existed. Maybe a shell company hiding another company's participation? But why? These thoughts intrigued Marco. He decided to tell Simon everything except the fact that the company did not exist. Later perhaps once he had learned about Simon's connection to the company.

Next, he wanted to open the second hard drive. The drive was more difficult to unlock but Marco persisted. That persistence was rewarded when he learned it belonged to Andrew Riccardi, a vice president at the company.

A Google search of Andrew's name brought many hits. The most interesting was the latest. A news story in the Virgin Islands Daily News reported the drowning death of one tourist, Andrew Riccardi, on his honeymoon, under circumstances that were still under investigation. His bride, Collette Corrigan Riccardi, had returned to the United States.

Marco's mind traveled several paths finding only questions at the end. Was Simon in harm's way? Did he know about the drowning death? Did he know about the business with a non-existent Turkish company? How did this Turkish company receive the payments noted in the ledger? And, what did the payments buy? Of course, he knew? Simon was nervous about these hard drives. He knew something was on them that would harm him and his boss.

"Who are these people?" Simon asked aloud once Marco presented his findings.

Marco shrugged and looked with increasing scrutiny at Simon sitting behind his desk. Simon's face blanched when he heard about the investigation into the drowning. He rose and walked to the window and the panoramic view it offered of New York City.

"Simon. Simon are you okay?"

Simon turned to Marco, his friend, his lover and now his confidante in what might be a dangerous time to come.

"Sit down."

Simon stood, waiting for Marco to sit.

"Listen to me very carefully."

Marco sat forward.

"I might be ... *we* might be in deep trouble."

"I don't under…"

" Just listen," he demanded.

Marco nodded.

"My boss has been buying special prized artifacts from the Middle East."

Marco blinked and shrugged ignorance.

"These artifacts, I believe, come from Syria."

"Syria? What about the Turkish company?"

"I pay them up front and they ship the artifacts to my boss through me. They are shipped to me. I pay for them with my boss's money through a business account that I set up with that accounting firm. He doesn't know about this account."

Simon turned to the window again.

"He believes the payment is made after the delivery of the artifacts."

"I don't understand."

Simon turned toward Marco.

"He pays me. I'm supposed to pay for the artifacts, but I keep the money. My boss can't get the artifacts unless I pay upfront. But he is adamant about paying on delivery only. As adamant as the broker is about being paid first."

"Broker?"

"A Turkish broker of sorts. My boss found him and then put me in charge of all purchases. At first, I felt good. He was trusting me with the purchase of these artifacts which he prizes very highly. You should see him fondling these coins, and little statues."

Marco took out his cell phone and began punching the digital keys. Simon noticed.

"What the hell are you doing?"

Marco kept thumb stroking his cell phone.

"Marco!"

Marco looked up at Simon.

"I'm trying to get you answers." He went back to clicking until he stopped abruptly to read.

Simon walked to Marco's chair and looked over his shoulder at the screen. He bent very close but could only read the headline of a story, "FBI Investigates Black and Grey Market Sales of Ancient Antiquities Stolen from Palmyra by ISIS."

Simon walked back to the window to digest what he had seen.

"He set you up."

Simon's back stiffened as did his resolve to protect himself.

"He used me! Like some stupid lackey, fool! It looks like I'm the buyer. Like I'm selling to a broker for ISIS."

Marco rose and walked to Simon. He put his arms around Simon who leaned back against Marco.

"I will protect you."

Simon pulled away. "How?" He stared at Marco as though he was the cause of the new problems.

"Not sure, but I will try to cover your ass ... somehow."

Simon softened and reached out one arm beckoning Marco. The men embraced, each deep in a personal reverie that would benefit self.

Chapter
14

"When can Andrew's body be released for burial?"

Dieter knew the process in New York, but he wasn't sure about getting the body released from the St. John police. He looked at Lindsay sitting at the New York City West Side bar, her glass of Malbec surrounded by both hands, and her eyes aglow from the first glass she had finished too quickly.

"I'm not sure."

"Can't you speak to the St. John police?"

Lindsay wanted to help Collette and to assuage all the emotions which hacked at her about the murder. Somehow, magically, if Andrew's body would be returned, she might begin steps toward closure.

"Yes, I can, and I will." He realized his response was too sharp and he softened. "In the morning."

Lindsay did as well. "Thank you." She pulled the Malbec to her mouth and sipped.

"Lindz, there's a lot more to this case. The forensic accountants found some anomalies in a few files that are … "

"What? What are you saying? Is - was Andrew an embezzler?"

Dieter looked at Lindsay and was sorry that he had brought up the possibilities which were previously discussed by the head of the forensics group on site.

"No, it doesn't look as though he was, but it might be that he didn't fully recognize or investigate these anomalies."

"These two years were challenging for him. Our marriage ended .... "

Dieter leaned in toward Lindsay, "Because he cheated on you."

Her face paled, her eyelashes fluttered, and her head bowed in regret. "Yes, I know what he did. I know it very well."

"Lindz, I'm sorry."

"You are right, that happened, followed by the murders in my living room and much more. Even so, he stayed in touch with me."

Her eyes searched Dieters.

"Okay." He sat back on his bar stool. He gulped the glass of Scotch.

"Karl, I know Andrew. He didn't drown by accident."

"That's been established," Dieter interrupted, fighting anger.

Softening, she reached for his hand, "And he wouldn't embezzle, steal or cheat anyone." She felt foolish since he had cheated her. "He was an honorable businessman." She let that sit as Dieter felt her hand tightening on his.

"Nevertheless, there are anomalies that have to be explained. Until they are, I should keep all possibilities open. It's my job, my responsibility to dig up the facts and follow them to a logical conclusion. Right now, all we have are the anomalies."

"Anomalies? I don't understand."

"Money, from a client, was sent to a shell company in Turkey for purchases or services of ... we don't know. Collette found these anomalies right before their honeymoon. There is a note to ask Andrew about them once they return. We think they stumbled onto something that got Andrew killed."

Lindsay sat erect, "What did Collette say about this?"

"She's going to be questioned tomorrow morning."

"Questioned? Is she a suspect? No, she's genuinely grieving."

"Joe Lane, head of our team investigating the books at their company, will interview her for background information."

Lindsay's eyes sought the bar's vintage metal ceiling tiles. She allowed herself a silent, cleansing breath then slipped from her bar stool and moved to Dieter. One hand went to his face and held it. The other grasped his arm. He pulled her close and they kissed.

"Get a room," a drunken male voice declared farther down the bar. The woman at his side slapped his shoulder reproachfully. His response was to grab her and kiss her roughly, which she returned in kind.

The bartender, ever watchful of surrounding drama, shook his head mockingly while pretending to focus on drying a wet wine glass.

Bertram Alan Thompson Googled the Turkish broker's name with no results. Not surprised, he continued his Internet search. *Palmyra* brought many results explaining the ancient city, the fighting there and the destruction of large ancient monuments. One site, detailed the sale of smaller ancient artifacts, dating back to the Roman era, that was sold to wealthy buyers worldwide. This made Bertram feel even more special. It made him proud to be among the elite of the world who now owned pieces of ancient history. Wealth allowed him a place of power, if not distinction in his entitled world, but something was missing. He wanted to rule like the despots of long ago and enjoy the undying adulation of the ancient crowds that he imagined lined the streets as the powerful paraded past.

Research uncovered news stories about the FBI's ongoing investigation into the sale of antiquities and the link to ISIS. That ISIS profited from his money did not concern him; however, the possibility of being connected to the purchases concerned him greatly. Simon would be an initial connection he thought. Simon would plead innocent of wrongdoing by implicating his employer as the final source of the collections. Certainly, the collections would have to be moved or hidden. Bertram smiled feeling comfortable that Simon would be held accountable or dispensed with if need be.

Dieter entered Captain Grover's office. The big man was buried in paperwork that his intelligence and formal education allowed for rapid decisions. However, when Dieter entered, he smiled and slid his chair back waving Dieter to a nearby chair.

"Busy work?" Dieter asked.

"Hell no, all my work is absolutely necessary," with a self-deprecating laugh. "Okay, let's hear the update."

"We know for sure that Andrew Riccardi was murdered. His apartment and his new wife's apartment were broken into and computers stolen. We were able to get an image, but the guy who did both is not in any database we have."

"You sent his picture to all the other databases – overseas too?"

"Yes, waiting results. The info on the two hard drives is being evaluated now."

"Any connection to Riccardi's death?"

"It looks like there might be a company somehow connected to both the wife and the husband."

"Meaning…?

Dieter shrugged, "No idea."

Grover reached around for his basketball perched on a sculpture of two hands. He rolled it in his hands feeling the ribbed stitching. It had become his method of thinking deeply.

Dieter noticed. "Listen, Captain, Riccardi's murder seems to be the tip of an iceberg. The guy was a straight up and up guy, who may have gotten taken out."

"Isn't he the guy who was married to your lady?"

"Yes, how did you know?"

"Same name, I do background too, you know."

"Did you do background on the new wife too?"

Grover carefully placed the basketball into the sculpture's waiting hands. He stood and walked to a nearby filing cabinet, opened the top drawer, pulled out a file folder and handed it to Dieter.

Collette's maiden name was typed on a white sticky tab. Dieter opened the folder and read the one-page report. He looked up.

"She's clean too."

"Yes, so what did they stumble on that got him killed and caused her to run from St. John back to New York and hide?"

"With the one person who she hurt."

"Your lady."

"Exactly."

Grover, as was his way, sat on the front of his desk facing Dieter.

"This feels like an important case to me."

Dieter nodded but was unsure of what Grover was alluding.

"Whatever you need to solve this case...to get anything, I promise I'll sign off on it."

Not like Captain Whitehead. Dieter rose, "Good to know Captain."

"I have your back, as I said."

"And I've got yours," Dieter answered.

"I know."

Grover moved around to his pile of papers as Dieter left evaluating the Captain's opportunistic comments.

Chapter
15

Lindsay's last patient of the very long day arrived on time and slightly out of breath. Frank Davis, thirty-one, a tall handsome and highly successful Wall Street Trader had come to Lindsay at the behest of the Human Resources officer at the hedge fund where he began right out of the Wharton School at the University of Pennsylvania. It was the first business school in the United States now with the largest alumni network in the country.

Frank had dreams of 'big money success' as he called it a young boy in the Howard Beach section of Queens, New York. His friends, sans his natural intelligence, had opted for far more mundane lives. Mother and father labored long hours to keep Frank and his older sister clothed, fed and reasonably secure. One summer's night he heard them discussing money. They had to make a choice between paying the mortgage on time on their tiny house along 78th Street or the medicine for big sister's asthma. *A rock and a hard place,* he heard his father say several times. He was not going to be in that predicament.

After graduating from Wharton with enormous debt, he landed his dream job at one of the City's top hedge fund offices. From day one he worked longer, better and smarter than anyone else until he paid off his college debt. That's when the good times with colleagues, clients and lovely ladies who enjoyed his good looks and money began. The pace of the work, the play and the death of his father from lung cancer put a damper on his normally positive nature. A variety of drugs to keep his mind sharp, to help his mood swings allowed him to work and make the big money; but, it took a toll on him. Beth Krause, the Human Resources Director, had a chat one day that led to his visit to Lindsay's office.

Frank sat facing Lindsay in the comfortable chair that Lindsay had recently acquired. His body relaxed as did his demeanor.

Lindsay had no such luxury. She was tense, tired and concerned about Collette.

"Doctor Riccardi, this was a hell-of-a-day for me. Can I cut class a little?"

Lindsay smiled at this humor. "Okay," she smiled, "but don't make a habit of it," she continued the joke.

The fifty-minute session ended after thirty minutes. Frank rose, stretched and asked, "Doctor, how much longer for these sessions? I know they are not binding, and I've learned a lot about how I drifted away from me that used to be, so what do you think?"

"Well, what do you think? You're not required to come to a session. It's up to you."

Frank suddenly was overcome with a need for sleep. "You know what...can we discuss this next time...I'm really not up to speed right now."

"Good idea. Same time next week, then."

Lindsay too was tired and needed sleep, but she remembered Frank's comment from his first session about his parents being between a rock and hard place. There she was, between that rock and hard place, along with Collette. She had a choice. She could support Collette during her hard time or just lay back, but she knew she couldn't because she was in her own rock filled place. For a moment, lately, life had taken on a new direction. Karl was contemplating retirement and perhaps something new for him, less dangerous, nevertheless challenging. They had discussed the possibilities and then that phone call up-ended everything. Timing is everything he had said once regarding an investigation. He was correct.

Andrew was dead, and it pulled on her heartstrings with great force. They had shared a love and a life early in their marriage. The possibilities seemed limitless. Work and their desire to succeed and do good work somehow outranked their marriage. She felt culpable because she was the psychotherapist who should have seen it coming. She should have made allowances for them over their work as they did in the first two years of marriage when that carefree spark still burned. But, the rigors of New York City life and the energy it took to complete each day slowly changed everything.

Collette's presence in Lindsay's apartment at first seemed a heavy intrusion that she didn't want to carry. Guilt dallied troubling Lindsay. *This is my work, my chosen career to help people in distress.* Her guilt arose from a well-spring of anger at what Collette and Andrew had done to her…forming Lindsay's personal rock and a hard place.

Collette's initial fear and anxiety had been replaced by anger and the need for retribution. Her raison d'être was to help find the people responsible for the murder of her husband.

The two women who, at different times, loved the same man were now allies.

While Lindsay sat adding notes to Frank's file, Collette appeared at the opened office door.

"I heard the patient leave. Is this a bad time?" Collette stood at the doorway.

"Not at all, come in," Lindsay closed the folder and pushed it aside. "I could use a glass of wine." She rose and left the office with Collette following.

Lindsay found a cold bottle of Chardonnay in the refrigerator. She pointed to a cabinet and Collette retrieved two white wine glasses and held each at the ready. Lindsay poured a substantial glass for each, with a bottle in hand she walked to the living room. They sat, sipped the wine while each allowed the wine to settle in.

"What happened at your office today?"

"I surprised the police, I guess, and probably most people in my office." She let that sink into her mind. "Yes, I sure did."

Lindsay waited and watched Collette's expression turn to resolve. "Did you find anything new?"

"Maybe, er, hard to say. I pored over the files that Andrew and I shared since our personal computers were taken. The police thought there might be a connection somewhere in the files to the people who...." Collette's eyes moistened. "I selected several names of companies, that we both had worked on. Only three in New York City. I gave the information to the police."

"What did they say?"

Collette thought for a moment. "Not much of a response. No, no response at all. He took the information that I had collected then his phone rang, he answered and left." She gave a long look at Lindsay.

"You want me to ask Karl?"

Collette nodded.

"I'll try, but he can be closed about an on-going investigation unless he needs..."

"Help, right? Unless he needs help?"

Lindsay simply responded with passive, non-committal palms upright.

Both women took a long drink of the Chardonnay.

Chapter
16

The sun rose slowly over the Syrian road that Abu Mustafa was taking. He had traveled this road before. The heat today would come soon and would stay all day and through the early evening until the winds came to lessen the heat's influence on the land and its impoverished people. He traveled this day as he had for two years because of his cousin.

As a child, his cousin was far more aggressive, a natural born fighter some said. Abu Mustafa did not inherit the same genetic codes. He worked hard with his hands while his cousin worked with his mind and his growing anger. It was the anger that brought his cousin to the doors of ISIS which he entered fully aware of the danger ahead.

However, Abu Mustafa fell onto hard times. The raging war around him destroyed towns, lives, and opportunities for making money – until his cousin had arrived one evening for a visit.

The two men met and shook hands followed by a kiss on each cheek, "As-salaam 'Alaykum."

"Cousin, would you like some tea?"

"Yes, thank you, Abu."

Once the tea was prepared and placed before the men Abu's cousin sat forward, his fiery eyes startled Abu.

"My Cousin, are you satisfied with how things are here?" he pointed to the meager home.

Abu Mustafa stiffened. "It's enough, for now, but I am…"

"I can help you get better situated."

Abu Mustafa thought he was to be offered a way to make more money. This need for money weighed heavily on him. The war scared him. The deaths scared him. The armies alternating control of his province kept him to himself afraid to even talk about the situation to others. All communication ended with others; but, the non-stop discussions that his mind held at each turn of an event were all the communication he had. And now, his cousin sat fiery-eyed, as he did in his youth, waiting for Abu Mustafa to speak.

"How can you help me?"

"I can help you earn money…if you are ready."

"Ready? Of course, I am ready."

Eager now, he too sat forward facing his cousin awaiting the next words.

"For this work, you must be ready for anything. Even to meet Allah."

Abu Mustafa was a proud Muslim. He had studied with the other boys when he was at the local mosque. He was not the brightest student. He learned to hide his confusion with the teachings when it arose. Now, equally confused he feigned understanding.

"I am always ready to meet Allah, my cousin."

"Yes, yes, you are. I know this. I have always known this my cousin. You have the heart of a warrior."

Abu Mustafa's heart was filled with trepidation, not war, however, he sat tall, puffed out his chest. "What is it that you ask of me?"

An agreement was reached after many long-complicated meetings with his cousin. Abu Mustafa would travel to Turkey, to sell the antiquities gained at ancient sites in Palmyra, Syria stolen by ISIS.

Two years passed since that fateful meeting. Many trips like the one he took this day. The money did start coming in from the sale of the ancient antiquities. He enjoyed the money even though fear arose when he realized he was selling stolen ancient antiquities that would profit ISIS and its efforts. His cousin had offered fifteen percent commission on the sale of all items. Life changed for the better. Abu Mustafa felt stronger, more confident with the money. For the first time in his life, he felt like a man. He enjoyed the feeling.

A gust of wind brought dirt from an open field across his car's windshield momentarily obscuring the view ahead. The dirt didn't stick and soon was blown away. This trip to the ancient Turkish city of Gaziantep, now the modern hub to sell antiquities looted in Syria and Iraq by ISIS, caused growing angst which became apparent to Abu. Sleepless nights followed by days without energy and focus were the norm. His resolve was being tested. *Allah needs me to persevere.*

Abu Mustafa met Emre, the Turkish broker, almost two years earlier at Tahmis Kahvesi cafe in Gaziantep where it has survived for three hundred and eighty-five years. The intense summertime heat gave birth to a cacophony of outdoor sounds and deep, sometimes overwhelming exotic coffee aromas. The long, galley-like sitting area, often filled with crowds of people standing over and around tables lent the exact air of frenzy that Emre enjoyed. It also covered all possibilities of being spied upon. Abu came to enjoy the smell and taste of Dibek coffee.

Emre was not a big man nor did he possess an imposing personality. However, he was astute at defining someone's character at their first meeting. Abu Mustafa was placed in the naïve, needing-to-please box with more than a soupçon of hunger for money. The perfect fool he decided.

The first ancient artifact he brokered went to a wealthy German banker who saw no problem with the purchase, asking no questions of its origin. The small coin dated back to the Roman Era, he told the German. Whether it was Roman or not was of no concern to the broker. His only concern was that the German believed it was Roman in origin, which increased its value and price. However, not all buyers were like the German; some very knowledgeable, egocentric collectors schooled Emre on the coin or statuette. This allowed him to increase the price of the object. The very savvy broker took advantage of every opportunity.

When Abu Mustafa reached the bustling street where he would meet with the Turkish Broker, he parked his car and began a leisurely stroll. The day was warm, the air dry. Sweet and aromatically pleasing smells from nearby shops wafted over him relaxing his body. However, his ever-present vigil for police was on autopilot.

"You must be aware of your surroundings Abu," his cousin cautioned him each time he left with a new valuable parcel in tow. "There are thieves who recognize strangers and prey on them. This is true my cousin. The police are to be kept at a distance at all times."

"Yes, Cousin, I understand, and I will be ever vigilant," he promised each time.

This day fate had another idea. As he strolled to a street corner looking left, a police officer approached from Abu's right narrowly missing a collision. Abu's fingers disengaged from the package he was holding tightly causing it to slide down his leg. Quick reflexes retrieved the package before it fell to the ground. The policeman never saw the potentially hazardous event, but Abu's heart began to beat rapidly. He stood trying to regain his composure. At that exact moment, Abu Mustafa hated what he was undertaking. Gaziantep had become an area where ISIL recruits have been very active. The increasing stress he felt on each trip to Gaziantep was overwhelming. He wanted to run, far away from his cousin, his new job and be left in solitude.

"Abu Mustafa why are you standing here. We have a meeting. Let's go." The Turkish Broker turned the corner and stood to face his courier, a head shorter, bald and indignant.

"Of course, let's go and finish the business of the day."

The Turkish Broker looked closely at Abu. He saw a weakness that might be used to his advantage. A wave and a few quick steps and the Turkish Broker was three strides ahead of Abu Mustafa who watched the man's bald head tip from side to side with each step.

Each time Abu left Syria he was given the price to sell the item in hand. This day he had a very valuable coin that he was instructed to negotiate forcefully. A weakness that he felt always.

"Well, my friend, this is an average coin. Its value is lessened by this deep cut in the face on the coin. I will not be able to get the price you've asked." He sat back offering a shrug and saddened countenance.

"There were others with similar blemishes. Their price was not diminished."

"True, my friend, you have a keen memory, but this one is so disfigured that one cannot recognize the face. Who is this? Without that knowledge, the value plummets. I'm afraid my buyers have gotten very sophisticated."

The duo haggled for one hour. Abu Mustafa finally acquiesced to a lesser price than expected by his cousin. *My fifteen percent commission will be less but enough for me.*

Once he reached home a fiery-eyed cousin bore hate-filled holes into Abu Mustafa. The deep brown eyes were fiercer and more dangerous than Abu ever experienced.

"That was not the price that I instructed you to sell!"

"But, he wouldn't..."

"You were supposed to make him pay my price!" His fist slammed down on the wooden table in Abu Mustafa's new, bigger but still modest house.

Cousin got up quickly causing Abu Mustafa to flinch. The man walked in little circles of anger bordering on rage. Abu Mustafa rose, but flashes from his cousin's eyes admonished him to sit down. Once Abu Mustafa was again seated, Cousin continued his circular path until he stopped and looked down at Abu Mustafa who fought the urge to stand and face his cousin; but he lost the battle. Cousin stood over Abu Mustafa. He bent down low, face to face then he exploded.

"You have cost me and my people much money. That cannot be tolerated. A price must be paid for your incompetence."

Abu Mustafa wanted to run.

Cousin rose and walked two paces away then turned and declared, "The loss shall be shared by you. Your commission, which has given you all this," arms expanded to the small house, "will be cut to five percent from fifteen."

Abu Mustafa rose feeling anger covered with fear.

"But, Cousin I have been faithful to you all my life. How can you do this to me?"

"To you!? You have done this to me and to yourself. Now, I must go back to the others and explain away your incompetence, so they don't kill you."

"Kill me? Why?"

"They will believe that you have stolen from the cause, that you probably did it all along these two years. It will take all of my abilities to explain that you are not a thief, but an incompetent fool, tricked by a smarter man in Turkey." He returned to his circular movements. "The more difficult question they will ask is why I picked such a fool. This answer must be carefully considered, or I will feel the weight of your incompetence."

"I am your cousin, your blood," Abu Mustafa pleaded.

Softening momentarily, "Yes, our mothers were sisters from the same mother. The same enemy killed both. Maybe they will understand that your incompetence comes from your anger toward our enemies – your mind was damaged in your grief."

Abu Mustafa was confused. He didn't understand the subtleties. All he could think of was the loss of money and the growing fear of being in the middle of such dangerous men.

Chapter
17

Joe Lane, a five-year member of the NYPD Forensics Accounting and Financial Investigations Bureau (FAFI) established in 2011, reviewed the file from Crawford and Bigelow Incorporated for the second time while waiting for Collette Riccardi to arrive. There were three common accounts listed that Andrew and Collette had reviewed for almost two years. No commonalities existed between the three accounts. One was a longtime healthcare facility in New Rochelle. Another was a Bayside, Queens, New York auto dealership showing questionable, but legal, transactions. Too small for major financial wrongdoing. The last, TB Inc., was a company that seemed not to exist. Unusual amounts were deposited then, soon after, an exact amount was withdrawn. It was easy for Joe Lane to track the depositor; however, the withdrawing company had no history. A shell company seemed obvious. What was the fictitious account shelling for and where was it? Who was behind it?

Joe Lane was a no-nonsense accountant. When Collette entered the offices at Crawford and Bigelow, where he decided to meet, he stood politely and offered her a seat.

Several stacks of neatly piled folders were on the table before them. A calculator and a phone centered on the conference table.

"I am Joseph Lane with the FAFI department, part of NYPD…"

"I know all about FAFI."

"Good, then let's begin." He shuffled the folders, opened one and pushed it across to Collette. "Look at these pages. Do you recognize them?"

"Yes, they are from a company that I came to question. I noticed peculiarities just before I left…"

"Left?"

"On my honeymoon." She became rigid.

"Yes, of course. I am sorry for your loss. What peculiarities did you notice?"

Collette's mind went into gear and she explained the strange deposits and withdrawals that she had come to see.

"I probably would have acted on them earlier if we weren't planning our marriage and honeymoon."

"I see. Life got in the way."

Collette held her breath, "Yes it did…and then it ended." She returned to the pages. "This list is not my list. I presented a list of names of people that Andrew and I worked for jointly."

Joe Lane pushed a second folder toward Collette which she opened.

"Yes, this is the list I submitted."

"Can you tell me about these people?"

Collette began a brief explanation about the people, their positions, as well as their level of control over funds. She quickly went through the list until she reached one name, Simon Winton. When she read the name, she stopped and shook her head questioningly.

"What is it?" Joe Lane asked.

"He's such a strange guy. A pompous, silly man. Harmless."

"Tell me about Simon Winton."

Collette's face screwed up in thought. "Not sure. He works for a local billionaire. We review the finances for one of his smaller companies…about half a billion in gross sales…I think."

"Who is it?"

"Bertram Thompson."

"Batman?"

"Who?"

"Bertram Alan Thompson, aka Batman, a very unusual character. We investigated him on criminal charges of fraud in one of his companies after complaints from suppliers."

"What happened?"

"Don't know. I was not involved, but people in my office were and they since labeled him Batman."

"Because he escaped prosecution?"

Joe Lane chuckled, "No, er, yes he escaped prosecution but because he had a closet filled with Batman costumes. Bizarre, but no concrete evidence found against him. They thought he was guilty, but they found no proof. Maybe Batman hid everything in his underground vault." Another chuckle.

"What now?"

"We're going to dig down into TB Inc. to start. Try to find out what it is and where the money is going and where it comes from. Easy enough."

"Then what?"

"I'd like to talk with this Simon Winton. Who knows, I might dig up the keys to Batman's cave."

Dieter dialed Sergeant Griffin's phone number in St. John.

"Sergeant Griffin."

"David it's Karl in New York."

"Glad you called. The toxicology report just arrived. Andrew Riccardi was clean. No drugs as cause of death. Our final determination is drowning. We believe he was held under water until he expired. Wounds found on his body indicate a struggle."

"Lindsay was right, he was murdered."

"Yes. How is his wife doing?"

"Not so well. We've opened an investigation that might lead us to the cause of the murder as well as the intrusion into the rental house that night."

"I'd like to know about that."

"Will send info, but I have a question."

"Okay?"

"When will the body be released and returned to New York?"

"On your dime or mine?"

Dieter thought about what Captain Grover had said, "...anything you need."

"The Department's dime. We need the body and so does his wife."

"I see. Okay. Let me see how that's done. Send me your updates?"

"You got it, David."

After the phone call ended Dieter remembered that Joe Lane was interviewing Collette Riccardi. Next call was to him.

"Joe, good morning, it's Karl. How did things go with Mrs. Riccardi?"

"Two names came up, not sure now if they are related to the St. John murder case."

Dieter reached for his notebook. "Go."

"Simon Winton and Bert Thompson. Winton works for Thompson."

"What does Winton do?"

"I'm going to see him. I'll let you know."

"You need help with him?

"Help? No, I want to see Batman's mansion."

"ASAP?"

"For sure."

Dieter rose, walked to Captain Grover's office where he was on the phone. Grover waved him off. He decided to try to reach Lindsay who usually had a minute before each hour. She answered on the first ring.

"Hi, handsome. I was just thinking about you."

"That's why I called," he joked, "I wanted to update you about your question last night. You know about Andrew's return."

"Thanks. Collette is at her office with a guy from the police."

"FAFI, a special division. Two things. One, you were right. Andrew was murdered. I spoke with St. John police. They confirmed the final autopsy. Two, his body should be released shortly. No time frame now."

"I knew it." A long silence.

Grover appeared at his door and waved Dieter to come back.

"Lindz gotta go, my boss..."

"Sure, sure, later."

Captain Grover was back at his desk scowling over some papers.

"Captain, you okay?"

"Hardly, come in. There's been more stuff flying around today than most days."

Dieter chose not to ask about the flying debris.

"We're going to need to bring Andrew's body back once he's released."

"You talking about department funds? Right?"

Dieter nodded, "Yes."

"Tell me what you know."

Dieter brought the Captain up to speed on all the new information including the discussion with FAFI. The Captain's demeanor grew more positive as each new bit of information emerged. Dieter thought it odd. Former Captain Whitehead would have been pissed.

"Okay, so you were right. This is a big deal case. Vice president of New York City major accounting firm is murdered in St. John. His new wife chased. She runs home in fear. Financial concerns may arise leading.... Where?"

"Joe Lane is on it, Captain."

"Didn't meet him yet. Capable guy?"

"Yes. Very. He's going to report back ASAP."

"Faster if possible. I need some good news to report up top."

"His widow needs good news too. Can we get him back here on our funds?"

Captain Grover got the message. "I'll do everything I can."

"Thanks, Captain."

Collette sat in Alex Francisco's office explaining the morning's events. He was confused and devastated by her account of events in St. John.

"Geez, Collette, I don't know what to say. You went through hell."

"Still there."

"Yeah, sure. What can I do to help?" half-heartedly.

"Protect my back...and Andrew's."

"I don't understand."

"Andrew never did anything wrong or unprofessional here...or anywhere as far as I know. He died for someone's greed or fear of being outed for financial wrongdoing. I just want to make sure nothing that is eventually uncovered hurts him."

"Sure, sure, nothing will. Listen, I know he was a good guy and all. No problem."

"Yes, he was a good guy, but he was an honest guy too." She flinched involuntarily thinking about their clandestine relationship and his divorce.

"Are you all right? Need some time off?"

"No."

"You're not all right or no time off?"

"Both. I need to be here to help uncover the one confusing account...TB Inc."

"Should be easy to get all the records."

"Yes, should be, if they lead somewhere. So far, a dead end."

"How? We examine all our clients before taking them on. There must be a record of that in the files."

Collette rose, "You're right. I'm going to check on their background."

Chapter
18

Joe Lane completed the initial investigation at Crawford and Bigelow, Inc. and decided to interview Simon Winton. Timing is everything he remembered the old saying. Grandfather Lane had begun to slide into the early stages of dementia. He often repeated it during Joe's weekly visits to the family's eldest and most beloved member.

When Joe arrived at Winton's address he displayed his credentials and announced his name to the attendant at the posh building's front desk.

"I need to see Simon Winton."

"I'll see if he is available."

"If he's here, he's available. Just tell him I'm here. Which floor?"

The attendant ignored the comments and dialed Winton's phone line.

The attendant turned away from Joe Lane, "There's a policeman here to see you." In a softer voice, "I don't know. Okay. Yes, I will."

"He asked to give him a few minutes…"

"Which apartment?"

The attendant stalled by looking through the listing of apartments.

"Which apartment?"

Joe Lane took the elevator to Winton's floor once the attendant gave up the information. On the ride up, Lane knew the attendant was calling Winton. His suspicions were raised, guiding him to take a sailor's tack - directly into the wind - with Winton.

The elevator opened onto Winton's floor. If Joe Lane was impressed it didn't show. Simon Winton stood five feet from the elevator door. He didn't move. Joe Lane, taller and much younger walked up to Simon and peered down. He took out his credentials allowing Winton to look carefully. His eyes scrunched while reading.

"What is the FAFI Bureau? Part of NYPD, I see, but never heard of FAFI."

Joe Lane very much liked this part. He announced the name slowly and with emphasis.

"FAFI is the Forensics Accounting and Financial Investigations Bureau...and yes, an arm of the New York Police Department."

Winton stepped back but held his ground.

"What can I do for you?"

"You can let me in to start."

"Of course," Simon turned and walked the long walk to his desk. He faced Lane.

Lane, over Simon's head, took in the view from the large windows that could have framed a painting's cityscape. He lowered his gaze and noted the anxiety that oozed from Simon.

Simon waited and fought off a slight trembling in his right hand which he casually buried in his pants pocket.

Into the headwinds went Joe Lane. "I'm investigating unusual accounting practices for a client at Crawford and Bigelow. They work for you? Right?"

"Well, yes and no. They represent Bertram Thompson. I am his employee...that's all."

"You don't have an account with them?"

There it is, Joe thought, a shot across the bow. He moved closer again. Simon stepped back nearer the desk.

"Me? No. I only represent Mr. Thompson."

"But, you are named as a client on their records."

"I have no idea why that would be. I do represent my boss. Maybe he named me...."

"So, you have never been to their offices?"

"No," *shit, too soon.*

"According to an employee there, you have been to the offices several times. This employee remembers you."

A long quizzical look from Lane got its desired effect.

Simon moved away from Lane and circled behind his desk to separate them.

"Well, yes, I've been there but only to bring certain documents to the offices on Mr. Thompson's behalf."

"Documents? What sort of documents?"

Simon attempted a self-deprecating smile, "I have no idea. Not privy to Mr. Thompson's business matters."

"Business matters? So, you know they were matters of business, but you don't know what they were."

"No, no. I don't get involved with his businesses."

"Businesses? He has many?"

"I think he does, but, again, I really don't know about his business affairs."

Joe Lane waited, allowing Simon's anxiety to grow.

"Then, what do you do for Mr. Bertram Thompson?"

"Do? I am responsible for all his personal world. His house here and other cities. I make sure each place is cared for, running well so when he travels to Paris, for example, his staff and apartment are alerted and ready for him. He is very particular." Simon stood nodding his head vigorously.

"I see, like a personal concierge."

"No. I oversee his staff and ensure he gets all that he needs when he needs it." Simon's anxiety was moving to anger.

Joe Lane saw the change and pressed even harder.

"That's interesting. In my experience, *people like you*," he paused to judge the effect, "who work for a very wealthy and important man usually are given certain privileges. Perhaps, you haven't worked for him very long."

"Ten years."

"Ten years and he doesn't trust you?" Joe reached into his jacket pocket and took out his notebook and pretended to write on it.

"He trusts me unconditionally."

Joe Lane pretended he didn't hear as he was writing faux notes.

"Sorry, what did you say?" His gaze fell on Simon fully.

"I said," he stopped, took a breath, "what do you want from me?"

"Well, I guess, nothing more." He returned the notebook to his pocket, giving Simon a final evaluative stare. "Okay, then..." and turned to leave.

Simon walked from behind the desk to follow Lane to the elevator. While waiting for the doors to open, Lane asked.

"You know, I almost forgot. Do you know of a company called..." he took out his notebook and flipped it open, "Here it is...TB Incorporated? Do you know this company?"

Simon froze. Joe Lane saw the recognition on Simon's face.

Gotcha.

"Do you?"

"No. Never heard of it. Why do you ask?"

The hook is out, the fish smells the bait. Time to haul him in.

"Nothing really."

The elevator arrived, and the doors opened. Lane stepped in holding the doors open, "We're starting a full-scale investigation of TB Inc. to verify that they may exist. So far, they don't. Thanks for your time."

Simon Winton felt faint. Blood rushed from his head.

Joe Lane pulled a card from his jacket pocket and handed it to Simon, "Here, if you have anything for me, you can reach me at this number."

He stepped in the elevator and the doors closed.

Simon rushed to his desk, took out a bottle of eighteen-year-old Macallan Scotch Whisky, poured a double into a crystal glass and drank it quickly. His heart raced, his hands shook, his stomach felt the warmth from the Scotch, but it offered no relief - he was terrified.

Simon struggled with his next move. He took out his cell phone and dialed. The call was answered after the second ring.

"Marco, it's Simon. I need your help. No, not my mother's old apartment, again. The special place...our special place. Soon...now if possible."

Simon left his building fifteen minutes later. He walked to the nearby subway station and took a train then transferred to the IRT and the 7 Train to Queens. He loved the subways as a kid. They were exciting for the young boy who at thirteen realized he liked the young boys more than the young girls. Later, he would only have disdain for the people who had to take the overcrowded subway. This day, the subway was his choice for speed, far too much road traffic for his anxious state of mind.

The train stopped at Main Street. He ascended the subway exit stairs and walked the three blocks rapidly. The once shabby, now upgraded building was their special place. The rent, always paid in cash and on time by Simon, was good enough to allow anonymity for the very occasional tenant.

Marco arrived earlier. He opened the door when he heard the keys rustling outside.

"Simon, what's happening? You need my help?"

Simon entered, closed the door and walked to Marco.

"I need you, right now."

Chapter
19

Dieter reread the reports from the forensics squad that searched Andrew and Collette's apartments. Forensics found nothing unusual in either apartment; but, both locks were jimmied open. Too many unconnected bits and pieces. There must be something big behind all this.

He read the reports from the St. John police a third time.

An unknown person drowned Andrew Riccardi. In salt-water submersion, the brine in the lungs acts through osmotic pressure to remove large amounts of water from the blood. In three minutes, 40% of the normal water volume in the blood is lost. This over-concentration of blood caused heart failure. Additionally, seawater chemicals were found in the bloodstream arriving through the lungs, disrupting normal fluid balances. Andrew's lungs were filled with sea water.

Dieter wondered what kind of information was on his computer. Did he know what he found? Maybe not...

Joe Lane entered the Detectives Squad Room. Dieter saw him and waved him over.

"Hey, Joe."

"Karl, I might have something for you."

"I'm listening."

"Met with Simon Winton. Got the name from Mrs. Riccardi when I interviewed her at Crawford and Bigelow. Spoke with her about him and others. He seemed right for a first look. I feel good about him. He got very nervous, very antsy. I got plenty of work to do on the books and background on companies, but he might be right for a second look by you. Your homicide badge might scare the crap out of him. I just think he knows something. Maybe he's not the perp, but there's something. Just a hunch, Karl. Okay?"

"Yes, thanks for stopping by."

Joe Lane turned to leave, walked ten paces and stopped. He called back to Dieter, "Karl if you mention a company called TB Inc., you might get a rise out of him."

"What's TB Inc.?

"No idea, but it smells bad, looking into it."

"Keep me up to speed on that."

"You got it."

Collette returned to her tiny office, sat in her swivel chair and looked around at a world that will never be the same. Her first day at Crawford and Bigelow had been exciting. The company had a big-time New York reputation which she wanted very much. Too much of her life had been second hand, second rate. The initial interview had gone very well. Things began to look up. She celebrated that evening at a local happy hour with a college girlfriend who was a working mom. They laughed and traded silly stories. The second interview was more challenging. A dismissive midlevel manager who, Collette would learn later, was jealous of Collette's good looks and the glowing report which got her to the second round of interviews. However, she was sent up for a final interview with the office manager. That day, Andrew Riccardi took over for the ailing manager. He didn't know it then, but he saw a happy, open, compelling personality. Months later, when his workload had become very heavy, and the office celebrated its seventeenth year in business, and he drank too much, Andrew saw Collette with amorous eyes. His guard dropped that evening as did hers. Too much champagne will do that she remembered later.

Their hands touched lightly, accidentally at first and then his hand sought hers surreptitiously a few times which she accepted. The ride down in the elevator, after most had gone home to families and loved ones, found them alone. She laughed too heartily at his talk as they descended. He noticed. When the elevator opened to an empty ground level floor he grabbed her hand once more. She stopped, crooked her head to one side questioning him. He answered the question by kissing her fully. He received her kiss too.

Andrew regretted his tipsy state of mind, but not the kiss which stayed with him even after Lindsay kissed him good night in bed. Sleep would have been elusive if it weren't for the alcohol which switched off his mind and senses. In the morning, he remembered the kiss while shaving and gave his mirror image a thumbs-up, "Still got it."

Collette's status rose from that night and the kiss. She was moved, months later, from the main floor of cubbies to a tiny office where she worked with midlevel management. Still, later, she was moved to a larger, albeit tiny office where she worked with the executives - especially, Vice President, Andrew Riccardi with whom a full-blown affair had begun.

There was chatter among the staff about them. However, more significant things held at the forefront of most staffers. One partner had been diagnosed with cancer and was fighting through chemotherapy, while the other had realized his mortality and began to travel – to complete his bucket list. Andrew spent more time at work, much less at home and frequently with Collette. Lindsay only knew that Andrew was needed at work. Her patients needed her to walk them through the rigors and stress of New York City life. She added more hours to her eight hours a day schedule. Some days blowing up to twelve hours of patient appointments followed by notes and exhaustion. Their lovemaking was less frequent and unsatisfying. The end of their marriage had begun without either's recognition.

Andrew was happier at work. The staff liked the new Andrew; he was funnier, more supportive of their work for which many gave him a pass on the growing obviousness of his feelings for Collette. She, on the other hand, was seen by some of the older female employees as a threat to their growth in the company. Backstabbing comments and smug looks became a part of the underworld at the office.

Collette swiveled left to right in her chair trying to deny the surreal state of things. The old feelings of abuse from her stepfather came forth. Feelings that stole her spirit and her self-confidence. It had taken much to move beyond those feelings over the succeeding years once she was rid of him. Now, as they came charging forward again, her stomach tightened, her resolve wavered. She felt defeated.

Alex Francisco appeared at Collette's door and took in her dazed look.

"Collette, what are you still doing here? Go on home. Really. It's okay. Take some time."

"Home? I have no home. They saw to that. Time? Time for what?"

Alex walked up to Collette's desk. "Collette, please listen to me."

She looked up at Alex who had been her friend, her supporter through the difficult times of her early relationship with Andrew and softened.

"What?"

"This is no place for you right now. There's nothing you can do or add. The cops are on it, I have the new kid working directly with me. If there's anything here to find, we will."

Collette considered Alex's comments. A new resolve was being born.

"You're right. There's nothing I can do sitting here."

She punched a series of keys on her desktop computer then typed into her phone. She rose and walked to Alex, squeezed his arm affectionately.

"I have things to do."

"Like what?"

Collette, was gone, striding across the office space toward the lobby and elevator bank. A simple task had risen to the top of her consciousness. She could do something. She could act. She was not helpless.

The late afternoon crush of people surrounded her as she exited the building. A cab pulled to the curb, only feet away, and let out its passenger. Collette rushed to the door and jumped in.

The cabby, never flinching, checked his new passenger in the rearview mirror.

"Where to lady?"

Collette pressed the keys on her cell phone and found Simon Winton's address which she gave to the driver. The cab pulled into the flow of traffic seamlessly. Collette sat back in her seat and planned what she would ask this funny little man about his dealings with TB Incorporated.

Chapter
20

Simon Winton took a long shower after he returned from the rendezvous with Marco. He was sated but deeply disturbed by the FAFI man's questions. *What do they know? What can I do?* He and Marco had lain in bed earlier exploring the possibilities ahead. Simon felt that his good life was coming to an end. He knew Bertram Thompson would never protect him.

No, he would toss me to the wolves to save his own ass. Who was I anyway? Who was I?"

The stingingly hot shower began to burn. Simon stepped out of the cavernous shower and reached for a towel. He paused at the full-length mirror that he had installed in his bathroom. He was still trim, and pleasant enough looking. He frowned to the mirror when he thought of the old woman who asked if he was that little boy who lived in his mother's building. At that moment, he saw signs of that little boy. Unsure in a world that seemed so absolute. A world where he didn't fit. Simon Winton shrugged off the burden of that image, as he shrugged off all deflating images he had faced.

The elegantly soft towel slurped up all the water from his body helping to renew, to reinvigorate. Simon perused his walk-in closet fingering the fineries that he came to love - to redefine him.

Once dressed, Simon poured another drink. He stood facing the window looking out on the greatest city in the world; he felt powerful above it all.

The house intercom rang.

"Mr. Winton, it's Frank at the front desk, there is a Miss Riccardi here…"

He heard a female voice, "Mrs. Riccardi."

"…Mrs. Riccardi is here to see you."

The walls seemed to crash down onto Simon. The city that lay proudly before him now looked dark and foreboding. A foreshadowing of ill things to come filled his mind. No sound, nor any vision was clear. Only a jumble of previous events leading up to this moment.

"Mr. Winton? Are you there?"

"Yes, I'm here. What does she want?"

Collette Riccardi's disembodied voice, at a distance from Frank's speaker, interrupted Frank.

"I want to speak with you privately, please, Mr. Winton. It's very important – to me."

Frank and Collette's voices were silent. Simon wanted to run across the streets below to be far away from her – from Collette Riccardi.

"Mr. Winton, please, I really need to speak with you."

Simon, turned to survey his office - his safe-haven - until now, to gather strength.

"Frank, please send Mrs. Riccardi up."

He bent to the desk's top with head in hands, then suddenly smashed his fists down onto its glass surface. The laptop jumped as did the small items that lay atop the desk. A pen rolled to the edge and fell. Simon didn't react. His fists ached from the desk's punishment.

The phone, with its receiver off the handle hummed. He picked it up, replaced it, then picked it up and dialed.

"Marco, I need you now. Come to my office right away."

Collette struggled to gather her thoughts on the ride up to Simon's floor. Once in the private elevator, she looked at herself on its mirrored walls. She didn't like the stressed, weak looking Collette that she had long ago overcome. That visage was back now. She steadied herself with several deep breaths, followed by slow exhales ending with an erect posture to steel both her spine and resolve.

The doors slid open. Simon stood only feet away, his small chest puffed out, hands clasped behind his lower back and feet spread slightly. Collette's first instinct was to laugh at his obvious posturing – she didn't. Instead, she took the two steps to face him, reached out her hand and gave a very firm squeeze. He responded in kind. The soon-to-be adversaries held onto each other's hand not wanting to be the one to back away.

Simon loosened his grip and stepped back.

"Mr. Winton, I am Collette Riccardi," she stopped at the sound of her new name.

"I know."

He didn't move.

"Thank you for seeing me – like this."

"You mean without an appointment?"

"Yes," was all he deserved. Not an apology.

Simon held his ground.

"What can I do for you?"

"Hopefully, you can clear up some confusion we have about an account."

"Confusion?"

"Yes, about an account related to you." She stopped, looked at his desk, "May I come in?"

Begrudgingly, he turned and walked to his desk without a single word. Collette looked around the sparse but elegant office space. No books shelves to herald education she thought. A feminine glass top desk. Then she looked closely at Simon. Beneath his posturing, her presence unnerved him.

111

Good. Okay, let's go.

"I'm here to learn more about TB Incorporated."

Simon stirred, moved around the desk where he stood glaring at Collette.

She waited for his response which didn't come.

"You are connected with this account, are you not?"

"I serve Mr. Thompson on a variety of issues and accounts."

"Is it possible you serve him on this account?"

"It's possible, but I really don't..."

"Your name is on the account, not his."

He shot daggers at her which she parried, "Is TB Incorporated your personal account?"

"It is not my personal account. Any account at your firm is on Mr. Thompson's behalf, not mine. No, not mine."

"I see. Do you know what the T and B stand for? We can't seem to find any record of its existence. Just an account where transactions have occurred."

"As I said, it's not my account. I merely process transactions as requested by Mr. Thompson."

He cocked his head to one side quizzically, "Why are you asking? I'm sure, if it's from Mr. Thompson, it's fine."

"Oh, the transactions are fine, all clear properly, but we need to know about the company for our records."

"Your records?"

"Yes, the police are asking us, so we need to know."

"The police? What do they want?" he feigned ignorance.

Collette knew he was hiding something. A spark of anger ignited which she subdued. *Was this little man, this lackey to a rich and perhaps overbearing man, involved in Andrew's murder?*

"They are asking about this company in relation to a murder." There it was. She felt faint. Anger sent enough blood flowing to keep her body upright.

"Murder? What are you talking about? Whose murder?"

Collette reached down to the chair before her and gripped its top for stability. Her gaze was clouded by the fading sunlight streaming in behind Simon. She took a slow breath, hoping it was imperceptible to Simon.

"Andrew Riccardi, my husband."

Marco entered the building and was immediately recognized by Frank.

"Gotta see Mr. Winton."

"He's got someone there now. I'll call him."

"Not necessary, he called me to join them," he lied.

"You sure, because he never mentioned…"

"I'm sure, It's okay. Really."

"Well, I'll call up and tell him you're coming."

"Fine."

Marco quick-stepped to the elevator. Pressed the button several times hoping it would react to his urgency. It did not. When it arrived, he entered and pushed the button to Simon's floor.

The ride to Simon's floor seemed a slow-motion version of previous ascents. Simon sounded very anxious. His message rattled in Marco's head since he heard it.

"I need you now," it repeated.

What could it be? Not those damn foreign antiques. That could be serious. He didn't do anything wrong…I hope.

Simon's eyes went to the elevator doors as they opened into the apartment.

Collette noticed and turned. Marco walked rapidly scowling toward Simon and Collette. It scared Collette. She stepped away from the desk and oncoming Marco.

"Who's this?" aimed at Simon. Marco shuffled back and forth releasing nervous energy.

"This is Mrs. Riccardi."

"What does she want?"

What do I want?

113

"Who are you?" Collette demanded. "I'm having a private conversation." Anger gave her bravery.

Marco stepped toward her ablaze. "I'm Mr. Winton's friend. That's who I am." He turned to Simon, "Isn't that right, Simon."

"Yes, Marco, you are."

Collette's fear dissipated as she realized the relationship between the two men was the issue for Marco.

"I'm here on business, that's all."

Both men's heads snapped to her. Then to each other.

"Yes, Mrs. Riccardi just told me a very sad story. Her husband was recently killed…on their honeymoon."

Marco softened.

"I'm sorry for your loss, but why are you telling us this sad news?"

"She told *me*, Marco."

Marco and Collette saw Simon's momentary glare. Marco stiffened. Collette decided to retreat.

"There is some confusion at her accounting company regarding one of Mr. Thompson's transactions."

"I'm going to leave now. Thank you for your time, Mr. Winton."

Simon moved around his desk and walked to Collette who felt fear again. She made a step back, turned toward the elevator.

"No more questions?" Simon asked.

"No, not now. Thanks."

"But, you see I have one question. A very important question."

"Okay…"

"What the hell are you doing here?" His voiced rose angrily. "What made you come to me to straighten out your confusion about that company? Who sent you? More importantly, what do you know that you're not telling me?"

Collette saw Marco move to the space between her and the elevator. Her eyes darted back and forth from each man. Instinctively, she reached into her pocketbook as her fingers

114

searched for the can of mace that she kept since her arrival from St. John.

Marco saw her anxiety and the hand searching for something. *A gun?* He rushed at her. Collette moved quickly. She found the mace and pulled it out. Simon had not understood her movements. As a result, he received a blast of mace which sent him screaming and scurrying around in circles holding his face. Marco grabbed Collette's hand and held it high and away as she pressed the spray into the room. In their struggle, she kicked him in the shins several times hurting him but pissing him off greatly.

Some of the sprays landed on her face. She screamed in pain and dropped the can. Marco kicked it away and punched her on the side of her head. The punch rattled her brain against the skull rendering Collette unconscious. Collette dropped to the marble floor with a thud.

Chapter
21

Lindsay completed her notes and patient phone calls at 10:25 P.M. and left her office. The living room was dark, with no lights, and no sounds. She assumed Collette was asleep in the guest bedroom which never held a guest until now.

The day had been long and difficult. Lately, most days seemed too long. Most days were certainly more difficult since Andrew's death. Collette's arrival was a constant reminder of his infidelity and her lapse into a relationship with deadly consequences. At first Jonathan, her lover was a necessary distraction from her feelings about Andrew. He was handsome, sexy and engaging - until he wasn't. The deaths that followed swallowed her into a seemingly endless abyss of grief, guilt and finally anger. Dieter had reached down and helped to pull her back up and out. She ascended willingly.

Lindsay entered the kitchen and rummaged around in the refrigerator. Nothing met her need for a bedtime snack. She shrugged, closed the door and the lights in the kitchen.

A hot shower would add the needed relaxation for her body. After disrobing in her bedroom, she slipped into the bathroom and entered the shower. She let hot stinging water splash on her back and shoulders. The water was like a hundred tiny fingers massaging tightened muscles that became stiff after sitting most of the day. When she turned to face the shower, it created another sensation and a memory when she and Dieter were together once in a large shower. Lindsay's mind became occupied with their lovemaking. The sensual flow of water on her breasts and lower body aroused her once more. She luxuriated at the moment letting it last until she turned off the water.

Lindsay was feeling aroused and she wanted to cuddle with *her Karl*, but he had stopped visiting since Collette arrived. Their new routine had ended, and Lindsay needed Dieter to return to a new life filled with possibilities that were now pushed aside.

The mirror displayed her body from the waist up. She stepped back to get a full view of the toned body that hours of gym time had produced. Her backside, once she turned, looked firm and youthful.

What the hell am I doing? Back to high school Lindsay, are we? Remember when you stood in front of the full-length mirror you just had to have like Suzie the cheerleader. Suzie was the first true narcissist you knew but didn't know it back then. Silly.

Lindsay sought a clean towel to vigorously dry her sensitive body. Moisturizer followed while her hands lingered on sensitive breasts. When she saw her image in the mirror she broke out into laughter.

"Enough. Bedtime."

She put on a silk nightgown and climbed into bed. The new book on her night table would sit once more unopened. Lights out. She stretched, turned on her side in the runner's position cuddling the full body pillow for comfort. But sleep didn't come.

At midnight, without any sleep, she sat upright. Ambient light allowed her to look around at the familiar surroundings that had been a part of her life for many years.

Time for a facelift in here. Yes, I need a project right now. Focus on me a little. Cleanse the room of its history.

Lindsay threw the covers back and bounded out of the bed. A glass of wine will bring on sleep. In the kitchen, she took a large bowl-shaped wineglass for the red wine that was already opened. Swirled it and sipped gratefully for the familiar feeling it brought.

She decided to stop at Collette's door to listen for the soughing sounds as she slept. The door to Collette's room was slightly ajar. Lindsay stood with one ear near the opening, listening. Nothing. Not a sound. Strange. Her right shoulder silently moved the door open allowing a view of the bed. Collette was not in bed. Lindsay entered the room, switched on the light, spilling a drop of red wine on the wooden floor.

There was no sign of anything unusual except Collette's absence. Lindsay moved quickly to retrieve her cell phone from the charger that she habitually used overnight. Once she retrieved the list of contacts, she pressed Collette's cell phone number. It rang four times, followed by her greeting and promise to return the call.

Lindsay looked at the phone. No text messages. No voice messages missed, and it was 12:16 in the morning.

Where was she? She's not out with anyone. Certainly, not now during these times. Where the hell is she?

 By the third time she checked her phone, it was 12:31. Lindsay circled the living room seeking her next move. Dieter was the only choice. He was often awake until well after midnight. The second ring brought his comforting voice.

"Lindz, you okay?" Dieter asked, fully awake.

"Sorry to wake you…"

"You didn't, what's wrong?"

"It's Collette, she's not here and it's after midnight. I'm worried. Where could she be?"

A long silence followed.

"Karl are you still there?"

"Yes, I'm going to send someone to her apartment. Maybe she's there."

"She would have called and told me."

"Are you sure?"

"Yes, of course, I'm sure. Could something have happened to her? I mean could they have found her."

"I don't know, but I'll find out. I'll be right over. Okay?"

"Yes, yes, thank you."

Dieter's first call was to the Sergeant on the desk.

"Monahan? Is that you? It's Karl Dieter."

"Yeah, Karl, it's me live and in color. What can I do you for?"

"I need someone to go over to an apartment and check on Collette Riccardi. She's part of an investigation and she might be missing."

"Address?"

Dieter gave the address from his cell phone. "You got it?"

"Yes, will do. I'll get back to you when I know."

Dieter's second call was to Collette's cell phone. It rang and went to voice mail as Lindsay had said.

Since he had been lounging in his underwear watching the Sports channel updates, he had to dress. Jeans, a tee shirt and a pullover sweater, keys, money, wallet, badge, and notebook, lastly his weapon holstered under the pullover.

The drive to Lindsay's had become familiar. He did it this time without much thought to the city traffic at midnight. His mind was on autopilot while driving which allowed him to multi-task. Collette's appearance in New York, running from people who wanted her dead, was more than a new case. It was too close and too personal. The things that touched Lindsay now touched him too. New feelings, new thoughts about another person had remained dormant for a long time. His job, his career was to protect the citizens of New York City; a job he had committed to long ago. Committing to Lindsay was more complicated. He shrugged it off with the cliché, *It is what it is.*

He pulled up in front of Lindsay's building and parked and entered the building. The man on the desk recognized him and simply waved him in. Two problems were ahead. Gathering information about Collette and where she might be; more importantly, he had to buoy Lindsay from the rocky seas that she faced.

Bleary-eyed Lindsay greeted Dieter, still in her silk nightgown.

"Karl, thanks for coming so quickly. I'm really scared."

She hugged him letting her head slip to his chest. He tried to step back to see her face, but she held on tightly. They stood holding one another until she recovered. On tiptoes, she kissed him and walked into the living room.

Dieter followed eyeing her body under the silk slip.

"Where could she be?"

He waited to answer, "I sent someone to her apartment. An officer will call when they have any information."

"Karl, do you think she went there?"

"No, I think she'd be too scared," Dieter responded.

"Then, where did she go? Where is she?"

"Where was the last place she went to?"

"She went to the office today. I thought she came back here, but there is no sign that she did."

"Ok, I'm going to call Alex Francisco."

"Who's that?"

"Her office manager."

"Isn't it too late?"

"I hope not."

Lindsay shivered involuntarily.

Dieter paused, pulled out his notebook, flipped a few pages, found the number and dialed.

Alex Francisco was sound asleep. His wife of twelve years lay next to him. She reacted first to the cell phone's chirping and shook his shoulder to awaken him.

"Alex, baby, your phone…it's ringing."

"Huh? What?" When he heard the cell ringing he sat up and reached to the nightstand and looked at the phone.

"Who is it?" his wife asked.

"Don't know."

"Don't answer it." He didn't and placed the phone back on the nightstand turning off the ringer. It lit up soundlessly. He looked at the same number and grabbed the phone angrily.

"Who the hell is this?"

"It's Detective Dieter."

He turned to his wife. "What is it, Detective?"

"Did you meet with Collette Riccardi today?"

"Yes, she came in and I told her to go home and get some rest. Why?"

"She may be missing. Any idea where she may go?"

Alex turned on the lamp sitting atop the nightstand. He rubbed his eyes to clear away the sleep. "Missing? What do you mean?"

Dieter explained the circumstances while Alex listened.

"Detective, she was agitated when she left, but she did say something strange."

"What?"

"She said that there was nothing she could do sitting in the office. She got up, and left."

"Where to?"

"No clue Detective." Alex looked over at his wife who sat up next to him, belligerent arms folded across her chest. "If there's anything I can do…"

"Yes, meet me at the office. Maybe there's something in the office that will help us find her."

Alex looked over at his wife, shrugged meekly. "Okay, Detective, I'll meet you at my office. Give me time to dress and get down there."

"How long?"

"Gotta drive from Queens."

"Step on it, Mr. Francisco. It's important."

When Collette Riccardi regained consciousness, her first impulse was to scream. She couldn't and choked on the gag in her mouth. Her bound hands, behind her back, wrestled with the plastic tie bands that held them immobile. She kicked her feet, also bound with a sturdy rope. Her breathing became labored. She couldn't gasp for air. Breathing had to be controlled. Inhale, exhale through the nose. Slowly, slowly. Controlled breathing.

Once her breathing became regular, and her body relaxed, her mind kicked in.

Was this how Andrew felt as he was drowning? Suffocating. Oh my god! Poor Andrew. Is this all my fault? Something on our computers? These people. That Simon Winton and the other guy…did they kill Andrew.

Collette struggled against the ropes at her feet. She pulled on her wrists, but the ties held fast digging deep into her skin. She pushed her tongue against the gag which was held closed by duct tape across her mouth. She banged her heels against the floor. Her eyes bulged with anger, not fear, just wild-eyed anger.

Where am I? What the hell is this place?

She was seated on a concrete floor, against a concrete wall. Her eyes were now accustomed to the slight ambient light filtering in from a nearby darkened window. The room was small, the size of a run-down gas station's bathroom, sans sink or toilet. The small basement style window was above her and to her right. It was painted black, but bits of paint chipped away to let in the light showing the empty room. The gray metal door standing straight ahead challenged her to exit. No way. Collette became still, listening for a noise, a sign telling her where she was. No car horns blaring their insistence. No fire engines blaring their emergency. Silence engulfed her.

She screamed, but only heard her muffled tones. She kicked her feet to hear any sound. The silence was threatening.

After a moment, she stopped moving. Her head ached where Marco hit her. A vein on her temple pulsed. No sound, no light, no way out. Her breathing became labored. Tears welled and slid down her cheeks. She slumped forward, her head bent toward her knees as convulsive crying took over her being.

Ancient feelings arose from the days of abuse by her step-father leading to anger, not sadness.

I'm not a victim. They can't make me feel victimized.

She invoked this personal mantra against the feelings of degradation.

I'm not a victim. They can't make me feel victimized.

The silence was broken by the clattering sound of footsteps on a hard surface growing louder. Collette sat upright, her back stiffened but her resolve waned as the door burst open.

Marco stood glaring at her. The space behind him completely dark. The light from a small, pocket flashlight aimed at her face, blinded her. He stood over her seething with anger.

She tried to speak. He slapped her face.

"You have no idea how much trouble you've caused with your snooping. No idea! We may all be dead very soon."

He smacked her across the face two more times, turned and slammed the door shut. She heard the lock click into place followed by retreating footsteps that ended with a new silence.

Collette pulled legs up to her waist while sprawled on the floor. She inched back toward the wall and pressed against it pushing her legs up to stand. Hands tied, legs tied she hopped to the door and banged her right shoulder then her left against it. Fatigued and hurting she leaned against the door for support. Her hands found the doorknob, but it didn't turn.

She slid down the door to her knees and turned facing the doorknob. Collette pressed her face against the doorknob seeking an edge of the duct tape. Her lips moved under the tape without benefit. She banged her mouth against the nob until there was a small tear in the tape. She pressed the tear against the nob spreading her lips and pushing her tongue against the gag. A portion of the torn tape stuck to the nob and she pulled against it releasing more of the tape from her lips. Collette pushed her tongue against the gag which filled the opening space from the duct tape. There it was, a chance to breathe. She could feel the air move over her lips.

Collette forced herself upright. She hobbled to the concrete wall where she rubbed the torn portion of duct tape against the jagged concrete. It held, and she pulled, at first very slowly, releasing the tape from her mouth. Finally, with enough of the tape released where it hung to the side of her face, she could spit the gag out of her mouth. Collette collapsed to the floor gasping in the air she had so desperately needed.

"Help! Help me! Someone help me!"

Her words went unheard through the window and beyond the door. There she lay, curled on one side until exhaustion took over and she passed out.

Chapter
22

Alex Francisco entered the twenty-eight-floor office building that had become his second home nine years earlier. The company's two principals treated him well, respected him and he rose to office manager as the company prospered and grew. When he saw the early signs of a relationship between Andrew and Collette, he kept thoughts to himself. He liked them both.

"Finally," Dieter called waiting at the nearby bank of elevators.

Alex looked at the security guard on the desk, waved and walked toward Dieter.

"I told you I lived in Queens."

Dieter didn't respond and pushed the elevator button.

"What is going on here? Is she all right?"

"We don't know."

"We?"

Dieter was sorry he added Lindsay but dismissed Francisco's question.

"Her whereabouts are unknown at this time. That's unusual under the circumstances."

"Is she in danger?"

Dieter allowed a long look at Francisco without a response.

"Shit!" Francisco felt the urgency and quickly left the elevator as the doors opened. He walked ahead of Dieter toward Collette's office. Inside, he switched on the lights.

"This is her office? No one else uses it?"

"No, of course not, she is a…"

"Okay, thanks."

Dieter walked around to the desk and opened each drawer. He tugged on files in her file cabinet looking for recent dates.

"Detective, what are you looking for?"

Dieter turned, "Not sure. Tell me what happened today…exactly, what happened before she left the office."

Francisco told Dieter about the last conversation they had while Dieter took notes.

"Was she upset?"

"Detective, I mean, wouldn't you be? Yeah, she was upset. Listen, I'm not with the police, but maybe she went to that guy's place."

"Which guy?"

"I'm not sure of his name, she called him the mousey guy."

Winton again.

Dieter's phone rang.

"Yeah?"

"It's me, Monahan. The officer I sent to that address found nothing unusual, and no one there. He says it was a previous crime scene. Right?

"Yes, it was. Still is. Post someone there for me."

"Will do, Detective."

"Thanks," and ended the call.

Francisco gave Dieter a questioning look.

Dieter shook his head negatively, "She's not home. I need a list of all her family members, names, addresses, and contact information."

"That's HR."

"Then get the Human Resources officer here."

"No need, I have the keys to all the offices."

Francisco left with Dieter on his heels.

Richard Gladstone's, Human resources manager's office was a jumble of files stacked on his desk and others on top of the three file cabinets against a wall.

Dieter looked at the files. "Where do we begin?"

"In the file cabinets." Francisco opened the top drawer of the first file cabinet. He scrolled through several files and pulled one out. The file belonged to Collette. Francisco began flipping through pages until he found one, pulled it and handed it to Dieter.

"The executives and management staff."

Dieter looked over the sheet.

"Is this the full list of the family?"

"As far as we know."

Dieter folded the page and was about to put it into his pocket.

"Detective let me make a copy for you."

Francisco fed the page into the copier and pushed the button. A clean copy emerged which he took and replaced in Collette's folder.

"How about friends here at work? Is she close with anyone in particular?"

Francisco's face screwed up in puzzlement.

"I don't know anyone who she's tight with. She has been working even harder since they got engaged. You know, like showing that she earned her spot in the company."

"Did people talk?"

"Well, sure, I guess the usual office chatter, nothing vindictive."

"Okay, thanks for this and for coming out so late."

"You mean so early."

Dieter looked at his watch. It was three-thirty A.M. on a workday.

"Yes."

Right on cue, Francisco yawned.

"Get some rest and stay in touch if you think of anything I might need to know."

"Not sure what that means."

"If it comes to you, you will know."

Dieter drove back to Lindsay's apartment feeling tired too. When he entered she saw his drawn face and bloodshot eyes.

"Hey, nothing new?"

"Nothing yet."

"Can I get you something, breakfast…?"

"I can use a power nap."

Lindsay took his hand and walked him back to her bedroom. He went into the bathroom, slapped cold water on his face. Toothpaste on his finger to brush his teeth then returned to the darkened bedroom. Lindsay was already under the covers, leaving room for Dieter. He took off his clothes and slid in beside her.

She moved to him, placed one leg over his as he embraced her. She patted his chest and let her hand linger making little circles.

"Get some sleep, Detective."

"Yes, Doctor."

Dieter drifted off to sleep, but Lindsay was wide awake wondering about Collette. *Could she have decided to leave? No, her things were still here. Besides, where would she go to be safe? Where would she go?*

Lindsay too drifted off to sleep comfortably in Dieter's arms. She relaxed feeling safe, for the moment.

Collette awoke with a scream. The dream, which took her back to St. John, had her underwater trying to push Andrew to the surface. She held him, kicked up toward the bright sunny surface, but each time, just before she could rise above water for air, Andrew slipped and slowly lowered. She would poke her head above the surface, gulp in air and return to Andrew's decent.

Awake with a heart pounding in her chest, she winced from the aching back that lay on the cold concrete floor. The bruise on the side of her head joined her pounding heartbeat with its slow rhythm. Once her eyes became accustomed to the darkness, she looked at the metal door wishing it would open and allow her to escape. It did not. The window joined the door in its indifference to her plight.

Collette scrambled to sit upright. She pushed back against the wall for support. Her jumbled mind, flip-flopped from one thought to another. Fear surrounded her mind and disallowed clarity.

I must think. I must get out of here. I must get control. Control. Must gain control.

Her eyes closed, blocking out her prison. She straightened her back and bent her legs, pushing her knees apart.

Breathe. Easy, breathe in and out. She sat for several minutes until a calm overcame her mind. She was no longer in prison, no longer tied down, she was free. Her mind raced forward to the possibilities. I must outsmart them. How? They are afraid of what I know and how it may get them killed. But, they don't know what that is. That's my power.

Collette, eyes still closed, and with her mind developing a plan to overcome Marco and Simon, lay down on the cold floor where she returned to sleep.

Sunlight entered through the slits in the painted window and spread across Collette's tiny cell. It brought no warmth to ease her aching body. The cold floor sucked out her body's warmth. She awoke shivering.

Before she could right herself, the door opened, and Marco entered followed by Simon. She didn't move nor did she show any sign of fear. They both looked scared. Marco moved nervously back and forth on his right foot then to his left. Simon looked exhausted. She gathered strength from their countenances. Her plan was about to take flight.

"Why the hell am I here?"

Marco stepped forward menacingly, but Collette held her ground staring daggers at him.

"I said, why the hell am I here? What are you afraid of?"

"Afraid? We are not afraid. You should be afraid."

"Me? You said we'd all get killed. Remember? What the hell are you afraid of?"

Simon shot a challenging look at Marco, who turned away.

"Come here, Marco."

Simon moved to the door and went outside followed by Marco. Outside and out of hearing to Collette Simon exploded.

"What have you done? You told her we could get killed? Why would you say that?"

"Because it's true, damn it."

"Listen to me. We need her. We need to know whatever she knows and get any proof that she has stashed somewhere."

"Proof? I have no idea what she could have."

"Transactions from that account, TB Inc., that's what."

"She doesn't have anything. I saw her computer hard drive and his too. Nothing specific. Besides, you said they were all legal transactions. Right? Couldn't you see how she didn't know anything for sure."

"No, I can't see that. Those transactions, the money that was moved around all gets traced back to me. Do you remember? Not Thompson."

"Then we have to get rid of the evidence before the police."

"It's too late."

Simon looked at the door as though looking at Collette.

"We have to create new evidence that points to Thompson."

"We can't...but, she can."

"Yes, and she will if she wants to live. Let her sit there for another day then we'll come back and see if she is ready to cooperate."

Chapter
23

Collette waited for the two captors to return to her prison. They did not immediately, nor did they return after several hours. Their departure decreased her resolve and the lack of food and water decreased her energy. She wondered if this would be the end of her. Would they just leave her to die?

The pain on the side of her head throbbed more insistently interfering with her focus, her thinking, and finally blurring her vision. Still, she gathered her strength inching upward against the wall hoping the throbbing would subside. It didn't. Her breath came in arrhythmic bursts. Darkness swallowed her consciousness and she fell to the floor.

Tommy's grandfather had bought him a drone for his eleventh birthday against his parents' wishes.

"Dad, he's too young for a drone," Tommy's mother had said.

Tommy's father agreed. "He needs to spend more time doing homework, not flying a drone around, spying on everyone."

"It's not spying," grandfather George said, "it's educational. There's so much he can learn and see."

"Dad, please, don't buy him a drone for his birthday. Promise me."

"I promise," George lied. The drone was boxed, wrapped and in the trunk of George's car.

Tommy's first drone adventure was nearby at George's home in rural upstate New York. He biked to grandfather's house where the drone was kept, secreted from his parents. Tommy practiced flying the drone above the trees, over hillocks leading down to the lake.

Once, while exploring on high, he spotted the chimney of a house in a clearing a distance away. Naturally, he wanted to check out the house. The drone flew under the control of a hand-held device while Tommy watched the land drift by on its screen. He stumbled once on the uneven ground, lost his footing, recovering as the drone dipped, but he righted it and continued his exploration.

Following the drone's lead, he approached the house. The land around it seemed scrubby as Mom would say. The house was settled in a tiny clearing seemingly uninhabited and a little scary to Tommy's imagination. Nevertheless, he approached the house, flying the drone around its perimeter recording no sign of life.

He flew the drone to each of the windows, hovering long enough to see into the rooms without a curtain. A tiny, upstairs room, whose window was uncovered, showed a bed but he could see little more. The windows in the downstairs living areas were covered offering no views at all. A small basement window, along the rear of the house, caught his attention. Its blackened face, with paint, chipped away might hold a secret, a mystery to be uncovered. But, he was nervous. Lots of things made him nervous since his parents moved to a more remote area seeking peace and quiet, as they always said. His new bedroom faced a tall tree whose branches flicked against his window on windy, rainy nights disturbing his sleep and scaring him awake too often.

His curiosity would win out. First, he would send the drone to scout out the window hoping to see through the openings in the darkened window.

The maneuver was tricky. He tried hovering, moving right to left but the light merely showed a concrete floor and the bottom of a wall. Then, just as he was about to give up, two bound feet appeared on the monitor. Tommy almost dropped the monitor from fear. The feet, he saw, were tied but moving. He sent the drone close to the window. Momentarily, the feet moved to bring legs, body and the face of a woman into view.

Tommy froze, then dropped the hand-held and the drone fell to the ground outside the window. He recovered, retrieving the device and drone and ran from the house into the adjoining wooded area.

He ran and stopped only when he heard a car's engine throttling up the slight grade into the clearing. That was enough for Tommy. He ran as fast as he could back to grandfather George's house only to find him out cold on the recliner, with a half-empty bottle of Gin on the small table nearby. Grandfather held an empty glass in his right hand. His head was back against the recliner, mouth agape snoring contentedly. Tommy had heard his parents talk about Dad's drinking. His mother had defended her father saying he was all right now. Tommy's father had said, "Hope so."

But Tommy had never seen his grandfather like this before. Grandfather George was a loving, generous man to his only grandchild. He spoiled Tommy like he never could spoil Tommy's mother. Times were always too hard.

Tommy didn't know what to do. He couldn't call his parents, who lived nearby, they didn't know about the drone. He needed his grandfather. That lady, down there in that basement was tied up. Maybe kidnapped.

Tommy walked to the kitchen and put on the video he had just taken. Maybe it was a mannequin or something he hoped, discounting its movement.

There she was, on the floor, feet bound, hands behind her back. The face that appeared briefly, before he dropped the controller, seemed frightened. He stopped the video and focused on her face. Not a mannequin. A real person. His hands began to shake. *This is really happening. I did see this lady. Grandpa George, I don't know what to do.*

Tommy hurried back to his grandfather's recliner. He was still snoring softly. An empty glass was perched on top of his palm, balanced against his fingers. Tommy reached down to take the glass. George's fingers tightened on the glass. Tommy held it and pulled gently, the fingers surrendered the glass as grandfather's eyes opened.

"Tommy! What are you...?" He sat up in the recliner. Blinked a moment seeking composure. George was embarrassed to be seen in such a state.

"I guess I took a nap, Tommy," rising from the recliner. He noticed the bottle and his embarrassment rose. George decided to ignore the bottle and the obvious. He walked to the front door and out onto the front porch away from the evidence with Tommy on his heels. George took a deep breath. "That's better." He peered down at Tommy who was clearly excited.

"Grandpa, I saw something over there," he pointed toward the house.

George turned and looked. "Where?"

"The old house down there."

George waved Tommy off, "There's nothing down there. That house hasn't been used for a long time."

"I saw a lady there...in the basement...tied up."

George fixed his eyes on Tommy evaluating the news. He cocked his head to one side, "A lady you say?"

"Yes."

"Tied up?"

"Yes, yes, tied up."

George stepped back, rubbed his face and looked in the direction of the house, "Are you sure, Tommy? A lady tied up in that old house that hasn't been used in a very long time?"

Tommy showed the monitor to his grandfather. "Look, see this window, now nothing, then suddenly...watch this, please."

George looked at the small screen but the reflection from the sun diminished his ability to see clearly. "Can't make it out. Come back inside."

The duo walked back inside. Tommy held it up and started the video. George's eyes bulged when he saw the lady and the ropes.

"I gotta call the police." George lifted the receiver of the ancient wall phone and dialed 911.

Marco and Simon hefted the travel trunk out of the house, sliding it into the small SUV. It had taken only minutes to sedate Collette, gag and duct tape her mouth again, and put her into the trunk before they exited the house to drive off initiating their new plan.

Chapter
24

Captain Grover's tall body almost filled the doorway to his office. He waved Dieter over and returned to his desk.

Dieter rose from his chair and stack of paperwork. He took one sip of no longer hot coffee and walked to the Captain's office knowing full well that Grover needed a better update than he was about to deliver.

Grover pointed to a chair and Dieter acquiesced and sat facing his boss. The Captain's face screwed up in thought.

"This thing is getting very complicated. First, an apparent drowning turns out to be a murder of a New York City resident on his honeymoon in St. John. His new wife is threatened, then she disappears…and now there's a financial connection to this too."

His puzzled stare at Dieter asked the unsaid question, the very same question that he had been asked. Where is this investigation going? We need an end to this.

Deputy Inspector Rodrigues had pushed for his friend and longtime Homicide Lieutenant, Victor Ortiz, to be the new Homicide Captain. Ortiz was a good cop, a good friend and experienced in homicide, but this guy Grover, from narcotics, gets assigned over protestations by Rodrigues. Grover had inherited the animosity and was trying to reduce it by doing a good job and strengthening his path to advancement. He didn't need someone blocking his ascension.

"Listen, Karl, I don't have to tell you that a case like this, which seems to get bigger each day, gets the attention of the people upstairs...know what I mean?"

"Yes, I do, it is getting more complicated, but I think there's more to go on this one."

"More? What more?"

"Collette Riccardi didn't just disappear, Captain. She was kidnapped." Dieter waited for the reaction...and it came quickly.

"Kidnapped? Damn, what's next. How do you know she's been kidnapped?"

"We received a report from an upstate police department responding to our alert for Collette, the picture we sent out got a hit."

"Go on. Did they find her?"

"No, they found evidence that she was kidnapped at a house in their district, but she is gone now."

"Gone?"

Dieter detailed all the information regarding her sighting by a drone flown by a young kid.

Grover stood not knowing where to move. He looked down at Dieter.

"What's next? Aliens?"

Dieter's shrug signaled no need to respond.

"And now?"

"We're going up there, see if we can dig up something more than a drone video."

"Be nice to the locals. You go up there, poke around with any neighbors who may have seen or heard anything out of the usual." Grover paused, "Give me something to point toward an end to this. I need it."

"So does Collette." He didn't add Lindsay's name to the comment even though he knew she was deeply troubled.

"What about the financial connection?"

"We're working on it." Dieter hated to leave hanging in the air but he had no choice. Forensic accountants uncovered one company, TB Inc., with a dead end after that. Money was paid or laundered, but who owned the laundromat and what was bought was still elusive. Follow the money."

New York City's heavy traffic, aided by never-ending construction, never lessened on the Henry Hudson Parkway heading north. The directions given by the digital GPS device, *fastest route, despite the usual traffic* led Dieter and McClure to the George Washington Bridge then North on the Palisades Parkway.

The New York City landscape of tallish residential buildings on the west side ended when they entered the Palisades Parkway. The roadway widened each mile north and brought hints of trees as they followed the instructions of the dulcet digital voice.

"This is a strange way to get up there," McClure mused as he drove. Dieter agreed but his attention was on his phone checking a text message from Lindsay.

Karl, please call me when you get there. Please. I must know if she is alive.

Dieter knew they wouldn't be able to know if she were alive from the report the local police had filed. He hoped there would be something to explain her kidnapping and how she was held. The house had to have neighbors, he hoped. He'd want to talk to the kid and grandfather and see the drone video up close.

The Palisades route took them past Doodletown, an old Dutch name, *doodle*, meaning dead valley. Hikers were the only inhabitants, albeit transitory.

The GPS announced their arrival at a stand of trees leading into a wooded area. *You have reached your destination.* They were a few miles from the Bear Mountain State Park recreation area.

"I don't think so, no house in sight," McClure looked at Dieter. "No road in sight."

Dieter punched in the phone number of the local police contact and asked for help finding the house in question. The officer said, "There's one of our cars nearby. Be there in a few minutes. Stay put, please."

A police car arrived in three minutes. The six-feet-six-inch, giant-sized officer left his car. Dieter exited to join him. They chatted after displaying shields. The local police officer drove off and McClure followed.

They soon arrived at a dirt road leading up a slight grade. Officer Rick Rennels drove on the side on the dirt road around the cordoned off area careful not to drive over the tire tracks of a vehicle under investigation. Dieter and McClure followed and met Rennels outside the house at the road's peak surrounded by the fallen branches from nearby trees.

The two creaky steps up the front porch led to a door in need of paint and repair. Signs of an investigation were evident to Dieter. The notice on the door warned to stay away.

"Detective, I was told to stick with you while you investigate the scene of the kidnapping."

"Got it. Your crime scene. No problem. The woman kidnapped is part of our investigation, so we'll work together."

Officer Rick Rennels had never been part of a crime scene like this one before. Nothing of this nature happened in his district during his ten years on the job. He was interested to see the scene since he was not part of the first batch of officers and forensics folks who came to the house.

The officer opened the front door and entered first. The small living area was empty. Dust covered the floors except where the officers and perhaps the kidnappers had trod. Several outlines where furniture once positioned were visible on the stained carpet centering the room. The mouth of the small fireplace was covered in unbroken cobwebs declaring its long disuse.

Rennels saw a door marked by police. "That must be the basement entrance."

He opened the door to find stairs leading down. The trio descended to a small concrete basement. A boiler on the left of the stairs no longer hummed. One darkened window held the sun back. McClure pointed to a door in the rear of the basement farthest away from the stairs. It too had a police marker on the doorknob.

They entered to an unremarkable, tiny, eight by eight-foot room. The window that had afforded the view from the drone was intact, rivulets of light flowed through the areas where the paint no longer hide the sun.

Markers on the wall and interior doorknob displayed the local police logo. Where the duct tape from Collette's mouth had been attached to the wall there now was a police marker.

Rennels pointed to a spot on the floor, "This is where a gag was found. Should be able to identify the woman."

"I'd bet the video is Collette Riccardi."

Rennels looked at Dieter, "You know her?"

"Interviewed her as part of a continuing investigation."

The three men left the basement and conducted a tour of the house. An old wood-burning stove faced the kitchen sink. No modern appliances here. An icebox, its door ajar, showed longtime neglect and filth.

"Officer, can you take us to where the boy and grandfather live."

"The boy lives with his parents, but George's house is about a quarter mile away. Follow me."

"You know the grandfather…George?"

"Nice older guy, but a bad drinker at times. No DUIs but sloppy in public once or twice at the local drinking hole."

The men drove to George's house, seeking the roadway rather than the trek through the woods to the open clearing near the house.

George stood on his porch holding a mug waiting for the cars to stop and the three men to exit.

"George," Rennels called out, "were you waiting for us?"

"No, didn't know I'd have visitors. Sitting out here with my coffee." George held up the mug.

The four men met at the bottom of the steps to the porch.

"George, these are New York City detectives. They'd like to have a word with you about the sighting at that house back there."

"All right. Happy to help New York City's finest."

The comment, a joke, Dieter thought, was ignored.

"Can you tell us what you saw?"

"Me? I saw probably what you saw, that video is all."

Dieter didn't like the clearly dismissive answers he was getting.

"Do you have the video?"

George's face screwed up into a scowl.

"Wish I'd never bought that damn drone for Tommy. The kid is now scared and his mother, my daughter, is pissed at me for getting it for him behind her back."

Rennels stepped. "Listen, George, the detectives need to see the video for themselves. Can you help us with that?"

George blinked, clearing away confusion and guilt for putting Tommy at the center of this craziness.

"Yes, I have it. My daughter refused to let it back in their house."

"We collected the data from the device, but it's in the station."

"Let's look at the original. I need to see it for my investigation, George."

George ascended the steps to the house, stopping at his door.

" Be right back with it."

Dieter looked at Rennels, "Is he okay?"

"Yeah, I think so. He got in trouble with his daughter. She's one tough person."

Rennels moved close to Dieter looking over his shoulder at the front door.

"Let's give him some credit for finding this. He's sick, cancer, and he hasn't told anybody."

"Not his daughter?"

George came out of the door, "Here it is." He descended the stairs and handed the device to Dieter who took it.

"Thanks, George for your cooperation...calling the police. You may have saved this woman's life."

George smiled broadly. Rennels stuck his large hand out to George who took it. They pumped a handshake for a few seconds.

Dieter fumbled with it and eventually turned it on and saw Collette's face just before the video's end.

"Pretty gal," George mused. "Hope she's all right. Got any idea who took her?"

Rennels was interested in the answer.

"Possible suspects?" Directed at Dieter.

"She must be in big trouble. I mean, why else would someone take her? Right?" George added.

Dieter returned the device to George, shook his hand and thanked him.

"But, I need to talk to your grandson."

Dieter waited as George's face went through several changes.

"Okay, I'll go with you to my daughter's house."

"Come with me George," Rennels said.

George went with Officer Rennels on the drive to Karen Reynold's house. A tidy looking two-story house with an unattached garage visible from the driveway on a road with few houses separated by several acres was Tommy's home. His bike leaned up against a bush near the stairs to the house. He hadn't left the house since he returned from the first drone ride.

The men ascended the stairs to the front door and knocked.

Thirty-four-year-old Karen came to the door wearing blue jeans and a blue button-down shirt. Her long blonde hair was pulled back into a ponytail. She held a cleaning rag in her left hand and stood behind the screen door waiting.

George, trying to ameliorate Karen's present state of anger asked, "Karen, how are you? How's Tommy?"

Karen's stoic face gave no sign of emotion. She did not answer.

"Mrs. Reynolds, I'm officer Rennels and these are two New York City detectives investigating the lady who's gone missing."

"Kidnapped."

"Yes, ma'am, kidnapped. That's why we're here. The detectives need to talk with Tommy."

Karen shot daggers at her father.

"It's very important that we have all the information, so we can find that woman." Dieter offered. "It'll take a few minutes and we'll be on our way."

"And Tommy? What about Tommy? When is he gonna be on his way back to being a little boy who is not scared?" Arms folded against her chest hid shaking, angry hands.

George moved to his daughter. They shared a look and he hugged her. She returned his hug.

"Why the hell did you buy that thing?"

An awkward silence fell on the men as they watched father and daughter struggle.

"Ma'am, that drone may be able to save someone's life. This may be a good thing for her. But, we need Tommy's help. He's important to our investigation."

"Mom, can I help?" Tommy asked from the nearby living room.

Karen flashed looks from her father, to the police and to her son who had moved to her side.

"Mom, can I? I'm okay now. I want to help."

Karen surrounded her son with a protective arm.

"Okay." But, it was easy to see that it was not okay.

"Karen, can we come in?" George asked.

"Sure, Dad, all of you...come in."

Karen led the men into her living room where Tommy plopped himself on his special television chair. George walked to the recliner that Karen's husband used. He looked at Karen questionably. She nodded approval. The three police officers sat scrunched on a lumpy couch with Rennels in the middle. Karen paced.

"Tommy, thank you for agreeing to help us. We're trying to find and save the lady you saw. Your help could be very important."

Tommy fidgeted. Karen saw it and frowned.

"Can you tell everything that happened and everything you saw that time at the house? Take your time. Okay?"

Tommy did take his time. His face screwed up in thought. A furrowed brow vanished when he began to speak.

"Grandpa gave me the drone for my birthday," a quick glance at George, who nodded his approval.

Karen crossed her arms across her chest and stiffened. George saw it.

"Go on Tommy." George allowed.

"Well, I was really excited about the drone, you know. It is very cool. I mean, I was like flying above the ground, over the trees and all." A look at Mom who softened a drop at seeing his joy.

"I took the drone up higher as I walked around. It showed a house way over there," he pointed. "So, I decided to explore because I didn't know there was a house over there. Not sure what I expected, I just went is all."

"That's good Tommy," Dieter said.

"Well, I got closer and guessed it was empty. The grass was high, uncut and weeds were everywhere. I help my Dad cut and weed here. Right, Mom?"

"Yes, Tommy is a big help around here. Very proud of you."

Tommy smiled and blushed a little too.

144

"I flew the drone around the house. It seemed empty, but the windows were all covered so I couldn't really tell. I went around to the basement windows where the paint was coming away from one letting the drone see inside. That's when I saw the lady's feet and then she moved."

He stopped remembering that moment. Karen came to his side, putting her hand on his shoulder.

"What happened next?" Dieter asked.

"I ran, I mean after picking up the drone, I ran to the front of the house and into the woods." Tommy sat back in his chair.

"Good, very good Tommy. You know there are tire tracks coming up the driveway. Did you see a car?"

Tommy jumped up. "Yes, I saw a car and I ran faster to get away. Right back to grandpa's house."

All three police stood.

"Tommy, did you see the car and who was in it? Think very hard. You know the memory is in there," Dieter pointed to his head. "Close your eyes and look for it."

Every eye in the room watched Tommy as he did what he was asked. Expectations grew as Tommy became quiet.

"I did, I saw the car, no, a small SUV, is that what you call it? Mom, like my friend Jimmy's Mom's car?"

"Yes, it's a small SUV."

"That's very good, Tommy. What color?"

"Black, or dark blue, maybe."

"Dark blue or black SUV. Very good. What about the driver?"

"Drivers, there were two."

Dieter turned to McClure who added to the notes his taking.

"Can you see the drivers?"

Tommy closed his eyes, then squeezed tightly. He shook his head as though trying to overcome the challenge. A small smile crossed his face. Eyes opened.

"The driver was older."

"How old?" Dieter asked.

"Like you maybe."

"And the other guy?"

"Like him," pointing to the younger McClure.

McClure stifled a chuckle.

"Okay, what else?"

"I don't know. Can't really describe them. Just regular looking guys."

Karen intervened, "Okay, that's all." She put a protective arm around Tommy who involuntarily hugged his mother.

"One last question?" to Karen. "Tommy, did you see them leave?"

"No, I ran away. Never went back there."

"Okay, we're going now. Tommy, you may have helped solve this kidnapping. You've been a great help to the New York Police Department."

Tommy looked proudly at his Mom as the police left the living room.

On the drive back to the City, Dieter called in the new information asking to check all bridge and tunnel videos into New York City that shows a small, dark SUV with two men, a driver in his forties and a younger man as a passenger. His second call was to Lindsay.

Chapter
25

"Karl, thanks for calling. What did you find?"

"Lindz, I'm in the car with my partner heading back to the office."

"Is she alive?"

Dieter shook his head to the conflict that raced around inside. He felt responsible to help Lindsay through this. His feelings for her demanded it but those same feelings clouded his investigation. This was too close to him. Other cases were placed at a distance from his personal life. Collette's connection to Lindsay made it difficult. Murder cases were difficult enough, this was far more complicated.

"Don't know. A small SUV came to the house and left with her we believe."

"What does that even mean? Was she alive?"

Dieter sat taller in the car seat. "It's possible."

"Possible?"

"Listen, Lindz, I'm working on this case and it's getting more complicated each day. I will tell you what I know when I see you tonight. Okay?"

"Yes, of course, sorry Karl. I just…Be careful."

Lindsay needed answers that were not on her horizon. If not there, then where? Who could she ask? She left her office and moved into the kitchen. Her hands went to work cleaning the countertop and face of the refrigerator, refilling a fruit bowl and puttering with the placement of the round kitchen table. Idle hands were at work allowing her mind to regroup and find a path to an answer. She didn't like the answer that came. She didn't want to return to a place filled with memories of Andrew before Collette.

The first time she went to Crawford and Bigelow was to meet Andrew for dinner in their first year of marriage before he rose to vice president. She was greeted warmly by the women and even warmer by the men who found her attractive. Alex Francisco was a smart, kind guy who was always professional and affable. He might have some information that could clear away some clouds.

Lindsay decided to drop in on Alex at Bigelow and Crawford. No call for a meeting, just a drop-by to chat. The afternoon free of patients and light traffic allowed her to taxi over to the office in thirty minutes. A new office receptionist asked her name and who she wanted to speak with.

"Lindsay Riccardi, I'd like to see Alex Francisco."

The receptionist asked, "Oh, I'm so sorry. Are you related to Andrew?"

Am I related to Andrew? How do I answer that question?

Fortunately, she didn't have to answer.

Alex was walking toward her.

"Lindsay, hi, what are you doing here?" Alex asked.

Lindsay's face hardened.

"I mean, nice to see you." He moved to her and offered his hand. They greeted with a limp handshake.

"Can I talk with you?"

Alex looked over to the receptionist, nodded to her, "Katie, I'll be in my office with Doctor Riccardi."

Several employees recognized her and smiled when eye contact was made but immediately huddled into gossip mode once they entered Francisco's office.

An awkward moment of silence began the meeting. Alex began first.

"I was shocked to learn about Andrew's passing. My condolences to you."

The awkward moment continued.

"Thank you, Alex. He still meant a lot to me. I came here today to seek some answers."

"Answers?"

"His death, Collette's return and her being missing now."

"That Detective was here, he told me. I don't get it."

"Neither do I. Karl, Detective Dieter, said there is a connection to work here. Some company. Do you know what I am asking?"

"I do. But, I'm not sure of the connection. The detective was looking into it," Francisco paused, "and maybe Collette was too."

"What do you mean?"

"Well, last time she was here she seemed to have an idea, a way to do something that she needed to do, to be a part of the investigation."

"What was that?"

"I don't know for sure, but maybe it has something to do with TB Inc. and that funny, little guy Winton."

"Winton?"

"Simon Winton. The detectives know all about that, I think. I know one thing for sure…"

"Yes?"

"When she left here she was revved up like a stock car."

Sergeant Griffon called Dieter's cell number from his desk in St. John.

"Karl, it's David Griffon, I have news for you."

"David, I hope it's good news. I could use something positive today."

"We can release the body any time now. Just need to know where to send it."

"David, it turns out to be a little tricky."

"How so?"

149

"Collette Riccardi has been kidnapped."

"What happened?"

"Not sure, still investigating."

"You sure she's been kidnapped?"

"Oh, yeah, very sure. Saw a video of her tied up."

"Hey man, what's going on with this case?"

"Working on it. Any leads to Andrew Riccardi's murder?"

"Maybe. Two teens came in about Andrew being murdered when the story hit the television news. They saw a man leave the water in full diving gear near where it happened. The girl said he looked suspicious, just a feeling she said. They gave a good description of the man and the rental car, but probably not a resident. Following up on that. We're finished with Andrew Riccardi down here, like to send him back, so tell me where to do it."

"I'll get back to you on that."

"Today would be good."

"Today, sure thing."

The first sensation Collette had after the sedative wore off was olfactory. A smell of coffee wrapped around eggs and bacon wafted to her nose. The second sensation was physical. She could move her hands and feet which were no longer bound. But the next sensation was visual, and it brought fear. Marco stood above her holding a tray of food as she lay on a comfortable bed. Frozen, she looked up at Marco.

"Breakfast in bed. How's that for service?"

Collette pushed herself back away from Marco, but the headboard stopped her progress. She sat upright.

"Let me go!"

"Eat something. Then we'll talk."

Collette folded her arms across her chest in defiance, but the smell of the food tempted her. She hadn't eaten in days and dehydration had set in. Marco bent toward her and she recoiled. He placed the tray on the bed.

"Eat. I'll be back, and we can talk."

He watched her all the way to the door, nodded and left locking the door behind him.

Collette pulled the tray toward her. There were no utensils, so she dug into the scrambled eggs with her hands, scooping up eggs with three fingers while taking a piece of bacon with the opposite hand. She ate rapidly ending when she had licked all the food from her fingers. A cup of black coffee lingered on the tray waiting to be held. Unsteady hands held the coffee mug luxuriating in its warmth. For a moment, after her first sip of the coffee, she sat back and relaxed. The moment was fleeting. She pushed the tray away and stood on unsteady feet. The hot coffee spilled on her hand, but she was unmindful of its heat. She walked to a curtained window and drew them back letting in the fullness of the sunshine. Her eyes, sensitive to the light, closed briefly. Opened, they saw a small manicured yard, heading toward a beach. Its waters were calm with only scattered white caps flopping onto the shore.

"Where am I?" to the empty room which only returned indifference.

She looked down from the window on the second floor onto a slate roof jutting out several feet. Beyond the roof, was an expansive driveway that held a small, blue SUV. Collette unlocked the window and tugged to pull it up. It gave no release.

"Let me out of here!"

She banged on the locked door until footsteps brought Marco to the door. He unlocked it and flung it open.

"No screaming." His stern face was serious.

He looked at the empty tray atop the bedcovers.

"Take a shower, calm down and we'll talk." He pointed to the small hallway leading to a door. "Go ahead, you'll feel better."

He took the tray and left locking the door once more.

151

Collette spun around once. The room was elegantly appointed. Lush beige carpeting, under her bare feet, spread across the room to the bathroom door. The queen-sized bed, its white down comforter over white sheets contrasted with the dark wood antique headboard, was centered between two antique nightstands each held matching lamps. The wall displayed three large murals of the ocean in bright, light colors. Under different circumstances she would have enjoyed the quaint elegance, but not under these.

She walked to the bathroom which continued the elegant antique theme. A large mirror topped the ivory colored sink. A woman's hairbrush and long comb, toothpaste and a toothbrush huddled next to each other. One lone ceramic drinking glass with an ocean motif painted on its face was placed by itself away from the others. Collette put the coffee mug down on the sink's counter. She sat to relieve herself. Next, she shed her clothes and stepped into the large updated shower deciding against the bathtub on legs. The hot water felt very good. She stood under the water feeling her muscles relax. Her eyes closed as the water cascaded onto her head and body. But her mood evaporated as visions of her capture returned and breathing became labored. She bent forward sucking in moist air then straightened stretching her arms upward expanding her chest. Tears formed and mixed with the hot water running down her face. Collette sobbed, then cried, finally losing control and collapsed to the floor with legs pulled into her chest and her head flopped onto her knees.

Chapter
26

"Where's the body going to be shipped?" Grover asked Dieter.

"Working it out now," he lied. In fact, there was no place but the morgue to send Andrew, but he knew that wouldn't sit well with Lindsay and Collette was out of the picture. He decided to ask Lindsay.

"What else?"

"Well, TB Inc. seems to be a shell company for someone or some company. I think for someone."

"Who?"

"This guy Simon Winton who works for Bertram Thompson seems to be the logical link, but..."

"What?"

"We haven't made a solid connection yet."

"Are you looking into Thompson?"

"No, should we?"

"Why not?"

"He's a billionaire, a public figure, in hiding anyway. Stays out of the light. What we do know is that he's eccentric but apparently clean."

"Clean? And a billionaire? Don't match. I'll make some calls to folks I know downtown and in finance. See what I can dig up."

"Good. Listen, Captain, I'd like to put eyes on Winton. Do we have detectives available?"

Grover shook his head with incredulity. "This case is growing each day. We got a dead body coming to NY, an officer on Collette's apartment, videos of her kidnapped body..."

"Moving, still alive..."

"...a billionaire in the mix, a shell company with no history."

"And the guys who stole the computers from two apartments."

"That too. What's happening with that?"

"Dead end, so far. The license plate was from an abandoned car we found in the Bronx. Still looking for the license plates. Probably in a dumpster. My guess is the car they used is registered but no way to know."

Grover reached for his phone, "I'm going to call some people, see what I can find, keep me up to speed."

Grover punched in some numbers on the desk phone as Dieter left the office.

He returned to his desk, looked around for detectives nearby and decided to call Lindsay. The call went to voicemail on her office phone which meant she was in session.

"Lindz, hope you're free and feeling hungry about eight tonight. I'm going to make a reservation at our place for dinner. Let me know."

Dieter was wrong about Lindsay working. She was on the phone with her father.

"Dead? Andrew is dead?"

"Lindsay, what happened?"

"A long story Dad. I guess I just wanted to hear your voice."

"Ok, then, how are you handling his death? I mean, I know you've both moved on and all, but ..." he searched for words that didn't come.

"I've been thinking about home lately. My high school days of all things."

"Yes..."

"Are you questioning yourself?"

"Dad, you always get to the point so fast."

"Can't help it, that's me. You, on the other hand, analyze things a lot. Sometimes, I thought, too much. Some things just are the way they are. Probably why you chose what you do. Helping people. We all question our actions, but you seek answers to our motives. Isn't that right?"

"Yes, all day long with my patients. They ask me why they do the things they do."

"And you try to help them discover the answers if you can."

"I try, but not always successfully."

"Nothing is always successful, Lindsay. Nothing. Especially my golf game lately." Dad chortled heartily.

A smile rose on Lindsay's face. She loved her Dad. When she and Andrew broke apart and were divorced she'd speak with her Dad. He was a good listener after a while. At first, he was the fixer, trying to solve all the ills that lay at her feet. Once he realized that was not what she needed, he learned to listen. She needed a safe place to vent. It wasn't easy to hear her cry. It cut into his heart. He did feel sorry for Andrew. He had liked Andrew at first. Good guy, smart guy and he seemed to love Lindsay. Athletic and successful too. But, later, he wanted to punch his lights out for his infidelity to his daughter.

"You still playing with your friends twice a week?" Lindsay welcomed the departure.

"Oh, yes, wouldn't have it any other way. Eighteen holes, weather permitting."

Lindsay noticed the red light on the office phone indicating a message had come on.

"Dad, I got to go. Thanks for chatting. Love you."

"Love you too, Doctor," more chortling.

Lindsay pushed the code to retrieve the voice mail. She listened to Dieter's voice which lately had become her anchor to reality. Dinner at eight? She checked her patient schedule. The last patient ended at eight. She had to see this patient. The next patient would arrive at any minute. Lindsay needed a bathroom break, so she sent a text to Dieter's cell asking to make it for nine instead. Then she quick-stepped into the bathroom.

Dieter arrived thirty minutes early to chat with Victor the restaurant's owner. They sat at the bar populated by Thursday night singles hoping for that someone special to arrive. Their friendship began with Victor's need for help. It lasted for more than ten years because of each man's loyalty to the other. Dieter would always have a table when he needed one with Lindsay.

"How is your lovely lady these Days?"

Dieter thought for a moment. "Always lovely but facing some difficult times."

Victor knew about difficult times. He had come to the United States from Romania after 911. They had little money but grand hopes. Hard work, scrimping on luxuries with which American television peppered the airwaves allowed him to sit at his bar in his restaurant with his eldest son at an American college while his wife kept a beautiful home in Flushing, Queens - the most diverse community in the United States.

"Ah, sorry to hear this," he waved the white-haired bartender over. "Top off my friend's drink, Petre."

"Of course, cousin." Petre gathered a bottle and poured a very generous amount of scotch.

"Okay, that's good. Thanks, Petre." Dieter's glass was half full when Petre topped it off.

"Of course, Detective. Anything for you. Isn't that right cousin?" Petre didn't wait for an answer. He attended to the others at the bar.

"He is right, you know. If there is anything I can do for you or Doctor Lindsay, I am at your service."

"I do know. She's just fine."

"Who are you two talking about?" Lindsay approached from the crowd.

Dieter rose, she greeted him with a kiss. She gave Victor two kisses, one for each cheek. Victor offered Lindsay his seat at the crowded bar.

"Thanks, Victor."

"I'll see to your table." A quick look at Dieter for agreement and he was gone.

"You look lovely."

"Oh, this old outfit," she joked. Lindsay had come directly from her home office, stopping only to freshen up her makeup and hair.

"Good evening Doctor. Wine tonight?" Petre asked.

"No thanks Petre, we're going to be seated first."

"Of course."

Right on cue, Victor arrived and took them to their table in a quiet section of the busy restaurant. A busboy arrived with water, bread and whipped butter.

"How was your day?"

"Better than Collette's." She was sorry the moment she said it. "I spoke with my Dad today. Felt the need for some Daddy-time. He made me laugh."

Dieter took her hand. "That was good."

"Yes, it was. So, what's up?"

"What do you mean?"

"I mean, you probably had something to tell me that was going to be tough and you picked Victor's place for the news." She held his hand tighter. "So...?"

Dieter smiled appreciating her keen powers of observation.

"The St. John PD is sending Andrew back..."

Lindsay frowned at the thought of his body being flown back to New York.

"I see."

"We don't know what Collette would want to do..."

Lindsay's eyes blinked confusion.

"We could send it to a funeral parlor..."

"It? When is *he* arriving?"

"Probably tomorrow or the next day at the latest."

A waiter brought a glass of wine for Lindsay and set it on the table. "Victor's compliments."

Lindsay took a sip, then a long drink. She cupped the glass in thought.

"Can we wait a little? I mean until we know about Collette."

She gulped the remainder of the wine and set the glass on the table.

"Sure, okay, I'll work something out."

Lindsay pleaded with Dieter, "The morgue?"

"No other choice, until we know about Collette."

Chapter
27

The call from Abu Mustafa's cousin initially scared him but eventually made him feel assured that all was going to be well. Overwhelming insecurity was present after his last encounter with his cousin. The anger and threats scared him almost to the point of running. But, running to what? Where could he go? He put his faith in his cousin's loyalty to him and their family. The phone call was cordial, almost like the old days. No threats causing anxiety.

The money that Abu had earned selling to the Turkish broker, Emre, afforded him minor luxuries that he now wanted to maintain. This was his motivation to continue working for Cousin. This would have to help overcome his fears.

Abu would serve his cousin's favorite tea and food. As children, they often ate dinners with the family, before the bad times changed their lives.

"Abu, may I come to see you today? I have a good bit of news for you."

"Yes, yes, of course."

They settled on midday for the meeting. Abu, never a good cook, went to the local market for kibbeh with bourghul. He added yogurt and dates but decided against rice. Simple would be fine.

"Abu, you honor me with such a meal," Cousin said, pointing to the table set with the food and hot tea.

"It is I who is honored that you have come to my home," pointing around, "such as it is."

The cousins ate, sipped tea and talked about old times with the family. Abu relaxed and slipped into familiar feelings about his cousin.

"Abu, I must apologize to you for the way I spoke last time we met. You are an innocent in this new world. I know this. You cannot be faulted for things beyond your knowledge." He sat forward, "But you must learn to be more aggressive with your sales. This Turkish man, Emre, is not the only one with whom we do business. He is shrewd. You must learn to be more shrewd."

"Yes, yes, I understand. You are correct. I am learning much from your teachings. I will do better if you give me another chance."

The words came out of Abu's mouth, but his heart still felt the fear that these meetings always brought. And yet, he wanted to please his cousin.

"Good, very good. I am here to give you another chance. I know you will do well."

Two days later, Abu was driving the familiar route to Gaziantep to meet with Emre. This time, he resolved, he would do better.

While Abu and Emre negotiated on the least significant of all the objects he had brought for sale, a man dressed as a beggar lay sprawled near Emre's car. He was unnoticed by the few pedestrians on the side street where Emre had always parked his car. No one noticed the small package he took from his jacket. No one noticed the bomb that he placed very gently attached to the undercarriage of the car. It would be triggered by the engine's start and detonate immediately.

Abu Mustafa steeled his back when he met Emre at a small coffee shop. I will not be outmaneuvered by this man, who is no better than me, he told himself.

As was their custom, they met, exchanged pleasantries and ordered coffee. Abu decided to focus on the coffee dismissing Emre's entreaties to get down to business. He liked the power he felt being in charge of the moment.

But, Emre, has used this tactic with others, so he sat back and waited.

"I drink tea at home," Abu declared to Emre. "Only here do I drink coffee. It is very good." He held the glass of coffee up in salutation.

"I'm glad you enjoy our Turkish coffee. We are known for this all over the world."

Abu Mustafa, however, could not outlast the Turkish buyer. His resolve diminished. Instead, he would take another tack. He looked at his watch.

"I have a long drive home and a busy evening."

He unfolded the small package and unwrapped the paper encasing a tiny statuette of a man with his hand on a sword still in its scabbard. Cousin had told Abu that the man was a warrior king from long ago. A man who conquered many lands and was known for his bravery. In fact, Cousin had no idea who this figure was nor if he truly ever existed.

"This man is a warrior king. See the scabbard holding the sword, ready for battle."

Emre smiled. "Yes, I can see it. Who is he? What kingdom did he rule?"

"His name is not known. Only his deeds. He ruled one kingdom in the south of Iraq many centuries ago. Legend has it that he had so many wives that his progeny lives today." Abu shrugged, underneath his façade, he felt good, proud of his negotiations.

"I'm not sure that I can sell him, this warrior king without a strong history behind him." It was Emre's turn to shrug.

Abu's heart fluttered. Cousin told him to be strong, be aggressive and most of all to wait for the moment to come that would bring the sale in his favor. He looked at his watch, shook his head, rewrapped the statue and stood.

"Perhaps another time."

Emre chuckled, "Sit down, sit down. We are just beginning. I see you have learned much since our last meeting."

Abu was flattered but suspicious. "If we are at an end to our meeting, then I must go. I will present the warrior king to my next buyer."

"Okay, okay, you win. Please, sit down."

Once Abu was seated, Emre asked, "How much are you asking?"

They negotiated for several minutes allowing Abu to feel he got the best deal. Emre knew that if he gave into a small loss of profit on this sale he would make it up on others. He'd let Abu win, this time.

When the two men left the small coffee shop, they were noticed by the beggar who held a position at the end of the narrow street where Emre's car was parked. He watched as the two men strolled to the car. Emre and Abu shook hands and Abu walked away while Emre fumbled with his car keys. Once the door was opened, he sat in the car reviewing the purchase, making mental notes about possible buyers.

The last thing he did on Earth was to start the engine, which ignited the explosive killing him instantly. A second, larger explosion followed when the gasoline ignited sending flames into the air. The first blast brought Abu to the ground at a safe distance from the car. The second caused bits and pieces of the car flying through the air. Several fell onto Abu as he lay curled in a fetal position covering his head and ears.

The crowd that emerged at the corner was soon met with a policeman who saw the carnage and ushered the people away. The beggar melted into the crowd invisible as all beggars are, watchful of the event that he had created.

Abu's ears were ringing, and his vision was blurry. He struggled to rise from the ground, the heat from the blaze pushing him away, toward the police.

The policeman moved to Abu and spoke, but Abu heard nothing except the ringing in his ears. His eyes searched the street, locked onto the car fully engulfed in flames. Abu never heard the siren from the local AMBULANS that had come to the scene. He was puzzled at the emergency personnel who escorted him into the ambulance and spoke to him in their native tongue. Soon, he lay quietly in the ambulance rocking side to side as it traveled the roads to a nearby hospital. By the time the ambulance reached the hospital, Abu had lost consciousness.

Abu Mustafa's cousin received the phone call for which he was impatiently awaiting.

"It is done," the voice of the beggar said.

"Both men?"

The beggar waited a moment too long.

"Both men?" Cousin's voice was filled with anger and grief.

"No. Only the driver, a little man. The other was injured and taken to the hospital."

Cousin ended the call. His fists pounded the thick wooden table, causing its contents to scatter and run from his force. He stopped only when the pain was too great.

Chapter
28

Collette dressed in the jeans and sweater provided by Marco. Socks and running shoes completed her ensemble. She wondered why she was brushing her wet hair. What difference does it make? *Am I going through the motions of life or is this my new life? The life of a captive is not for me. No.*

The bright room soaked up the ambient sun that intruded from a window facing the southwest. When she was finished dressing, combing and presenting Collette as she is now, she knocked at the locked bedroom door. She stood facing the door fully ready to meet anything that this man, this captor, brought.

She heard a key enter the lock, tumblers clicked, and the door opened. Marco stood in the doorway. Collette studied this man who had the power of life in his hands. He was taller than she, thin and young. His features were symmetrical allowing for a pleasant face when he smiled. Curly, tightly cropped, dark hair topped his head. Collette noticed he was very neatly dressed. Pants and shirt pressed. A whiff of men's aftershave greeted her. Strange. Weren't kidnappers supposed to be part of the great unwashed, the evil doers? Who is he? Why did he come to Simon Winton's assistance?

"You look well."

Collette didn't respond. She would stick to her plan to cooperate and get answers.

Marco looked at her seeking a sign that would give him an understanding of this woman. He already knew she was resilient. What more was she? What more can we learn from her?

"Would you like to leave this room?"

A little too quickly, "Yes."

"One rule and you may."

"One rule?"

"Yes. You must do everything I say. If I say *sit down*, you will sit down. If I say *stand*, you will stand. Understand?"

"You are in control."

"Yes, I am."

Marco stepped aside and waved her into the hallway that leads to a beautifully decorated beachfront cottage.

"Where am I?"

"Not important."

"Is this place yours? Simon Winton's?"

"Also, not important?"

Collette pretended to take in the room for its luxury. In fact, she was scouting it out for exits and entrances and windows that led out to the balcony. Where was the doorway to the balcony? An adjoining room? One door, farthest from the windows, was closed.

Marco pointed to a gleamingly white linen couch, "Sit down."

He walked to a similar chair between the couch and the closed door. Collette sat on the couch and Marco sat in the overstuffed chair.

"Why am I here? Why did you kidnap me?"

Marco merely looked at her.

"Why are you afraid of me?"

Marco flinched, and Collette saw it. He recovered and smiled.

"Believe me, we are not afraid of you. We are concerned about things you may know that are troubling to us."

"TB, Incorporated?"

"That is not him."

"Who?"

165

"Simon, that company is not Simon."

"Then it's you?"

"Me? No."

Collette stared at Marco fighting off the urge to leap at him like a leopard.

"Who killed my husband?"

"What? Your husband?"

"Yes, my husband, on our honeymoon. Andrew Riccardi. Someone killed him and now you kidnap me. Why did you kill him?"

Collette stood seething with anger and pain.

Marco bolted upright, "Sit down. Now." He remembered reading of Andrew's death by drowning. Was he really murdered?

Collette saw the confusion in Marco's eyes. She sat allowing for her breathing to return to normal.

Marco sat. He waited a moment, "What happened to your husband?"

"He was murdered, drowned while snorkeling."

"Lots of people die snorkeling."

"He was a competitive swimmer in college. The police said it was murder."

Marco rose and took out his cell phone. "Do not move." He walked to the farthest end of the room. His hand went to cover the phone and his whisperings to Simon, while his eyes never left Collette. She strained to hear but could not.

Marco ended the call and strode purposively to Collette. He stood over her. "Stand."

She stood, "What happened?"

"You're going back in there. I will get you later and we'll sort this thing out."

"This thing? You kidnapped me. Just let me go."

"Not now…"

Minutes later, Simon's sports car nimbly raced toward the Queens, Midtown Tunnel where he was met with a wall of traffic. His cursing to each car, truck, and soccer-Mom ladened mini-van that stood between him and his mission to get quickly to the Long Island's East End fell on deaf ears.

By the time Simon reached Exit 70 on the Long Island Expressway, he had been driving almost two hours and he had spoken to Marco three times.

"She thinks we killed him."

"*We* killed him? That's crazy."

"Simon! What the hell are we into?"

"Not us. It's got to be Bertram and that Turkish guy."

"Simon, this is serious. Maybe we should go?"

"Go? If we go it'll look like we killed him. No. We got to turn this thing back to Bertram."

"How?"

"Don't know."

Collette had been locked back in her room for almost three hours when Marco opened the door. Behind him stood an ashen Simon Winton. He moved around Marco and faced Collette.

"We have to talk."

Bertram Thompson met the swarthy man at the American Natural History Museum on Central Park West and 79th Street. He enjoyed the many exhibitions that heralded the mighty from centuries past. These were his idols as a child and now, that child still within Bertram longed for all the power that the ancient mighty enjoyed. His fantasies were fed by the antiquities that he bought via circuitous routes until they landed in his hands. His fortunes sated his need for money; but, his fantasies could not be sated. It was this unbridled passion that brought him to the museum.

The swarthy man waited patiently near a bank of elevators as people entered and exited. Bertram eyed him standing fifty feet away. When an empty elevator opened, the swarthy man entered and held the door for Bertram who scurried in before the doors closed.

"The Turkish Broker has been killed, sir."

Bertram had learned in his business negotiations to show no emotion.

"How?"

"Car bomb."

The elevator stopped and a mother with two young boys entered. The boys stared openly at the swarthy man. Bertram busied himself with his cell phone partially covering his face. The family left on the next floor.

"We have to clean things away. Understand?"

A fleetingly perceptible nod from the swarthy man ended the conversation. Bertram left as the elevator doors opened. The swarthy man stayed until the next floor where he left the elevator and took the stairs down to the building's exit.

Bertram strolled downstairs near the entrance of the Museum, where he turned left. He took the stairs down into the lower level and into the exhibits. There was where he had found the long gone Egyptian Gilded Lady exhibit. Her sarcophagus beautifully displayed in its full color intrigued him. He especially liked the forensic artist Élisabeth Daynès's rendering of the Gilded lady's bust which seemed to look directly at him with exotic dark eyes. Here she was, still important after many centuries. He was envious of her longevity and purpose. Anthropologists at the museum pored over her using a state-of-the-art CT scanner to see inside without disturbing her. She was important centuries ago and was still important, perhaps even more now.

"Cool, right, Mister?" A dark-skinned boy about ten asked.

Bertram looked down at the boy, but his gaze only returned to the Gilded Lady.

"She reminds me of my mother. A lot."

Bertram allowed a brief look.

"She is very pretty like my mother was."

Bertram turned to look at the boy. The boy's features were not unlike the Gilded Lady. He too had large dark eyes. His were filled with innocence but hers were strong, even distant, but compelling.

"You like the Gilded Lady?" Bertram asked.

"Oh, yes, a lot. We studied her in school and then my Dad took me here and I saw her face, like my Mom's. She must have been very special."

Bertram's gaze returned to the Gilded Lady.

"I suppose she was."

A tall angular, dark-skinned man walked to the boy, "Here you are. Come on we have to leave."

The boy turned and left with his father. Bertram never looked back at them; he was consumed with the Gilded Lady's eyes.

Anthropologists labored to learn who she was. Was she nobility? They thought she was not, but how did she get to be mummified? What set her apart from the others?

The Delamain de Voyage bottle in a Baccarat decanter sits inside a beautiful fan-shaped gift box styled after an old-school camera's bellows. Bertram liked that old school melding with his taste for Cognac. He once told a man that Cognac has substance. What he meant was that it was royalty like himself.

Bertram stood holding the crystal glass of Cognac in the center of his private room which held his special collections. The collections were special because he deemed them so. If he liked it, owned it and cherished it - it was special. The Cognac was special in the way it warmed his insides as it trailed down his throat into his stomach. It made him feel alive. It heightened his sensitivities to all things.

He took another sip as he began to walk around the room. Hard thinking, he called it, was necessary when difficult problems arose. The Turkish Broker's murder was a problem and it demanded hard thinking. It also demanded a calm, centered mind that could make hard decisions with full clarity. However, more information was necessary. Why was he murdered? Who murdered him? Am I in jeopardy? I can be protected. Jeopardy can easily be deflected to Simon. He and his lover are vulnerable. The swarthy man understood this.

Bertram needed to see the last coin he received; the bearded man of great significance would help.

Chapter
29

Abu Mustafa was taken by ambulance to Sani Konukoğlu Hospital's emergency rooms. There he was sedated and his minor head injuries from the blast were treated. It was determined he was not injured critically and he should be held until he was able to leave on his own.

News of the blast was on Turkish television. An American broadcast journalist, on assignment, decided to investigate the lone injured person taken to the hospital.

It didn't take much for Robert Collins from a world-recognized American television network to get permission to see Abu Mustafa. By the time Collins met Abu Mustafa he was sitting up on a gurney and sipping tea. A small bandage was on his upper right forehead resulting from the moment he turned to see the blast as bits of metal fell on him.

"How are you doing?"

Abu blinked with confusion.

"You were obviously there when the blast occurred?"

Abu's confusion turned to a harsh stare at the stranger. A pain shot to his temple and he winced. He placed the tea on the gurney.

"You okay?"

"Who are you?"

Collins took out his press card ID and held it for Abu to see.

"I heard about the blast and the death of the man in the car." Collins pulled out his cell phone and scrolled around. "Here it is, his name is Emre Arslan. Did you know him?"

Abu Mustafa's face clearly displayed recognition and fear.

"You knew him? Yes?"

Abu nodded.

"Were you with him? You know, before the blast?"

"I was."

"It could have been you also."

Collins knew there was a story with Abu Mustafa.

"What is your name?"

"Why? You don't need my name."

"Okay. It's easy enough to get…"

"I am Abu Mustafa."

"Thank you. I see you have a bruise. Can you tell me what happened?"

Abu fingered the bandage. He looked at his hand for blood.

"Were you walking with him before the blast?" Pressing.

"Yes, yes. We had just met for coffee nearby."

"I see. Two friends meeting for coffee?"

"No, no. Not friends. Not friends."

"A business meeting then?"

Abu looked very carefully at Collins. "What are you doing here with me? What are you after?"

"The truth. People want to know why this man was killed with an explosive that blew his car to pieces…and almost killed you. If the street was filled with people, more would have died. It's important."

Collins waited for the significance to sink into Abu Mustafa's brain. The response did not come.

"You could have been killed. Do you know why anyone would want to kill you?'

"Me? Kill me?"

"Maybe? Weren't you near his car."

"Yes, but…"

Abu's cousin's face flashed before his troubled mind. He remembered the rage and insults hurled at him after his return from meeting with Emre. Threats of death for being cheated by Emre resurfaced along with palpable fear. Abu swung his legs to the side of the gurney. He attempted to stand but fell forward. Collins grabbed him and held him upright.

"Hey, maybe you better stay here right now. Sit, please."

Abu sat because he couldn't stand but also because he hoped for a way out of his troubles.

"Can you help me?" Fear tortured his face.

"Absolutely, I will do anything you need."

Abu looked around at the hallway where his gurney was placed. Only staff and patients lined the corridor. He looked for men who didn't belong.

"I need to leave but I have nowhere to go here in Turkey. Will you help me?"

Collins offered his hand to help support Abu as he rose from the gurney and walked unsteadily with the journalist's help down the corridor and out of the hospital to his rental car. Abu entered the car and sat back with eyes scanning the area while they left the parking area and blended with traffic.

Twenty minutes later they entered the hotel room where Collins was housed for his assignment. The single room looked out over a busy street filled with early evening traffic.

Abu sat on a comfortable couch letting his legs flop forward as his head leaned back. His eyes wanted to close, but his mind wanted order restored.

"I'm going to order something to eat. What can I order for you?"

The slow service eventually brought the meal to the room for two. Collins decided he'd wait for Abu Mustafa to eat and gain strength before he asked questions. They ate in silence. When he had finished eating, Abu sat back, sighed and allowed resolve to take charge.

"I need your help. In exchange, I will tell you everything I know, but you must promise to protect me and relocate me."

Collins felt the journalist's surge of energy when a great story was at hand.

"I will bring all the resources of my network to your assistance. Take your time. Let's begin at the beginning."

"Okay, good. Let's begin."

"Who are you working for?"

Cousin sat passively contemplating his next directive to the man seated before him. He knew Abu Mustafa had survived the blast. He wasn't sure how to proceed nor could he afford to wait to learn about Abu's fate and whereabouts. The photo of Abu Mustafa that Cousin held weighed heavily on him. It displayed Abu smiling his innocent, childlike smile as though the world was a safe place. The photo, taken years before the difficult times, still looked like Abu. It would do for the man sitting before Cousin.

"This is the man."

"He is my target?"

Cousin glared at the man. "Yes, he is your target. Do not fail this mission."

The man stood, with the photo in hand, "I will not fail."

"I must know when it is done."

Chapter
30

Collette sat in the living room that the Hamptons crowd might call elegant chic. The brightly lit room looked out over the ocean less than a hundred yards away. The sun, setting in the west, colored the right side of windows with an orange glow. Some would say the setting was idyllic. Collette would disagree.

Marco and Simon sat on a white linen couch that sagged too deeply. They seemed smaller than the threatening duo who caused her such pain. She liked the visual of the two lovers sitting side by side shrunken into the couch. She sat tall in her chair facing them, separated by an ultra-modern glass coffee table.

"I can assure you that we did not kill your husband," Simon began.

Marco winced at the word *we* wishing he had never been a part of this dangerous situation. He had only wanted to help and protect his lover. Murder and kidnapping were never part of his desires to be with Simon. But, a protective reactionary moment for Simon brought him to this couch on this day that could never be taken back. He would try to be more self-protective.

"Really? Then who did? Did you hire those men in St. John who killed him and then came after me?"

Marco's face blanched all its blood. Simon's face reddened with anger.

"No, no. We had nothing to do with any of that. Nothing"

He looked at Marco for confirmation, but Marco looked away.

"No? Then why am I being kidnapped? What the hell are you afraid of?"

Collette's strength had returned, and she felt its power.

Simon took several moments to respond, mulling over each word that would show he too was a victim.

"My employer has been buying rare, stolen antiquities from the Middle East."

"That's illegal."

"Yes, yes, it is. We didn't know this."

Marco stood ablaze with anger. "We? I had nothing to do with these antiquities."

"I know. I meant, *I* didn't know this." Gazing up at Marco. "Please, sit down."

"What does this have to do with me and my husband?"

"I'm not sure. Someone alerted the killers that your company might have compromising information about the sale and payment for the antiquities."

"Someone? The Killers? Who would do that?"

"My employer is the only one with the direct knowledge of the sale and payment procedures that he had me put in place. He set me up. No finger points to him."

Marco felt a fleeting twinge of pity for Simon.

"Are you saying that your employer bought these antiquities, used you to buy and sell and he covered himself, and he's the one who had my husband killed?"

Collette stood abruptly causing Simon to react in kind. Marco didn't move.

"It makes the most sense to me. Believe me when I say that I had nothing to do with your husband's death. My crime was to cover the money he sent to pay for the items."

"You laundered the money for the sales?"

"Laundering? No, not mafia stuff like that."

"Worse! Terrorism financing!"

Marco rose and strode away from the couch. Simon looked at Marco but brought his attention back to Collette.

"Terrorism? Financing?"

"Yes, the sale of those stolen antiquities helps to finance terrorism. Millions and millions of dollars of antiquities sold to wealthy collectors all over the world are financing part of ISIS and other groups."

This was much worse than Simon already knew. He knew Bertram was illegally receiving coins and other objects, but he had no idea the money was going to ISIS until Marco brought it to his attention. Now Collette knew. Simon sat back down on the couch and seemed to shrink away. Marco noticed and sat next to him. He encircled an arm around Simon's shoulder.

Collette saw their compassion and knew this was her opening.

"Listen, Simon, we must turn everything around and aim it at your employer. He is the real criminal here."

"Yes, he is. Not me."

Collette took charge of the moment. She rose and strode back and forth as she had seen Andrew often do in meetings.

"The first thing we must do is find out about TB Incorporated. That must be the link back to your employer."

Simon's shoulders sunk.

"No, it is a direct link to me."

"You?"

"I set up TB Incorporated to pay for the sales, so my employer wouldn't know I was paying in advance. He refused to pay until the items arrived at his satisfaction. But, I had to pay the broker in Turkey before the items could be shipped."

"So, you set up the company, paid for the items and then he paid you?"

"Yes, he gave me the money."

"And you put it into TB Incorporated?"

Simon looked at Marco for support.

"Simon put most of it there since the price TB Incorporated paid was always less than the amount he told his boss."

"You skimmed money from the sales?"

Marco looked at Simon for his response.

"He has so much money. Billions. I thought there was something unusual…he didn't want to know about the transactions, the correspondence and all. He was adamant each time I made the mistake of talking about where or who it came from. Don't you see? I had no choice."

"So, you had no choice but to steal from your employer because you felt…what?"

"I felt I deserved the money. I deserved it for the risk I was forced to take."

"You were not forced. You made a choice. A bad choice."

"This is not news to us about ISIS," Marco began. Simon glared at Marco.

"Simon, it's time for the truth. You can't keep hiding."

Marco walked around to Collette.

"Simon is the victim. He didn't know that the money was or may have been going to ISIS or whatever group is behind this."

"He didn't know?"

"No, I told him that there may be a connection to the sales."

"You? How would you know? Were you involved?"

Simon rose, "No, he acted on my behalf when we took your computers on a tip that your company found a connection to the sales.?

"You! You took the computers? That's why Andrew was killed?"

Simon fell silent. Marco couldn't.

"Someone thought there was a connection to them that your company, maybe your husband, maybe you had found. They acted on that possibility. I only found out afterward…after I saw the computers' hard drives. By then, it was all about covering the tracks to Simon…nothing more."

"Until you knocked me out and kidnapped me."

Collette struggled with her next words. "I'm leaving. You too are criminals and will end up in jail."

Both men stood. Marco moved between Collette and the door. He looked at Simon for directions.

"You're not going anywhere until we reach a decision."

"To kill me too?"

"No. A decision to untangle us...me from all this and help you get the person who killed your husband."

"That's what the police will do."

"Not without our help. There is absolutely no connection to Bertram without my help."

"What about the stolen antiquities? That is evidence. That is proof."

"Yes, it is, but only of the illegal purchases...not the murder. Isn't that what you want...the murderer?"

Simon pointed to Collette's chair. She eyeballed him with a complete ferocity which he ignored. He pointed to the chair again,

"Please, sit down, let's figure this out."

Chapter
31

Dieter reached the Office of the Chief Medical Examiner on East 29th Street hours after Andrew Riccardi had arrived. Captain Grover had pulled myriad strings to get Andrew there, even temporarily.

With his Detective Shield displayed on his jacket, Dieter entered the lab where Andrew was stored.

"Detective, I'm Susan Dolan, Forensic Lab Administrator. Follow me."

She walked down a string of rooms and entered one. It was lined with chambers housing bodies. After I quick look at her notes, she took him to one, opened the case and displayed Andrew's wrapped body. A tag listed his name, age, and New York City address.

Dieter could tell from the wrapping that Andrew was not whole any longer. The funeral, if there was to be one, would have to be closed casket.

"The relatives might want to think about cremation for this man, Detective. Ocean flesh eaters have disfigured his body. It's kind of unusual that an officer comes down here. Are you related?"

"No, I know two of the deceased's family."

Strange he thought. Two of the deceased family members. Only one may be alive.

"Are they going to arrange to have him moved soon?"

"Yes, some complications, but very soon."

"Good, we're a little full these days. Unfortunately, we'll need the space."

Dieter's phone chirped.

"Dieter. How long has he been gone? All right, stay on it. I'll meet you there in thirty minutes."

"Work, Detective?"

"Yes, I will help sort this out."

Dieter drove uptown to Simon's building where he met Detective, JB McClure at the concierge desk in the posh lobby of the residential building where only multi-millionaires lived.

"Karl, this is Gabe. The man's the front desk."

Dieter eyeballed Gabe, aka Gabriel Rojas, a prideful middle-aged man who took his position very seriously. Gabe's attention was diverted to an elegantly dressed woman with an older man who strode to the desk.

"We need a cab, Gabe." They left and waited at the exit doors as Gabe picked up his phone and called the outside doorman.

"The Johnson's need a cab right away." His attention returned to the detectives.

"How long has Simon Winton been gone?"

"Hard to say. I came on early this morning. He was not at home yesterday for a part of the day."

"How do you know he wasn't here part of the day?" Dieter asked.

"His employer asked for him."

Dieter and McClure exchanged looks.

"Is his employer here now?"

Gabe sighed reluctantly. "His employer is a very private man, Detective. He would not be happy if he knew that I mentioned him."

"He won't know. But if you don't tell me whether he's here or not, I will not be happy."

Another sigh and a definite change in his posture from confident to vulnerable became evident.

Bertram Thompson never suffered intrusions from irrelevant sources. When Gabe called to announce that two of New York City's Detectives would like to speak to him, he normally would have been dismissive. However, circumstances have changed, and he allowed the detectives to ascend to his world.

Dieter had seen opulent apartments before, but McClure hadn't. When the elevator deposited them to a large foyer surrounded by statues of great men from centuries past, McClure stared openly. A male servant appeared and signaled them to follow him. They were taken to an office whose windows faced east. The rising sun shone brightly into the room and into the eyes of the detectives. Bertram Thompson stood facing them with the sunlight at his back framing him in its light.

"Detectives, what brings you to me?"

Dieter smiled at the comment. "We actually came to see Simon Winton, your employee. But he's vanished."

"Vanished? That seems mysterious."

"Yes, he has been gone for more than twenty-four hours. Didn't you know?"

"Detective, I don't keep my employees on a leash." A smugness wrapped around his face.

"I see, he's got free reign around here then."

It was Bertram's turn to smile. "Not exactly, but he is available when needed."

"How is he needed?"

Bertram stepped away from the light which shone directly into the detective's eyes.

"He is my personal representative. He takes care of many of the day to day things...ordinary things."

"Like?"

"Like my personal affairs, detectives. Personal things. What do you want with him? We went over this before."

"We're investigating a string of events that might be connected to him."

"Events?"

Dieter liked the hook that Bertram had taken. He'd reel him in slowly.

"Those are personal to him at this point. But, one bit of confusion might relate to you."

"Me? Really? I don't think so."

"You're probably right. It's a company that he's related to."

"If he's related to this company, I'm sure I don't know it."

"TB Incorporated, it's called. Then you don't know this company?"

Bertram's face screwed up in faux thought.

"No, never had any business with this company."

McClure moved forward, "It's close to your name. TB reversed is BT, Bertram Thompson. Strange coincidence."

Bertram resorted to the tone when speaking to an underling who has stepped beyond his boundaries.

"That is quite a stretch, Detective."

"Is it?" Dieter asked.

"Yes, it is. I have no business connections with Simon. He is my employee. I don't mingle the two worlds."

Dieter took a long look at Bertram Thompson seeking something in his demeanor. The light from the sunshine defeated a clear visual.

Dieter pulled a card from his jacket pocket and offered it to Bertram who looked down at his desktop. He placed the card in the center of the desk.

"Call me if you remember any connections to TB Incorporated."

"There is definitely no connection to that company."

In the elevator ride down, McClure offered, "He knows more than he's saying."

"Yes, he does. We've got to find Simon Winton."

183

Simon was holding on to every bit of focus he could muster. Too much had come undone. He was vulnerable and scared. Fearful for his future. Jail would never be an option, he thought. We could run to another country. Hideaway from the possibilities that lurked around the corner. *I could run away. Leave Marco. He's done nothing…really. Taking Collette. That would bring him trouble. We could run. Money is no longer a problem; so much hidden and safe.*

"Simon are you all right?"

"Yes, fine. Just thinking is all."

"Lots to think about. I'm not sure we can trust her. She blames all that's happened to her on…"

"Me? Yes, I know."

"If we let her go…."

"What are you saying? Kill her? Are you crazy?"

"No, not that. But, what? We have to find a way to incriminate her too."

"Makes no sense."

"Maybe not, but what else do we have?"

Simon knew she was a liability. However, he also knew that he needed her to point the finger at his boss. Maybe she could help through the accounting company and his holdings. But, how? All the possibilities were far above his head.

Collette emerged from her bedroom.

"I have an idea. It's a little tricky, but it might work."

Simon and Marco exchanged questioning looks.

"Your boss has to be spooked enough to do something foolish."

"Never going to happen. He has no feelings, no fear. He thinks he's the king of his world."

"What are you thinking?" Marco asked.

"I'm telling you both. He can't be spooked." Simon walked away from Collette.

"What is the one thing he protects most of all?" she challenged.

184

"One thing? There is only one thing - himself. Nothing else matters."

"Exactly. And if he is threatened publicly?"

"Publicly? What the hell are you talking about?"

Collette walked to the window to arrange her next words.

"Okay. There are news outlets that would pick up a story about a New York billionaire who is buying stolen antiquities from ISIS and hiding from the public."

"Is he hiding them?" Marco asked Simon.

"Yes, probably. They get delivered, but what he does next I don't know. I mean he always cuts me off when I mention the buyer or anything that could hurt him. Maybe he doesn't really know."

"Don't be naïve. He knows exactly what he put you up to do for him. He knows the risk of buying from ISIS. His reputation as a businessman would be ruined."

Simon laughed. "Do you think he's the only one buying these objects?"

"No, there is a worldwide market for these artifacts, I'm sure. What about linking the purchases to my husband's murder? Would that get his attention?"

"Yes, but we don't know if he was involved?"

"Don't we? Let's lay it at his doorstep anyway. Listen, I can go to the media…"

"No! What about us?" Marco barked. "You can't go to the media."

"I can. I can call into a network station in New York City from here. You can hear everything I say."

"He won't hear it," Simon said.

"He will when the media comes knocking at his door."

"What about us?" Marco asked.

"What about you?"

He steeled himself, "We kidnapped you."

She paled, "I know you did, but I'll say that I never saw the kidnapper's faces. You can hear me say it. Leaving you out of it."

"I don't get it. How is this helpful?" Simon whined.

"It will put the spotlight on him. The police will get involved directly. The story will be a daily event on all the networks and cable outlets. Don't you see? It puts him where he should be…under the microscope."

"How do I stay out of it?" Simon was not convinced. "I accepted the packages. I met with a scary guy at my apartment."

Marco flashed Simon an incredulous look.

Simon returned Marco's puzzled look. "Not like that. I collected the boxes and gave them to my boss. That's all…"

Marco shrugged, "Okay, how do we protect Simon. This doesn't sound good."

Silence surrounded the trio. Marco searched and found a decanter of liquor in the bar. He poured himself a drink and downed it quickly.

"Simon, you want one?"

Simon didn't answer. He sat on the couch, head bowed in thought.

"I'll have one," Collette said.

Marco pulled another glass and poured a little into it.

"More."

He added to the drink which she took, but only sipped gratefully. Her eyes closed, allowing a temporary escape.

"I don't like it. He'll find some way to blame it on me. He's a convincing liar." Simon sat shaking his head. "I don't like it."

Collette took advantage of the moment.

"How could you know how he set you up? You were doing your job…for him. Making things easy for your rich, entitled boss. That's what we all do, isn't it? We work for the rich. We protect the rich and they give us pennies."

"She's right, Simon."

"There comes a time when we must fight back."

Simon stood, "You don't understand! Neither of you. I can't go to jail. I can't." Simon walked deliberately to the hallway bathroom. He closed the door and locked it with a resounding click.

Marco went to the door, "Simon, are you okay?"

No answer. Marco tried the doorknob. He used two hands to try and turn it open. He banged his shoulder into the door, again and again.

"Help him. He might hurt himself."

Marco banged his shoulder into the door repeatedly, fully focusing on Simon.

Collette raced to a door, opened it and ran down the stairs through a large living area which led to the front door. She opened it and ran for her life.

Chapter
32

Dieter pored over online business news stories heralding Bertram Alan Thompson's success in hotels, transportation, and technology. Thompson Suites was a small chain of hotels aimed at vacationing families. Although Bertram had no interest in families doing anything, an advisor had argued that he needed this chain to help rebrand him from elitist businessman to a friendly entrepreneur who liked children. Nothing could be further from the truth. Bertram had no feelings about children. His only connection was his fascination with Batman. When he was a kid he became, at first, enamored with the capes and masks that allowed him to step into the fantasy world of power and invincibility. Later it was the secrecy and power that washed over him in all things that he did. It allowed him to move forward with all projects without regard for anything but his desired results. *Win at all costs* was his inner mantra.

The stories outlining his businesses discussed his keen mind for growth areas in technology. He invested in start-up technology companies that some called foolish. Their success proved the naysayers wrong while lining his pockets with millions. Transportation was a no-brainer for Bertram who knew that people liked shiny new cars with lots of gadgets. He invested in gadgets and international car manufacturing. Millions were made from a new device that enabled windshield wipers to clean away any built-up grime. It didn't work, but the advertising campaigns around the world made it sell. The message, he learned, always outweighed the product.

"What are you doing, Karl?" McClure asked.

Dieter broke away from the computer screen which had taken him into an hour of research.

"This is one smart guy."

"Thompson?"

"Yeah."

"Did you find a connection to TB Incorporated?"

"No. Doesn't mean there is none."

"Right."

"Funny, his big money colleagues don't seem to talk about him, there's nothing by other billionaires saying he's a good guy, or a bad guy or even a good businessman."

"No good old boys club connections?"

"Fellow billionaire, Arthur Carfaro, once answered a journalist's question about Bertram by saying that he was probably a private guy."

"Probably?"

Dieter shrugged. "He never married, father and mother died in their late fifties in an auto accident. No siblings. An uncle, on his mother's side, died ten years ago. That's it."

"Women?"

Another shrug from Dieter.

"High end paid escorts?"

Dieter looked at McClure. "Worth a look."

"Ok, will do."

Dieter rose and stretched his aching back. He walked to the coffee pots where Captain Grover was pouring a cup.

"Karl, how's it going with Batman?"

"In circles. It's almost like he doesn't exist."

"Oh, he exists, we just have to dig up more stuff."

"Can you help?"

Grover poured lots of sugar into his coffee and then a drop of milk. He looked at Dieter.

"You mean my friends in finance, right?"

"Well, yeah, you know people talk here."

"Man, people talk everywhere." Grover chortled, sipped some coffee then added more sugar.

"You know a guy?"

"Yeah, I know a guy...I'll give him a call."

"Thanks, Captain."

"Listen, Karl, I've been thinking about what you said about moving on...retiring and all. The more I think about it, the more I'm going to try and talk you out of it. We need you here. Hell, I need you here...but you know that. Right?"

Dieter chuckled, "Bringing down the curtain of guilt?"

Captain Grover choked on his coffee while suppressing a laugh before his expression morphed to serious.

"If that's what it takes."

"Hey, Karl, phone call," McClure shouted from his desk.

"To be continued," Captain Grover stated.

Dieter quick stepped to his phone, "Detective Dieter."

He listened scribbling down notes standing over his desk.

"Thanks, Sergeant be there asap." He hung up the phone.

"Be where?" McClure asked.

"Montauk Precinct. Collette has been found. That was a Sergeant Coyne, East Hampton Town Police. She's all right. Give me a minute to make one call."

"Sure, whenever you're ready."

Dieter took out his cell and punched in Lindsay's cell number. When she didn't answer, he began a voice mail, "Collette's been found. I'm leaving for Montauk to get her now."

He hung up the phone. McClure followed him out of the station to the parked cars.

McClure asked. "Was that Lindsay you called?"

"Yes."

Collette sat in an uncomfortable chair switching positions, seeking comfort in the Montauk sub-station where the police officer had taken her. She had run from the house, along private uninhabited beach front, finally feeling safe enough to seek the main road. She walked up to a hilly, winding road where a few cars went by. Since she didn't know what car to look out for she didn't wave anyone for help until she saw a woman in a minivan. The woman stopped when Collette jumped up and down waving her arms frantically.

"Hey, you all right?" Constance Hebert asked from an open window.

"No, no I'm not."

Nurse Hebert had just finished a shift at The East Hampton Healthcare Center and was heading home to bed.

"I need the police. Can you help me?"

"Get in," Constance said.

She drove Collette to the Montauk Station listening to Collette's retelling of her ordeal.

"You're going to be all right. Sergeant Coyne is on duty now. I know him. He will take care of you. Are you hurt? Injured?"

"No, just want to get away from them."

Collette turned to Constance, a plump fifty-something woman with a no-nonsense attitude, and she felt secure for the moment.

"Thank you for stopping...for saving me."

Collette slumped forward into unconsciousness.

The three-hour drive to Montauk frustrated Dieter and McClure. Once they left the Long Island Expressway and eventually reached the two-lane roads heading out to Montauk they fell behind local slow-moving traffic. Traffic slowed further through the towns of Bridgehampton, Easthampton, Amagansett leading to Montauk.

The police sub-station was a series of small connected portable buildings topped by solar panels. An American flag waved in the wind.

"Different from our house," McClure observed.

"Come on, let's get inside."

They entered the building and scanned the space. A middle-aged officer sporting a slightly bulging midsection walked over to them.

"NYPD? I'm Sergeant Coyne."

He stuck out his hand to Dieter then McClure.

"Where is she?" Dieter asked.

"She's resting in our coffee room. There's a couch back there. Follow me."

They walked into the room where Collette lay on a couch. Her eyes were closed. Dieter noticed that she looked peaceful.

"How is she?" he asked Coyne.

"Okay now. She was passed out when she arrived. We gave her something to eat and water. I guess she's okay under the circumstances."

"What about the kidnappers?"

"She told us the whole story. We checked out the place based on her description and simple direction to a beachfront house."

"Empty?"

"Oh yeah, but they left in a big hurry that's for sure. I called for forensics folks who went over and are probably still there."

Collette awoke to see the trio standing a short distance away. She rose quickly, stumbled slightly and righted herself.

"Detective, hello."

Dieter walked to Collette, she straightened and attempted a smile.

"How are you?"

"Fine, no…okay, I guess."

"Let's sit down."

Dieter motioned to McClure toward Sergeant Coyne.

"Sergeant, will you get me up to date?" McClure asked.

"Yeah, sure, come to my desk."

They left the small coffee room. Dieter and Collette sat on the well-worn leatherette couch.

"Who kidnapped you?"

"Simon Winton and his partner Marco."

He thought it was finally going to get around to some people directly involved in the murder. Dieter took out his notepad.

"Take your time. Start when they first kidnapped you."

Collette did exactly that. She detailed each moment of the kidnapping, the place in the basement where she was tied and all the following events and their discussion about Andrew's murder. The fact that Collette believed they did not kill or have Andrew killed didn't persuade Dieter. He'd get a warrant for Simon's apartment and find out about his partner Marco. He knew they were probably gone. He also knew they'd be found. And then there's Batman.

The call that Dieter had been expecting rang with Lindsay's signature ring. He stepped away from Collette.

"Hi, you got my message, right?"

"Yes, yes. I had an emergency with a patient and just listened to the message. Is she all right?"

"Yeah, pretty much. Talking with her now. I'll get back to you. Okay?"

"Yes, and thanks for the heads up."

Dieter smiled, "Heads up? You're doing cop-speak now?"

"Shut up," she teased. "See you tonight."

Lindsay was relieved that Collette was alive. Death had been stalking her for far too long. It was beginning to be part of her life and she vowed to fight it off. Her time with *my Karl*, as she called him, was filled with many things that life had not brought her until they met. Her emotions overflowed, and she understood their effect as never before. It would help her empathize and understand more deeply the needs of her patients. But, her mind, after Karl's phone call, focused on Collette who was safe again. She wondered whether Karl would be able to reach the bottom of the case and find Andrew's murderers, and why he was killed.

Chapter
33

Simon drove his sports car at high speeds over the winding roads out of Montauk away from the Route 27 which connected each town throughout the Hamptons. He decided to snake his way back to the Long Island Expressway and East to New York City where he would get all the money he stashed at his late mother's house. There he secreted information for foreign bank accounts including his fake passport.

"We'll be okay, I promise. We must get out of the country. Where is your passport?" Simon asked.

"Passport? I don't have a passport. Never left the country." Marco responded accusatorially.

Simon knew Marco would now be a burden. As much as he came to rely on Marco, Simon knew he could find another Marco wherever he landed. Money could buy anyone.

"We'll work it out and get you a passport."

Simon glanced at Marco whom he had almost loved. His need for himself always topped loving another person. Marco had come the closest. Not even his mother or sister achieved love from Simon. His father, gone before he was able to walk, was never part of his life. He reached out a hand to Marco to seal his loyalty. As Marco took his hand and looked at Simon, eyes meeting, a car slammed into the rear of the tiny luxury sports car.

"What the...?" Marco yelled.

Simon looked into the rear-view mirror to see a large black SUV as it slammed into his car. He sped up and so did the SUV.

"What's he doing?" Marco screamed. "Is he drunk?"

"No. He's come for us. Hang on."

Simon pressed the gas pedal and tried to maneuver the small, winding two-lane road. He slid into the oncoming lane several times but had to retreat as a lone oncoming car cursed him. The black SUV rammed his car each time he had to retreat to his lane and slow down. Simon fought to control the wheel while his eyes switched from the road ahead to the rear-view mirror. He thought he had seen the face of the driver before. Simon slowed on a very winding portion of the road. The SUV slammed into him, pushing his car until it left the road, taking flight along the road's edge that fell off ten feet. The sports car hit the decline, flipped and rolled into trees and brush. The SUV stopped, blocking the view of a car that drove by in the opposite direction but allowing the driver to observe the sports car. When the car had passed, Simon's car exploded into flames. The swarthy man checked his rear-view mirror and drove off leaving the road empty and the nearby woods in flames.

Bertram Thompson's private cell number rang. He answered the cell number that he'd been anticipating.

"It's done."

"Are you sure?"

"Yes, very sure."

Both men hung up.

The sports car's flames began to engulf the low brush that populated the woods near the road. It was spread to other trees by the gasoline that washed over the area surrounding the car. A well-worn pickup traveling on the opposite lane, pulled over to see the car in the center of the inferno. He jumped out of his truck and approached the edge of the road, stopping when the heat pushed him back. He entered his truck, put on the flashers and phoned

911. By the time the fire trucks arrived on the scene, several cars had stopped along the road to witness the blaze. Three teens who stopped to gawk took out their cell phones and took videos which they immediately posted to a social media site. Local police blocked the area causing consternation to drivers who had to seek alternate, out of the way, routes to their East End destinations.

The black SUV reached the Long Island Expressway heading west and joined the traffic at a legal speed. No drivers noticed the front of the SUV's bumper damage. The swarthy man decided he was hungry and would stop to eat somewhere near Long Island MacArthur Airport, far away from Simon's car.

Dieter and McClure drove west on Route 27 missing the traffic caused by the accident on a northern road which increased traffic for Route 27 going east.

"Can we stop soon? I need a restroom." Collette asked.

They pulled into a nearby fast food restaurant. She went into the lady's room while McClure waited at the outside door. Dieter called Lindsay.

"Hi, how is she?" Lindsay asked.

"She's fine. We stopped for a bathroom break. How are you?"

"Me? I'm fine. Is she hurt physically?"

"Doesn't seem to be."

Collette exited with McClure leading the way. Dieter saw them.

"Lindz gotta go." He ended the call.

A team of East Hampton Town Police moved through the rooms of the beach-front house where Collette had been held. They found the clothes she wore when kidnapped, dirtied from the concrete floors. A soiled blouse was atop a bra and panties. Scuffed low flat shoes were piled nearby. The team collected the towels, and bedding for evidence to be examined later. Glasses in the upstairs living area were retrieved, placed in plastic bags and tagged. The photographs taken earlier would detail the position of each item found.

The house they quickly determined was owned by Bertram Alan Thompson of Manhattan.

"Who is this guy?" Officer Angelo Franzese asked

"Beats me, probably another super rich guy from the City." Officer Bradford said.

Both shrugged and moved on.

"Looks like no one has been here for a long time."

"Yeah, the last time neighbors saw a car here was more than a year ago."

"It's good to have money," Officer Franzese mused.

"You got that right."

The officers went to the three-car garage which was pristine. Its painted floor had no sign of a car ever having been inside. Interior shuttered windows were closed.

"Empty, nothing here, probably never been used. Weird?"

The officers walked to the rear of the house to observe an empty patio facing the ocean.

"No patio furniture. Not even a barbecue. Nothing back here too."

"Strange," Franzese said. "If I owned this I'd be here all the time."

"Man, this guy must have tons of money to let this place sit empty like this."

"Wasn't empty when he kidnapped that lady."

"No, it wasn't."

"Who is she?"

"No idea."

Chapter
34

Captain Grover and his longtime friend Patrick Ferguson, Vice President at Gleason Capital, were seated at *Florianópolis,* a new trendy, Brazilian restaurant near Ferguson's midtown office. A lone guitar player offered a light background of music for the happy hour crowd that had begun to assemble. Harried employees of banks, financial companies, and law firms assembled regularly to reduce stress and enjoy the Brazilian style ambiance.

"James, this guy Thompson is a real mystery, even for the folks who do business with him."

"How do you mean?"

"Well, it seems he's given up all the daily decisions to his Chief Operating Officers, his COOs."

"He's not a hands-on guy?"

"He was until a couple of years ago. Actually, he let out the power slowly, but essentially, the daily decisions are made by his people."

"Is that unusual?"

"For a guy like he used to be, it is very unusual."

"Okay. What does it mean?"

Patrick sipped his drink. "Maybe he has other interests."

"Interests? You mean like new companies, abroad somewhere? The last trips he took were to the Middle East and Turkey. What business could he have there?"

Patrick leaned into the center of the table. Grover followed his lead.

"Some of my investors have been interested in buying things from there. Ancient coins and the like. James, these men are interested in buying bits of history not for its history, but for its potential value. They ask me if it's a good investment. I really don't know the law."

Patrick sat back.

"The thing is, some of it is legal, some not at all legal and some in a gray area. The FBI has set up a division to investigate."

"Yes, I know. Did any of these investors buy…?"

"You know, once I told them it was risky, they backed off…I think."

"But, you're not sure?"

"Not really. These are very independent minded men. You don't get to be millionaires, even billionaires without cutting corners."

Captain Grover needed all the information he could get from Patrick Ferguson. Dieter's case could be that one giant step up, something he's longed for since the early days on the beat. When he was a kid playing basketball with much shorter students in elementary school, he knew he was special. Later, in high school, he proved his worth on the court which translated into a college scholarship to a Division I team. His college basketball career ended when he broke his ankle in a practice session. With his scholarship lost he couldn't afford to stay away from home. He returned to New York City and entered Brooklyn College where he studied in the School of Business. Upon graduation and the realization that he was not interested in the slow pace of growth that he saw, he entered the police force. It came at a time when he was considered a positive attribute for NYCPD's department. He rose quickly from officer to sergeant and captain. Most of all, he enjoyed the successes that had eluded him at college. He planned a career that would take him to the heights of NYCPD and perhaps more...the New York City Mayor's office.

"Why are you asking about Thompson? He's pretty much a recluse these days. Not much in the game...."

Captain Grover sipped his drink seeking time to answer his friend without seeming deflective.

"We're looking at one of his employees who is involved, we believe, in some shady business."

"You see, that's what I mean. He's divorced himself from business."

"Yes, maybe, you're right." Captain Grover needed to change the subject. "So, when are we going to a Knicks basketball game?"

"It's been a while. I still have season tickets. You tell me who you want to see."

They returned to talk of basketball and old times. But, Captain Grover was waiting to hear from Dieter about his trip to Montauk and the kidnapped woman.

Dieter had insisted that Collette is checked out in a hospital against her wishes. She went along and sat waiting for the doctor's examination. Doctor Gilbert Amundsen, on duty in the emergency room, was a young man from Sweden who studied medicine in the States. In his last year at the hospital, he was planning to enter private practice. After the examination, he spoke with Collette and then to Dieter in private.

"She is bruised, but remarkably healthy and slightly dehydrated. No sign of sexual assault. Some trauma to her head. Basically, she's okay. However, she might want to see a therapist to help her deal with the trauma she's been through. I can recommend a doctor if you need advice."

Dieter shook his head, "No, I know someone and so does Collette."

Nurse Tabitha Jackson came to Doctor Amundson, "They need you in another room. Okay?"

Amundson shook hands with Dieter and followed the nurse to the next patient.

Dieter took out his phone and called Lindsay.

"Lindz, hi, she's all right. Doctor checked her out in the emergency room. I'm going to bring her to you, with an officer to watch over things. Okay?"

"Of course, I'll cancel my last appointments…if I can. Are we in danger?"

Dieter didn't have the answer. Was Lindsay in danger too? If she were to be near Collette, then probably.

"An officer will be with her at all times…I'm sorry that you're in the middle of this; but, I need your help."

Lindsay felt a slight rush of pride mixed with growing anxiety. She was the one who leaned on *her Karl* for support when things were rough. His presence was often all she needed to regain control of roiling emotions. Andrew's death brought more to her plate than she'd ever felt. Even the murders by Jonathan paled with the ramifications and feelings since Andrew was murdered. When Collette showed up at her door, a new whirlwind of emotions engulfed Lindsay. One question centered the storm. Why was Andrew killed?

Norbert Billings took the opportunity to check with the gaggle of police outside the house next door in Montauk. He walked the several hundred yards to the stone packed driveway where several East Hampton police vehicles were parked.

An officer stationed at the door approached Billings, "This is a crime scene, sir. Do you have business here?"

"Officer, there has been a small SUV parked on the road near the driveway to my house for a few days. Just sitting there. Thought I'd tell someone…since I saw the police cars, I came here." Billings stood, palms upright. "That's it, officer."

"I'll have someone check the car. Can you describe it?"

"Yes, small, blue SUV."

"Do you have the license plate numbers?"

"Ah, no, but you can't miss the car. It's the only one there."

Billings walked away feeling that he wasted his time. He decided to call the local television station. When he returned home, he spoke to a young female voice. He relayed the message about the car and the crime scene next door.

Forty minutes later a local television reporter and cameraman pulled up the driveway as the police cars prepared to pull away. Sandy Campbell, newly out of the Newhouse School of Journalism, approached an officer asking to speak on camera. Billy, her cameraman was eager to take a video but held off.

"Sorry, we are in the middle of an investigation," the officer responded.

"What happened here?"

"Still under investigation." He walked off.

"Officer, please, can't you tell me what it's about?"

He walked back to Sandy, "Okay, there's been a report of a kidnapping here. More than that, I can't say." He smiled at Sandy and walked away.

"Wow, kidnapping. Billy, take a video of the house, the police cars and then we'll go find that blue SUV the caller talked about."

In the car, on the way back to the television studio Billy asked Sandy, "You think this has anything to do with one of those super rich people who are out here all the time? I mean, that would be one hell of a story, right?"

Sandy considered the question and the possibility that she'd be seen by the networks and maybe get an early jump on her career.

"I'm going to check out a few things first. Want to know who owns the house, and that SUV parked on the street. Maybe the car is connected to the kidnapping. Most of all, I got to find out who was kidnapped."

"Then what?"

"We tell Edie Baron and see if she'll go with the story on the next newscast. But, first, I have a lot of research to do."

"Sandy, you know, my sister's husband is on the police force in East Hampton…maybe he'd give me some background."

Sandy nodded to Billy and fully enjoyed the excitement of the chase for the story. This would top covering the polo matches, fundraisers by the super-rich and the cat up a tree story.

Chapter
35

Abu Mustafa awoke in the hotel room that Robert Collins, his journalism savior, had arranged. The two men spoke often in the time that Abu stayed hidden in the hotel. He wanted to be safe from his cousin's long reach.

"Mister Collins, if my cousin could reach out to Turkey and find someone to blow up the car of the broker, then he could also find someone to end me. I can't leave this place right now. No, no, I cannot."

Robert Collins could record the interviews with Abu Mustafa if Abu's face was not shown, and his voice was disguised. Most importantly, his motivations to come forward were the money he was promised and the exit from Turkey to a country of his choosing.

This journalist, this man who saved me is my only chance to survive, Abu told himself. I don't know if I can trust him, but I have no other choice.

Abu Mustafa luxuriated in the bed and sheets that engulfed his body. He enjoyed the hot shower each morning and the fresh fruit and his favorite Turkish coffee for breakfast. The money that he had saved was gone now. There was no way to retrieve it. He would easily be found and killed. It would be the price he paid for his life. Now, he would bargain with the journalist for the information he gave. Money for each interview. The raging fear that his cousin brought to every fiber in his body was being overtaken by the possibilities of a safe, wealthy life. The raging fear brought on by the bomb blast that blew up the car with Emre was ever-present. It was also, his ever-present sense of caution.

Edie Baron, the supervising editor of Montauk's television affiliate, went over the story ideas for the morning ahead. Sandy sat at the table with two other reporters, each vying for the top spot on the news. Traffic reporter, Francine Johannsen, presented her story about the sports car that burst into flames on a road a quarter of a mile from a popular bar. Two men died in a fiery inferno. There might be a connection to drinking and driving she mused. Edie was not impressed with the possible connection. Sandy's story of the kidnapping, still not officially verified, was of paramount interest.

"How do you want to lede into this Ted?" she asked Ted Vaughn, the morning news anchor.

"It is a potentially big story for our area. If Sandy has nailed down the facts, we go all out with it. If it is still fuzzy, well, we offer a good lede with more to come."

All eyes went to Sandy.

"East Hampton Police Department spokesman verified a kidnapping. A woman was found wandering a road. She was picked up by a local nurse."

"Do we have her name?" Edie Baron asked.

"The nurse or the victim?"

"Both, Sandy, both," Ted interjected.

Sandy blushed but flipped through her notebook to deliver the names of the nurse and the victim.

"Is the victim a local?"

"No, Manhattan, New York City resident. Apparently, she was brought here and kept in hiding."

"What about the kidnappers?"

"Nothing. Montauk Police Sergeant Coyne is not announcing any names until the joint investigation with NYPD is complete. He did say that there were two suspects, both men."

"There whereabouts?"

"Not known at this time, he said."

Edie smiled at her new, young reporter. She had answers for all the questions which meant she did her work.

"Okay, here's what we're going to do. Ted, you lead with Sandy's story and follow with the car crash then on to the local stuff. That's it. Let's get to work."

"Okay, one question for Sandy." Ted looked at her, "Where is the victim now?"

Collette looked out of the police car which was transporting her to Dieter's office. The city was bustling with almost four million commuters and residents during business hours. The traffic was comprised of cars competing for space while trucks delivered the goods to its one million six hundred thousand residents. Her world was moving on as it always did. It was resilient and strong in all its challenges. She resolved to be the same.

The police car pulled up to the station. Dieter stood waiting for her arrival.

"Hello," Dieter said. No questions for her. He knew how she must be feeling. The information uncovered from initial interviews had been checked. Simon Winton and Marco were long gone. No sign of them at Winton's address. Bertram Thompson presented faux concern but hadn't heard from his employee.

He walked her up the stairs to the Detectives area and showed her to a small room where they were to talk. Collette looked anxious. Dieter noticed.

"You okay?" he asked.

"The room, it's small."

Dieter realized that she had just been confined to small spaces.

"Let's find another space."

Collette looked around the room, "Thanks."

Dieter walked to a not so small space with a window. He stopped at the door, allowing Collette to look inside the room.

"How's this?"

Her answer was to walk into the room. Dieter followed and moved two chairs near the window's light to reduce her anxiety.

Collette took a cleansing breath, "Detective, I have to thank you for all you've done for me."

Dieter decided on the truth, "What I've done is my job…and for Lindsay too."

Collette felt foolish for a moment. "Of course, for Lindsay. I intruded on her life by being with Andrew…and now I'm intruding on your obvious relationship with Lindsay by what has happened." She paused to let her own words settle. "I am truly sorry."

"You are the victim. Help me get to the bottom of this case. Fair enough?"

Collette choked out, "Yes, of course."

"Why did you go to Winton's apartment?"

Collette wished that she hadn't but now knew that was the only way to get the answers she needed.

"I thought there might be a connection to a shell company that Winton was named in. There was and that's what spooked him. They kidnapped me to find out what I knew, which really wasn't anything. All I knew is that he was part of TB Incorporated. But, not sure how or why at the time."

"And now?"

"He paid for stolen antiquities that Thompson received from a broker in Turkey. He got scared when I found out about the shell company because he was skimming money from the sales for himself. Stealing from Thompson."

"How do you know this?"

Collette knew her answer would not be enough for the moment. She also believed that once the two kidnappers were found she'd be proven correct.

"We talked about this." She looked at Dieter.

"We?"

"Simon Winton and his partner Marco…I don't know his last name. "

Dieter waited for Collette to continue.

"They wanted to prove to me that they did not kill Andrew. They were emphatic about that."

Dieter rose and walked away. He turned to her and came back.

"Perpetrators lie. Do you know this? They all lie at first. Why would they tell you the truth? More importantly, why are you convinced of their lies?"

Collette's immediate anger was replaced by confusion that erupted into tears. Dieter was glad Lindsay was not present. She would have complicated the interrogation with her empathy. Fingers wiped away the tears from eyes that now focused on a distant place. A memory of those moments with the two men who controlled her life. Were they still in control? She couldn't shake away the possibility that she was wrong about their denial.

"I don't know…they seemed so…fearful at the time."

"Fearful about what?"

"Not what they were afraid of. Who they were afraid of."

"Who is that?"

"Thompson. They were afraid of him. They wanted to make sure everything was pointing to him…Andrew's murder, the money for stolen antiquities."

"Where are they now?"

"How would I know? They kidnapped me. I'm not in any of this with them. Why are you doing this to me?"

"All right. Tell me everything from the moment you knew you could get away."

Collette reviewed the last moments and her chance to escape when Simon locked himself in the bathroom leaving Marco to try and get into the bathroom.

"So, you just walked out?"

"No! I ran down the stairs, out the front door, around the sports car parked on the driveway. I didn't want to take the road, so I ran along the beach for a short while and then back up to the road. When I was sure they were not on the road I walked out and flagged down a car. You know the rest."

"Okay, you sit here. Can I get you something to drink?"

"Water." Collette slipped away.

Dieter returned to his desk where he called Chris Handwirth.

"Chris, it's Detective Dieter, I need some information on a car registration. Check to see if there's a sports car registered to Simon Winton in Manhattan." He listened. "No, I don't know the make or model. Okay, call me back at my cell."

Chris Handwirth began his research. Dieter retrieved a bottle of water from the refrigerator near the coffee machine. He returned to Collette and gave her the water.

"Do you know the kind of sports care you saw?

She shook her head in the negative.

Dieter's cell rang. "That was fast. What did you find?"

"Simon Winton owns a Maserati Gran Turismo Convertible."

"Thanks," Dieter called McClure next.

"JB, it's Karl, I'm going to send you a text about Winton's car. Get a BOLO on it asap."

Collette looked at Dieter for an answer.

"We're going to find his sports car and then we'll find Winton."

Collette sighed and nodded.

Chapter
36

The police car pulled up to Lindsay's building depositing Collette and one officer who escorted her into the building and up to Lindsay's apartment. Their meeting was filled with guilt on both sides but for different reasons. Collette's guilt was for the anguish she brought to Lindsay, but mostly for the intrusion of the life-threatening concerns that she left at Lindsay's door. Lindsay's guilt was far simpler. She wanted all the chaos to end and get back to a life with *her Karl*. Lindsay knew the difference between being selfish and self-loving. The second allowed her to embrace her loving relationship with the man who made her feel good about herself. They had reached the point where they could share all the good, bad and ugly things in life as long as they had each other's support. Collette had intruded on that connection and Lindsay felt guilty that she harbored anger toward Collette. She also knew that it could be managed and that it was temporary until all the evil events were eradicated.

"Are you hungry?" Lindsay asked.

Hunger had not been a part of Collette's life since the kidnapping. Not much beyond her fears had taken center stage during the days of capture.

"Yes, I think I am." Collette mused.

The duo sat and ate the croissants and jellies that Lindsay had put out. A pot of Green tea was placed on a coaster in the table's middle. Collette ate hungrily and stopped when sated.

"Collette, you've been through so much...do you want to talk about it?"

Collette didn't want to talk about it, she wanted to scream about it to the world, to reduce the roiling terror below. Instead, she cupped the warm tea and let it settle her for the moment. A sip slid down burning away some of the angst momentarily.

"It's surreal. One moment we were saying our vows, flying off to our honeymoon being in love and the next...I'm here having tea with his ex-wife who is trying to help keep me alive."

The irony was not lost on Lindsay. Therapist Lindsay mirrored Collette's comments. "You've been on a steady roller coaster ride for some time now."

"Rollercoaster is right." Collette felt the jarring ride up and down. Her future with Andrew was ended by someone who was fearful of what they thought he knew...and what she might know. But a pity party was rejected once again.

"I want these men to pay for all they've done to Andrew, to me and...to you. I want them dead."

Collette felt no guilt for her pronouncement.

"That's normal," Lindsay said, "but, they hold the answers to all the questions."

"That's why I want to be there when they're found. I know what questions to ask."

Chris Handwirth's all-points bulletin for the Maserati sports car got a hit. He called Dieter.

"Karl, it's Chris. Listen, the car was in an accident somewhere near a place called Amagansett, Long Island."

"The East End. Go on."

"It was burned to a crisp. Two bodies were found inside. It is owned by the guy you asked about...Simon Winton, but the bodies still have to be identified."

"Thanks, Chris, send me all you got."

Dieter sat at the ancient diner-like counter of his favorite morning stop for coffee and....

"More coffee Detective?" Maureen Daley asked.

"Maybe a shot of Scotch."

"Oh, oh. One of those days?" She leaned a conspiratory elbow on the counter.

"Lately, it seems like a month of those days."

Dieter rose, left a hefty tip for Maureen, who said, "Off to work Detective?"

"Time to catch the bad guys."

Maureen smiled at the handsome detective whom she had learned to like a lot. He reminded her of Mikey, her Marine son whom she lost in Afghanistan.

Gregg Jackson called out, "Hey Maureen, can a guy get some service over here?"

She offered a faux scowl to Gregg, a regular morning customer, "Wait your turn wise guy."

"Yes, ma'am," he laughed.

It was Dieter's turn to wait for the autopsy report from the East Hampton Town Police. He knew the results and it stymied him. He also knew that it was not an accident and its passengers were murdered.

As Dieter entered the Police Station, Captain Grover was rushing out of the building.

"Captain, we got to talk," Dieter said.

Captain Grover stopped, and both moved aside to let the changing shifts enter and exit.

"You have something new?" His eyes flicked to his waiting car.

"Yes, but you won't like it."

Grover frowned. "Not much to like anytime lately. What is it?"

"Collette Riccardi has been found alive, her kidnappers, however, are not so lucky."

Grover did a little swivel around.

"You sure about this?"

"Just got some information, about to check it out, but it seems solid."

"Okay, okay, I'll talk to you when I get back from downtown."

Grover quick stepped to his car and it pulled away. Dieter entered the building as McClure caught up to him.

"Good morning Karl."

"Maybe not. Got a lot to catch you up on."

The swarthy man checked the transfer of money to his Swiss bank account with satisfaction. His employer always paid promptly, a quality he enjoyed. The present meager surroundings in his New Jersey apartment contradicted the possibilities for the future. His payments were building up abroad for the work done in the United States and the US Virgin Islands. Gratification came from the work, not from the killing but from his growing abilities to get away unknown and unseen. The swarthy man's bank accounts and ego were being fed and he enjoyed the feast. His hires for the killing in St. John did get the job done, but they were potentially traceable to him. The two men forfeited their lives when they let the victim's wife escape. Bertram Alan Thompson was the only connection to him...he would never be a problem.

Dieter called the officer on duty at Lindsay's apartment. An energetic voice answered.

"Yes, detective, I'll bring her right over."

Officer Raphael Ortega, in his third year on the NYPD force, knocked at the apartment door. Lindsay answered.

"Ma'am, I've just replaced officer Adams on the shift. I got a phone call from a detective asking me to bring Collette Riccardi to him."

"Was it Detective Dieter?"

"Yes, ma'am, it was."

"Okay, come in. Can I offer you some coffee while she gets ready?"

"Thanks, but not necessary. I'll just wait."

Ten minutes later police officer Ortega was driving Collette to Dieter's office when her cell phone rang indicating an unavailable name and number. Collette was suspicious, but she answered the call.

"Hello, who is this?"

A disguised male voice answered. "So, it's true...you're still alive...for now."

The call ended. Collette gasped, and Officer Ortega heard it. He looked in the rearview mirror to see her anguished face.

"Ma'am is something wrong?"

"I think my life was just threatened."

Officer Ortega hit the car's siren and gunned the engine. He called ahead to the police station and when he pulled up policemen quickly surrounded the car with weapons pulled. Before Collette exited, Dieter arrived at the car.

To Collette, "Stay inside."

"What happened, Ortega?"

"Someone called her and threatened her life."

Dieter and a gaggle of officers escorted her into the station and to a comfortable room where Dieter could update her on the investigation.

Collette grew pale from the message and the ominous voice which she heard repeatedly. Once she seemed more in control, Dieter began.

"Tell me about the phone call."

She told him about the message and the disguised voice and he asked to see her phone.

"Why? Don't you believe me?"

"Yes, I believe you, I'd like our IT guy to see if he can trace the number."

"There was no number."

"He might be able to get around that."

Reluctantly, she handed the phone to Dieter who got up and left the room. He walked to McClure's desk and handed him the phone.

"See if Handwirth can get the number of the last call."

McClure took the phone and left for IT.

Dieter returned to Collette. She looked frail compared to the moments when she was angry and strong.

"I'm afraid I may have bad news about the kidnappers."

Collette became resolute. "What is it?"

"Simon Winton's sports car was found on fire with two bodies in it in a nearby town where you were held."

She shot upright and stood. She looked at Dieter having nowhere to go. Confused.

"Were they in it?"

"We think so, but we have to wait for the bodies to be identified to be sure."

"What does this mean? You're never going to know who killed Andrew?" Collette's fists balled into fighting mode.

"Oh no, I will find his killers, that's a certainty."

"Really? How? Everyone is dead."

It wasn't long ago that she had wished them dead for all the pain they brought. Now, she wished she had been smarter and followed her plan to outsmart them. Simon was unnerved when he was talking about his boss. He wanted to get even with Thompson for using him as a shield. TB Incorporated was connected to Simon, not Thompson. Now what?

Chapter
37

The sun declared the end of another day. The moon waited for its curtain call after millions of years rising and offering its curtain of sleep.

Sleep was elusive for Collette. Even when she pressed her eyes closed, visions imposed their presence. Memories of the darkened concrete room where she was captive surrounded her. She lay encircled by the covers which gave no solace to her needs. Comfort was alien to her body. It had survived much since St. John, but the future, if there was to be one, was fogbound.

She sat upright in the bedroom...in Lindsay's second bedroom, in Lindsay's apartment. Collette had nothing. Everything was taken. Her husband of a few days, her safety, her joy for life which was Andrew's first connection to her; all gone, bound into a ball and tossed...who knows where. Her desperation was crushing. Her body was at war without a clear enemy to battle. Who were these people? Why did all this happen?

Collette threw the covers back, away from her limbs. She stood and walked to the window. The street below was still alive with light taxi traffic and delivery trucks making late-night rounds. Parked cars waited patiently, lined up in rows, one behind another until the morning demanded they be moved or driven to work. It all seemed so calm, so right. Nothing was calm and certainly, nothing was right within Collette's world.

A spreadsheet could be filled with numbers, calculated, summed to an answer or sometimes several depending on the question. Her world of numbers was orderly. Rules were established and followed to a conclusion. This horrible world was without rules, without order. Chaos reigned supreme. Her mind drifted to a college course where the professor discussed the concept of chaos theory as applied to management. This too became surrounded by fog.

The room was confining. She slipped on a bathrobe and left for the kitchen. It was darkened but ambient light allowed her to move around to find the teapot, fill it with water and collect an Herbal teabag. While she waited for the teapot to announce its result, she heard shuffling steps growing louder.

"Hey, can't sleep?"

"Sorry, did I wake you?" She asked Lindsay.

"No, I was only nodding off a bit." Lindsay looked at the teapot. "Is there enough hot water for two cups of tea?"

Collette wasn't sure. "We'll stretch the water if it's not."

Awkwardness filled the space between them. Lindsay turned on the kitchen lights as both women shielded their eyes briefly. Lindsay took two cups from the cupboard, some raw honey and two spoons which were placed on the counter near the stove top. The customary teapot whistle began. When it reached its crescendo, Lindsay reduced the heat and took the teapot off the burner. Each woman prepared the tea to taste. They stood allowing the cup's warmth to heal. Lindsay reacted first.

"I have a sweet tooth." Lindsay smiled. "How about you?"

"Sure, why not?" Collette observed.

"Yeah, why the hell not?" They both uttered a small laugh which broke the somber mood.

Lindsay rummaged around for something sweet to eat. "Chocolate?"

"Perfect."

Lindsay took out the bag of chocolates that was ever present in her kitchen. Almond covered chocolate would fill the need for something sweet.

They chewed and sipped in silence having been down this road before which was now filled with so much debris that silence was the best medicine along with chocolate, tea, and company.

"That phone call must have been chilling."

Collette nodded to herself and to Lindsay's words. Her brow furrowed in thought. Lindsay allowed the necessary contemplative time.

"Strange…"

"My computer, that's how someone got the number. It's the only answer."

"Didn't the men who kidnapped you have the computer?"

"I don't know, maybe…don't know where it is now."

"Karl will find it."

Collette looked at Lindsay searching her face. "You like him."

Lindsay smiled briefly, "I love him." She rose from the kitchen table to rinse her cup in the sink.

"You've been lucky."

Lindsay gave Collette a startled look. "Lucky? How have I been lucky? Andrew left me for you. Karl came into my life after people were murdered in my apartment. And now, Andrew is murdered, and your life is in jeopardy, and maybe mine. How have I been lucky?"

Collette joined Lindsay at the sink. She put her cup down into it and faced Lindsay.

"Everything you said is the truth. I was the spark that started this whole mess. If I never met Andrew…"

"He'd have found someone else."

Both women searched each other's eyes.

"We were finished, and I didn't know it. Maybe he didn't know it either. But it was over. You filled a need that I no longer could fill for him. We had separated by focusing on our professions and not on each other any longer. New York is a tough town. It can eat you up if you're not careful, or very strong."

Collette frowned and walked back to the kitchen table.

"He would have found someone else. Really? He didn't seem needy to me. He was very together. Smart. Loving and kind."

Lindsay walked to Collette and took her hands.

"Yes, he was all of those things. No, he wasn't needy in that way. Yes, he was kind to everyone."

Lindsay squeezed Collette's hands.

"When we met and fell in love we were full of life, as a couple. We did silly, impulsive impractical things. Then, time and our careers misled us to seek success...to run with the bulls. So, we ran and ran until we were both too tired for one another."

"But, he would have found someone else, you said." Misty-eyed Collette said.

"Yes, but he found you and you filled his need to be who he was once. You did that, and he didn't have to find anyone else."

Collette wrapped her arms around Lindsay and sobbed. They stood together until Lindsay slowly released herself from Collette's arms. Lindsay was serious.

"How am I lucky with all that I just told you? How?"

"You've been loved by two very special men...two men. Some never find one person to love them. You found two...and you still have one."

Lindsay looked at Collette with a new level of appreciation.

Bertram always awakened an hour before sunrise regardless of the time zone. His inner automatic clock triggered a rise in mental acuity and consciousness. The morning ritual had taken charge each day for many years. First, arise from the bed, followed by stretching and a bathroom stop. He enjoyed a cleansing, invigorating shower in the specially designed glass room with ten moving, rotating heads that sprayed hot water, mixed with a special Asian soap. He never shared this room with a woman.

Women were always paid for and dismissed. His shower room was one of the special places never to be shared by another.

Each morning, clothes were laid out according to his prearranged schedule by the single staff that he kept for such things. Bertram's mind needed to be clear of all interferences. Once he had followed the remaining rituals, he entered his office. The day's business would be reviewed. The CEO's of each of his companies sent a morning update detailing progress on all projects, sales, market status leaving no surprises to be uncovered. Bertram dictated replies to each CEO with instructions to be honored.

At precisely eight A.M., a specially prepared herbal tea was delivered in silence to his desk. For the next few minutes, he enjoyed the tea while he turned to the window and scanned the sky. This morning reverie was his favorite time. He wondered how he'd be remembered. Would he have the same glory as the ancient kings on the coins he so cherished? His world was certainly bigger, more extensive than even the greatest conquerors. Or so, he believed.

Bertram was a thoroughly modern man who invested in the most trending innovations...except one. He never used a digital device that would lead a trail to his personal, very private activities. Cell phones were fine for business communications that were legal or routine. High-speed computers connected to high-speed IP addresses were also regularly used for business, but never for personal, private use. His world had been overtaken by a growing paranoia which controlled more of his existence each day. Little slivers of conversation heard at the finest New York restaurants caught his attention. Once he heard a snippet that aroused momentary concern, "The rich are taking over the city," said one diner, to which another responded, "About time," followed by laughter. Bertram wondered whether they were talking about him and laughing at him. He never suffered ridicule very well. The very normal joking among friends during his adolescence unnerved him, but he pushed down the anxieties it bore. It was this distance from personal connections that allowed him to succeed in business. No risk was too great. No advantage over another was wrong. Their problem, not his if they couldn't cope with his ability to win. Winning was the ultimate connection to self. His ego grew high above the adolescent anxieties that were pushed ever deeper into his psyche.

With the sun rising onto his city, Bertram decided to search Simon's apartment for anything that might hurt him. He took the elevator down and used the keys he had to enter. The apartment, lighted by the morning's ambient sunlight, allowed him to search the office space easily. His search was about himself, not Simon. Were there things here which could incriminate him in the purchases that Simon made on his behalf? He searched the entire office and living quarters smirking at the hidden pornographic paraphernalia that he found in Simon's bedroom closet. Bertram knew about Simon's proclivities for men, but they had no interest nor concern for him. Once he was satisfied that he was safe from his connection to the ancient antiquities, he returned to his apartment. He would show the appropriate surprise and remorse at Simon's passing to the police questions.

His thoughts turned to the woman who might know too much. Time may be running out for him...and for her.

Chapter
38

Sandy Campbell continued her research on the house where the kidnapping occurred. It brought her to the East Hampton Town Tax Receiver's Office at 300 Pantigo Place. Her good-natured, easy persona helped to connect with the local government officials. Charmaine Robins, who arrived in the Hamptons from Saint Ann's Bay, Jamaica twenty-five years earlier was now a friend. Hard work and a stickler for honesty allowed Charmaine to rise to her present position at the Receiver's Office.

"Oh, oh, here comes trouble," Charmaine joked to Sandy as she looked up from a stack of files on her desk.

Sandy smiled and was familiar with the necessary chatter that had to take place each time she came for information.

"You know, Sandy, I'm not going to commit any crimes for you today or any day. Don't care how pretty you look. Nah, ah." Shaking her head but pleased to see the young woman.

"Well, that's good, because I'm only asking for a misdemeanor."

"Okay, maybe I can do a misdemeanor. What do you need?"

Sandy took out a slip of paper with an address and handed it to Charmaine.

Charmaine took it, looked at Sandy. "What do you need to know about this address?"

"I need to know who owns it. A crime was committed there."

"A crime? What kind of crime?"

"Kidnapping of a lady."

Charmaine shook her head disapprovingly. She turned to her computer, keyed in the address, and waited for the results. Once the name flashed on the screen, she wrote it on a Town letterhead and gave it to Sandy.

"Here it is? You going to help the police get this guy?" She returned to disapproving head shaking. "Is she alive?"

"Yes, she escaped."

"Listen to me, you do all you can to help get this guy arrested. Put his name out everywhere. Get him locked up...see how he likes that."

Sandy took the paper and held Charmaine's hand. "Count on it."

Detective Dieter knew that Bertram Thompson was the owner of the house where the kidnappers held Collette. Since Simon Winton worked for Bertram Thompson, and since Winton was the kidnapper, it was logical to pay the billionaire another visit. He and Captain Grover decided to keep the pressure on him until hard proof of connections to the kidnapping and deaths of the two men in the car could be nailed down.

Normally, Dieter would bring in the suspect, make him nervous and hope for a chink in the armor he put up that would lead to more information. He'd do it until he knew the suspect was either clean or guilty. It was tricky with one of the most powerful businessmen in New York. Bertram Thompson would not go easily if he were behind any of the crimes committed.

"Karl, listen, this guy has big-time clout in the city, especially downtown, if you know what I mean."

"Yes, I know. He could apply lots of heat to the case and to you personally. Right?"

Captain Grover, agreed, but he didn't like the ease with which Dieter connected the dots to Grover's career path. His timeline to ascend to Police Commissioner, then eventually to the Mayor's office would be halted permanently. Grover wasn't about to let that happen. Slow and steady as he had always done makes the best results.

"Karl be very clear about this if Bertram Thompson is involved I want to nail him, just like you; but, I don't want him to stymie our investigation with armies of lawyers shouting deflecting, time-wasting invectives to the media."

Dieter realized Grover just might have a point.

"Okay, we'll go by the book, no shortcuts…and no toes stepped on."

He looked long and hard at Grover to assure him of his words.

"You see, that's why I don't want you to retire. You get it; besides you could rise above the daily investigations to higher office in the department. Know what I mean?"

"Captain, I assure you, I have no desire to rise above detective work, and certainly not to have to deal with the political pressures."

"I know how you feel today, but things change. Life has a way of influencing what we believe. Am I right?"

"Not about this."

Sandy Campbell punched in Bertram Thompson's name to her favorite search engine. A long list of pages, websites, newspaper and magazine articles about the eccentric man filled her monitor's screen.

She sat back and realized that this might just be the story that would catapult her to the next level of her career. But, she knew that she'd better get it right or it might be the end of her present and all future careers. In ten minutes, she had a small stack of printouts from the searches. Her customary research was to print out the data, review it, make sense of it. Once finished with the research, she'd find the thread of the story and the lede paragraph.

Billionaire, Bertram Alan Thompson, resided in New York City with several investment homes and properties around the country, few of which he had ever visited. His mainstay residence is the lavish apartment in his "...favorite city in the whole world" read a quote from a trending financial magazine. Although he did travel overseas seeking investment opportunities in exotic, turbulent countries, his holdings in the U.S.A. were considerable and money making.

One news site showed photographs of the house in the Hamptons where the woman was held, hostage. It was published by a local magazine highlighting the rich and sometimes notorious owners of homes where the super-rich liked to play and be seen. Bertram Alan Thompson had no desire to be seen in the Hamptons scene. In fact, there is no record of him staying at the house. A local interior designer had decorated its comfortable traditional look as per his written request. He had not met with the interior designer, Claire Vandergarde. She had met with one of his representatives, she said in a phone conversation with Sandy. After rustling of pages, she said, "Simon Winton, a pompous little man."

"Simon Winton?" Sandy spoke to her reflection on the computer's monitor. "Hmm, let's see who he is."

She punched in his name, but nothing came up. "Strange." Urgency mingled with curiosity as her fingers flew across the keyboard. He was a ghost. She called Claire Vandergarde again.

"Hi, Claire, it's Sandy again. I'm researching Simon Winton, but nothing comes up anywhere."

"Really? Well, he exists, I know that. Maybe he gave me a false name."

"Maybe. Okay, thanks, Claire."

Sandy wondered what the connection to Collette Riccardi, Bertram Alan Thompson and a guy named Simon Winton could be that caused her to be kidnapped. Was Thompson a bystander, not involved? Was Simon Winton a spook, existing in some ethereal space?

"Stop it, Sandy." She complained to the monitor. "Back to work."

Her blue eyes pored over the pages until she began to formulate an idea, a lede for the story. "Could one of New York City's billionaires be connected to the kidnapping of a woman held hostage at his mansion in Montauk?" She smiled, sat back and considered the pushback from her editor, Edie. She'd want proof that he owned the mansion. Check. Got that. She'd want to know more. "What else do you have?" Edie would ask. That triggered Sandy to renew her search into the printed notes and more online research. "Just one little thread connecting the ghost, Simon Winton, to Bertram Thompson...come on."

Dieter entered Bertram Thompson's lair once again. This time he let his eyes linger on the room as he approached Thompson. Elegantly appointed, of course, he thought. Big money, big power. Even bigger ego. A dismissive attitude last time. Let's see how solid that ego holds up...go gently, he remembered. Not a suspect...yet.

"Officer, what can I do for you this time?" was Thompson's opener.

"Detective."

"What?"

"I'm Detective Dieter. Haven't been an officer for years." How do you like them apples Thompson? he thought.

"Yes, yes, I meant Detective. Nevertheless, how can I help you...Detective?"

Dieter took out his notebook and clicked open his pen with purpose. Thompson's eyes flashed to Dieter's hands poised with pen and notebook, but he remained outwardly contained.

Dieter flipped some pages, although he knew exactly the questions to ask.

"Can you please tell me, again, the relationship between you and," he paused again for effect, "a Simon Winton?"

"Relationship is not actually the correct word. He works for me. That is our connection. I pay his salary, give him an apartment downstairs, and he performs certain duties for me which I need to be concluded properly."

Dieter let a fleeting inquisitive look cross his face.

"Certain duties? Can you elaborate?"

"Detective, many of the duties he performs are inconsequential…"

Dieter cut him off, "You mean like taking your clothes to the cleaners?"

Thompson chuckled, "No, Detective, he doesn't take my clothes to the cleaners, as you say. My clothes are laundered and cleaned on the premises. I have people who do this."

"I see, well then, what duties does he perform?" Dieter wasn't liking the entitled, dismissive attitude.

"Detective, is there a point to these questions? Didn't we go over this once before?"

"Yes, we did, but circumstances have changed." He waited for a response or change of Thompson's expression.

"Again, I don't understand."

"You'll have to hire another person to perform your *certain duties.*"

Thompson knew the news about Simon was next. He'd try to look surprised, perhaps even sorry for the man's demise.

"Why is that, Detective?"

Dieter would make this last. He did the reading from the notebook look again, "Simon Winton and another man's bodies were found in a car that went off the road and exploded into flames not far from Montauk. The car was registered to Simon Winton. The bodies are still being autopsied."

"Really? Simon's car for sure?"

"A sports car?"

"I have no idea what he drove."

"Terrible. Sorry to learn of this."

"My guess is you'll be even sorrier to learn the next bit of news."

"More bad news about Simon?"

"Yes, he and another man, named Marco, were the kidnappers of Collette Riccardi who was held at your Montauk mansion."

"Can't be true. He is a meek, little man who never showed aggressiveness to me. No, no, can't be true."

"It is true. The woman identified them. Furthermore, she was kidnapped right here."

"Here! What are you saying?"

"They kidnapped her from Simon's apartment, right below yours. Seems there was a commotion. She was knocked out. Tied up and taken to another site and finally to your mansion where she escaped."

"That is difficult to digest Detective. Simon is…"

"Was, Mister Thompson, was…"

Thompson felt growing anger at the game Dieter was playing. Time to put it to rest.

"Do I have to contact my attorney?"

"I don't know. If there's nothing to hide, then you don't."

"I certainly do not."

"That's good, because, Collette Riccardi is working with the police and the FBI to determine the connection between TB Incorporated and the death of her husband. Simon Winton was somehow connected to that company. What is it called?" he mused. "Oh, yes, a shell company, that's it, a shell company. Isn't that what it's called?"

"Detective, I told you before that I have nothing to do with this TB Incorporated."

"Yes, I remember, but it is interesting that its name is the reverse of your initials…B.T."

"Detective, I think, your fishing expedition should come to an end. I have nothing to do with any of this. If poor, dead Simon was involved, I am sorry that he was even remotely connected to me, but none of what you've said today has anything to do with me or my businesses."

"Do you know of any next of kin he might have."

"I do not, but I will pay for any expenses incurred for the internment of any kind. He did work for me for several years."

Bertram Thompson moved behind his desk to a drawer from where he pulled a business card. He handed it to Dieter.

"Please, speak with my attorney in the future regarding any questions you may have. We will cooperate fully."

Dieter took the card, his eyes never leaving Thompson's eyes, and placed the card in his notebook. He closed the notebook slowly, clicked the pen closed and placed both in his sports jacket pocket.

"Good to know. We'd expect that from you."

Both men ended the interview with similar feelings of anger. Dieter for Thompson's arrogant, entitlement and Thompson for how Dieter how orchestrated his every response. Thompson never enjoyed being challenged. When he was challenged, he never forgot it.

Chapter
39

Major television network international reporter, Robert Collins, sat editing the footage of the meetings with Abu Mustafa. He'd protect this man who feared for his life, but his story had to be told. Collins researched and discovered that ISIS made great sums of money from the sale of the stolen antiquities and he wanted the world to know. He was unsure whether it could help to cut off the profits from the sales. Perhaps, he thought, it would chase the wealthy buyers from the thriving worldwide black market.

Collins scrolled to a section of the video and engaged the sound. The video showed Collins, seated, facing the rear of a masked head. He cut into one moment.

"Who are the buyers for these objects?"

"I never met any buyers. Only the middleman." The muffled voice answered.

"The man who was killed by the car explosion?"

"Yes."

"Did he ever speak of the buyers?"

"He said they were rich and powerful men from all over the world?"

"All over the world? The United States?"

"Oh, yes, definitely the United States."

"Did he ever speak of any one man?"

"Yes, but, not by name. He met this man in Turkey. They spoke and arranged to purchase small items."

"Small items?"

"Ancient coins, small statues, engraved cups. Items from the rulers of the ancient times. He was very particular about that, the Turkish buyer said."

"Where is this American from?"

"New York City. A very wealthy, powerful man, but I never learned his name."

"You are saying that a very rich, New York City man bought these stolen antiquities from your Turkish connection."

"Yes, that is what I am saying. Many items delivered to the Turkish broker and more before I was asked to deal with him."

"But, you refuse to tell who hired you to conduct these sales?"

"Refuse? I cannot, no never. That would be suicide. He has already tried to kill me along with the Turkish broker."

Collins liked this portion of the interview because it leads to a further investigation in New York and further television segments. It would be aired along with other footage, maybe a multi-part story. Once completed, Collins would dig into the lives of the rich and powerful men in New York City. He hoped his inquiries around the city would trigger a desire by some of the men to undercut their competitors. It was also possible that it would shut down all avenues to enter the good old boys' club.

His cell phone rang, and he answered the network producer's call.

"Hi, Cynthia."

He listened to her tell him that the spot should soon be ready airing.

"I can do that."

Cynthia asked how long the spot would run. Collins had an approximate run time depending on final edits.

"Are they thinking about a multi-part piece?"

He smiled at her response which indicated at least two parts.

"I can handle that. Thanks, Cynthia. I'll be back in the States by the end of the week."

The call energized Collins. He had seen much destruction by the terrorist group ISIS, and other newly formed and still growing in the Middle East and around the world. Innocent lives lost for allegedly religious reasons. He saw a naked sense of greed and power at the true core of the attacks. Money was, to his mind, the prime motivator for the killings. He wondered why rich and powerful men were interested in buying the stolen antiquities. What benefit could it bring to them? Who was this purchaser in New York City?

Abu Mustafa was hungry. He had slept well for the first time in many months. Sleep was difficult since the murder of the Turkish broker, Emre. His eyes had become bloodshot, anxiety crowded every corner of his mind. When will my cousin magically appear and come at me with a saber waving above his head? This fear stole all his energy and resolve each day. He took to prayer once again. It had been years since he prayed with others. He never prayed alone anymore. He had risen early, before the sun, washed and put on clean clothes. There was time for the morning prayer, Fajr, the remembrance of God. Now, with all hope vanishing, he set out a place to pray in the direction he believed to be Mecca. As he knelt and prayed, he was overtaken by a sense of calm which had been alien from him for so long. When he finished his prayers, he rose and noticed the hunger was still there. He looked out of the window to see the sun rising in a clear sky. A good omen he thought. Things will be good. Allah has heard my prayers. He picked up the phone to call for room service, and ordered, after many attempts to communicate with the Turkish speaking person on the phone. He paced the hotel room with renewed energy and strength until there was a knock at the door. The food has arrived, he thought and opened the door to two men who rushed in and threw him to the floor. One held Abu's hands behind his back while the other raised his head and slit his throat. Blood squirted from the carotid artery, pooling in a growing circle alongside his head. The men rose, straightened their clothes and went to the door where one opened it and looked right then left down the corridor and signaled the other to join him as they exited the room, closing the door quietly.

Later that morning, Robert Collins, had devised a plan. He would get Abu out of the country; Great Britain would be a good choice to start he believed. Things were working out just fine. He had fallen upon a story that would shed light on the sale of stolen ancient antiquities around the world.

Everything changed when he went to Abu's room to find a throng of police inside with the opened door cordoned off allowing a gurney to exit carrying a covered body.

"Oh, shit!" he uttered half aloud.

"You know him?" an English-speaking policeman asked.

"Yes."

"Your friend?"

Collins thought for a moment, "An acquaintance. I was coming to have breakfast with him."

The Turkish police officer looked suspiciously at Collins. He turned to point to the food cart inside the room.

"It is only set for one. Why is that?"

Collins had no answer to the rising sense of guilt that forced him to swallow. The policeman moved closer letting the others leave the room.

"What is your name and what is your business here in Turkey?"

Collette lay awake, in bed at two A.M., as Abu's body was taken to the morgue. Her mind raced toward a resolution. "Bertram Thompson must pay for all he's done."

Chapter
40

Collins spent the remainder of the morning answering questions from the local Gaziantep police.

"What business do you have here? Why was he killed like that? What did you learn from this man?"

Before he reported to the police, he had forwarded all his recordings to the New York television station fearing that they might be confiscated. In fact, his recordings were confiscated with the promise that they'd be returned in a timely manner once they were cleared. The likelihood was small for a timely return. Collins was on a deadline.

He felt the full threat of the Turkish police while answering questions from an investigative officer who spoke with a slightly accented English.

"You, Robert Collins, had all this information about the explosion of a Turkish resident and you never came to the authorities? Why is that?"

"I must first verify my sources. It is important to report the truth, not fabrications."

"And now, is this story that Abu Mustafa gave you the truth? He is murdered. Does that make what he said true?"

"Don't know for sure."

"I see. What will you do with the information you have at your disposal?"

"I will review all of it, try to verify all of it and determine if it is newsworthy."

"Should I assume the information was digitally sent to your offices in the United States?"

Collins frowned. "Yes."

The investigator rose and looked down at Collins sitting across from him at a table.

"Then, I won't keep you from your travels to the United States. You will not need a return of the copies we have now. Correct?"

Collins rose, smiled knowingly, and shook his head. "No, I won't need them returned."

Detectives McClure and Dieter entered Captain Grover's office as summoned by their boss.

"This case is getting some legs. I mean it keeps running to places that were not obvious. Why's that?" His demeanor was more concern than anger.

"One thing I'm pretty sure about Captain is at the bottom of all this is Bertram Thompson. He's connected in a round-about way to almost everything that has happened."

"The murder in St. John of Andrew Riccardi?"

"Yes, tangentially."

"What?"

"Riccardi and his new wife worked for an accounting company that reviewed some of his business affairs. The same company reviewed business dealings from Simon Winton on behalf of Bertram Thompson. We have no idea why Simon Winton was involved."

Captain Grover fidgeted in his chair and washed his hand across his face seeking clarity.

"Okay, let's get forensics to this guy Simon Winton's apartment. Get me the address and I'll get us a warrant."

"It's in Thompson's apartment complex."

"Simon Winton lived with Thompson?"

"No, Thompson has several floors in the building. Winton lived below Thompson."

"Weird, but okay let's look at both places."

"Thompson lawyered-up."

"Really? How surprising? Since it's part of a murder investigation of Winton, it should be easier to get a warrant for both places."

"Captain," McClure began, "this guy, Thompson, is like a snake. He's wiggled out of hundreds of lawsuits represented by some of New York's finest law firms."

Captain Grover looked at McClure then at Dieter, "Dieter, you were right about him."

"Told you. He's a good detective."

McClure suddenly realized they were talking about him and not Thompson, but he said nothing as both men looked at him.

"Okay, I'll find a judge who will get us a warrant into Batman's cave." His eyes glowed with the possibilities ahead.

The white van had entered the garage under Thompson's building at midnight the day Simon Winton was murdered. The driver had taken the private elevator to Thompson's floor. He was let in by Thompson who had placed all the stolen antiquities into a cardboard box labeled Thompson Industries. The driver had made this run many times before for Thompson Industries and thought nothing of the unusual pickup time, nor of the drop-off site at a secure warehouse in rural Pennsylvania. His generous payment eased all concerns.

Once, the driver left the underground garage, Thompson sat down and laughed for several minutes. He was safe again. His armor of invincibility would protect him from the police, he thought. All connections to the antiquities had been severed. First Andrew Riccardi, then Simon and his companion. Thompson had no concerns about the Turkish broker being connected to him.

Gaziantep is a world away, he thought. *He's a shrewd man. The connection is to Simon, not me.*

And yet, in the short time since his collection was removed from his premises, he felt alienated from those ancient worlds which the antiquities represented. Strange feelings overcame him. The coins and tiny statues had comforted him. The visages of the men on the coins were his equals, not his betters. There were no modern men like them. Not the totalitarian men who ravished countries and killed innocent people. No, they were merely ignorant tyrants who knew nothing of the world. He knew so much more. Science had taught him about things the ancient kings never could have dreamed. He was a better, smarter, far more educated man then they all were, but they had their faces on coins heralding their power and wealth for all time. Here he would sit fondling the coins that were made thousands of years ago. The kings were conquerors who ruled over thousands. He was merely a successful businessman like too many others who he had come to shun when he felt their power growing equal to his.

The only concern he still felt, albeit limited, was to Collette Riccardi. She couldn't reach him. The police couldn't reach him. No, he was far above them all. She and her husband had created all the problems that danced around him; however, an abiding concern lingered.

Chapter
41

Sandy Campbell hurried into the morning meeting at the television station. Editor Edie was hovering over a laptop and several folders. Morning anchor, Ted Vaughn, bedecked with makeup and a cloth around his neck to protect his collared shirt, was leisurely sipping coffee. Liz Fortunato, a young Long Island University graduate of its C.W. Post campus where she studied journalism, was the traffic reporter. Liz had stumbled upon a story of a wrecked car that burst into flames and she was eager to get the story out.

"Okay, people, let's go," Edie began.

Liz was first to respond, "A fancy sports car was involved in an accident. Two bodies were found in the car, burned from the fire."

"Names?" Edie asked.

Liz scrolled through her cell phone to her notes.

"Only one name, Simon Winton. The other passenger was not identified at this time."

Sandy's face light up. "Did you say, Simon Winton?"

"Yes. Why?"

"His name came up from the story I'm investigating."

"The kidnapping story?" Edie asked.

"Yes. He was the connection to…" more cell phone scrolling, "…Bertram Thompson, the owner of the mansion where the woman was held,"

"So?" Ted offered.

Edie scowled at Ted.

Sandy looked to Edie for support. "Not sure."

Edie sat forward and placed her hands in a steeple. "Listen, folks, it sounds like we may have two big stories out here. The thing is, we must get them right. Understand. Let's connect the dots to the mansion, the kidnapping and maybe this guy Winton. What else folks?"

The meeting ended in twenty minutes with the morning lead story going to Liz on the traffic beat then handed to Ted who added the knowing significance of something more to come later. Sandy caught up with Liz after the news spot was complete.

"Liz, how did you know it was Simon Winton?"

"The autopsy report identified him. I have a friend at the coroner's office who passed along the name after a happy hour stop at Crosby's Bar and Grille." She smiled conspiratorially.

"Gotcha."

Robert Collins boarded his plane at Istanbul Ataturk Airport after a flight from Gaziantep Airport over 500 miles south. He was grateful that the hour and the thirty-five-minute flight was uneventful. The next eleven-hour flight would allow him to rest and digest all that has happened. More importantly, he wondered where all this will lead. Abu Mustafa was a victim and a fool. He saw the man's weakness and understood his fear especially after the car bombing. Collins knew that Abu didn't have to die, especially not the way he was killed. The televised story would now be stronger due to his death. It would lead to the need for more questions answered about ISIS and the sale of stolen antiquities. Who would buy these items? Rich men probably knew the source of the items, but they didn't care.

His travels around the world acclimated him to delays and hurried dashes to make a plane. This time, the flight times and connection at Ataturk airport went seamlessly. Once the flight was in the air, he began to write notes, mostly unanswered questions. How much money was gained from the sale of these stolen antiquities? He knew the drug trafficking business in Colombia had fed the terrorists years ago. Did ISIS find a new income source when they ravaged sites in Iraq? The stakes must be very high since people were being murdered.

He stopped working for a drink of Absolut Vodka. He sipped it slowly letting it warm his stomach, enjoying the added taste from the slice of lemon. It relaxed him. The second drink relaxed him more and he dozed a while.

"Another dead end?" Grover asked.

"This time it's literal. The connection to Simon is obvious but without him, we don't know exactly how TB Incorporated is connected to Thompson, or if it is connected." Dieter shrugged.

"What about Collette Riccardi? Can she figure it out?"

"We interviewed her several times. She's more frustrated that we can't point to her husband's killer."

"You think she knows more than she's letting on?"

Dieter shook his head, "No. She's still in shock, angry and confused."

"How about if I speak with her?" Grover asked.

"Yes sure, but why?"

Grover leaned across his desk, "I spent a lot of time digging out things that people didn't know they knew. The world of narcotics is filled with angry, confused people." He stood, towering over Dieter, "Bring her in for a chat with your Captain. He'd like to offer his full support...tell her that."

"Okay, Captain, I'll get her in today."

"Make it tomorrow. I have a busy afternoon with the folks Downtown...again."

"First thing in the morning."

"Make it late morning, give her time to do whatever she needs to do first."

Dieter smiled, "I forgot, tomorrow is pickup basketball morning for you."

"Well, that too. Where are we with Thompson?"

"Same place. No forward movement." Dieter's expression turned to frustration. "I suppose no help is coming from the people Downtown?"

"Oh, they want to help for sure. But they must step very carefully until we can find something concrete on Thompson. He's a big contributor to bunches of them."

"You see, Captain, that's why I don't want to move up from my position. I don't want to give myself away."

Grover's face hardened. "Are you saying I've given myself away."

"You know, you seem kind of concerned about the folks Downtown. I understand they're pressuring you."

"I'm dealing with that…"

"But I don't want to…"

The two men stood silent until Grover shook his head and laughed. "You really are a smart guy…and honest too. Maybe those two characteristics will get in the way."

Dieter didn't laugh. "So are you Captain…smart and honest."

Another long look from one to the other. Grover's phone rang.

"To be continued." He turned to answer the phone.

The flight from Turkey to John F. Kennedy International Airport in Queens, New York landed as the sun rose. Collins disembarked with the other passengers and headed for the Men's room on the way to Baggage Claim. He washed his face with refreshing cold water. He tucked his shirt into his pants, ran a comb through his hair and called his office.

"Good morning, it's Robert, back from Turkey."

"Rumor is they threw you out of the country."

"Harsh words. Do you have all the information I sent?"

"Oh, yes, and it's getting hotter by the minute. We're preparing an intro to your spot to be aired on the morning newscast in about an hour. We're going to use your headshot – the good one – as background for the teaser."

"When is my spot going up?"

"On the news tonight, so you better get your butt in here right away."

"I need to edit it."

"Well then, hang up and get here."

In the cab ride to the television studio, Collins wondered who the New York billionaire buyer of the stolen antiquities could be. Lots of billionaires enjoyed the life of the country's largest city.

Collins punched in numbers on his cell.

His lead producer, Nancy Strong answered, "Hey, Rob, how was the flight?"

"I guess the whole office knows of my return. Should I be flattered?"

"Probably not."

"Listen, I need some background asap."

"Okay…"

"Get me all you can on the top money guys in the city."

"Money guys?"

"Billionaires. Make it the top five."

"All background? Anyone in particular?"

"No, hoping you will find a link to a collector of ancient things worldwide."

"Is this related to your piece coming up tonight?"

"Might be. But not for tonight. I need more hard information than background can probably offer."

"You want me to follow up any connection I might find?"

"Sure, also my source in Turkey was murdered, so keep an eye out for stories coming out of Gaziantep too. I'll text you the name of the deceased and a police investigator there in a minute. Might help."

"Got it. Is that all?"

Collins could hear Nancy chuckle.

"For the moment."

More chuckling from Nancy, "Later Rob."

"Nancy, wait, one more thing, find out all you can about the gray and black markets of stolen antiquities from Iraq and where the money goes."

"That's easy…to the terrorists like ISIS."

"Right, but let's get numbers, dollars gained, lives lost…the real cost of the ravaging of the ancient sites."

He couldn't see Nancy's smile, if he could, he would know for sure that she was fully on board with the research.

Nancy became his lead producer when she proved as dogged in questions and research as Robert Collins was known to be. He liked that, more importantly, he needed the professional backup that Nancy's questions always wrought.

Robert Collins settled into the cab ride wondering which one of the super-rich was buying stolen antiquities. He knew of several men in the upper world of big money; some ruthless bullies, some very strange, and entitled personalities. To a man, they would have the back of the other guys in the tribe. Not one would throw another under the bus, he thought. The ethereal world in which they flourished was always fraught with jeopardy that had to be overcome by any means. Did the buyer have an Achilles heel?

Chapter
42

Bertram Thompson sipped his morning coffee and used his remote to turn on the large screen television in his home office. His attention rose when the story about an Iraqi who sold ancient stolen antiquities to a Turkish buyer in Gaziantep were both brutally murdered. The tease got his attention. He never believed in coincidences. Bertram didn't want to call Emre, too dangerous for a possible connection.

Instead, against all instincts risking connections, he turned on his computer and did a search for Emre's name. It came up at the top of the choices. The story connected the two men, Abu Mustafa and Emre, by an American television reporter who was interviewing the Iraqi before he was murdered. He read several other reports, one from Al Jazeera and one video from CNN Turkey. The CNN report emphasized the connection to ISIS, as did Al Jazeera's report, but with a question about the name of the American buyer.

Bertram released his stranglehold on the television remote and dropped it on the desk.

Sandy's research had found the connection to Simon Winton's New York City employer. After several minutes of digging up the number, she called Bertram Thompson, but without a response.

She left a message asking whether Simon Winton, who was killed in a car crash, worked for him.

Law Clerk William J. Stratton called Bertram Thompson from his office adjoining Judge Mildred Stein's chambers.

Bertram thought about declining the call, the news about the murders soured his mood, but he answered on the fourth ring against his better judgment.

"Mister Thompson, it's Stratton from Judge Stein's office."

Bertram frowned, he didn't want calls seeking financial support this morning.

"William, how can I help the Judge?"

"Well, she doesn't need help, right now. Just calling to alert you that a warrant has been issued for your premises."

"What? My premises?"

"Yes, all the premises in relation to an investigation of your employee Simon Winton. Since you own the floors he lived on, it's for the full property. Just a heads up is all."

"Investigation?"

Stratton took a moment deciding whether he should give the reason.

"Ah, not really sure," he lied.

It didn't matter to Thompson. There was nothing to be found on either premise. But it did agitate him greatly. Too much happening at once.

"William, thank you for calling, I will cooperate fully with the police."

Thompson strode around his office reviewing all the details that might lead to him. All ties to the antiquities were cut now that the two men were dead. Simon's death brings a dead end to any connection to TB Incorporated no matter how coincidental the initials, he thought. However, that woman, that Collette Riccardi had survived the attempt on her life in St. John and now Simon's kidnapping of her. She must be stopped somehow. Her credibility must be challenged. He decided to call Darko Stevnich Horatio Horvat, a Croatian man willing to do anything for his American benefactor to help gain citizenship to the United States.

Darko had been a policeman in Croatia with a shady past. He left the country after being cleared of most wrongdoings. Darko had found, then shadowed Thompson until a meeting he planned found them alone in an office building's elevator with a third man hired by Darko.

The man triggered an altercation with Thompson allowing Darko to intervene by tossing him from the elevator on the next floor. The hired man received his pay from Darko and the connection with Thompson had begun. Darko learned that wealthy benefactors were important in Croatia. He knew that one would be important in a new country. He was correct.

"Good day, Mister Thompson."

"I need to have a chat."

"Anytime, anyplace, of course."

"I will get back to you later today."

Thompson felt anxious after the morning's events. He didn't like the feeling which he could easily overrule if only he had his complete precious collection of coins. All the coins had been sent away for safekeeping and his own protection, except the one he cherished most. He took out his wallet where the coin lay ready for his examination. The police won't ask to see my wallet he believed so it was placed there allowing easy retrieval when needed. It helped to both buoy and maintain his resolve to get through all things. The strong face with a prominent nose and chin was of a Middle Eastern king who had reigned over vast distances, many people and powerful armies. However, he missed fondling the other coins which gave him a sense of history and power. Total control was the foundation of power. The ancient kings' edicts were followed without question. The questions and events surrounding him had become a source of evaporating control.

Chapter
43

Collette Riccardi laid out the company's files for TB Incorporated and for Bertram Thompson Industries. No stone to be unturned. Thompson had many companies, Collette found records for three small companies in two states, one in Maryland and two in Pennsylvania. The Maryland company, Dorman HVAC, was the second largest heating, ventilation and air conditioning company bordering the Washington, D.C. area. Its clients were small hospitals and medical centers. Acorn Centers, a Pennsylvania company matched health caregivers to seniors needing home care. The last was a Pennsylvania warehouse, Thompson Industries, that reportedly stored equipment from the other companies in the Thompson group.

Collette organized each set of folders according to services, dates and income filings. The names of all CEOs and management personnel were listed, except TB Incorporated. The only link was dead Simon Winton. She'd ask Dieter to get his personal banking and financial records uncovered.

"Good morning roomie," Lindsay said from Collette's office door.

Lindsay stood with two cups of coffee from a nearby shop. She held up the paper cups, smiled and delivered one cup to Collette's outstretched hand. The two women, once enemies then acquaintances had become friends.

"Thought I'd pop by for a quick cup of coffee, catch up a bit."

Collette felt a slight rise in her ever-present guilt quotient. She'd been up and out of Lindsay's apartment at the crack of dawn for days, not returning until late. Their time together had dwindled as a result and Lindsay wanted to check on her roomie.

Collette looked tired and pale, yet her face lit up at the sight of Lindsay and her body relaxed with the first sip of coffee. Before the second sip, Lindsay reached across the desk.

"Cheers," with a mischievous giggle, albeit forced.

Collette's response was real, she laughed and clinked her cup against Lindsay's.

"Cin Cin Dottoressa."

The moment didn't last long. Lindsay scanned Collette's desk topped with file folders, some opened and some waiting to be opened. Collette noticed.

"Welcome to my world."

"How does it feel to be back at work."

"Not work. Research to find all I can about Thompson."

"Oh, I see. How is it going?"

"Not going. I'm looking for connections to all that's happened." Collette grew quiet.

"Trying to connect the dots as Karl says?"

"Exactly. There's got to be connections between Thompson and the men in St. John, my kidnappers and whoever stole our personal hard drives. More importantly, there must be a reason for all this to happen. Nothing makes any sense. My guess is that TB Incorporated is the link but there's no clue about the transfer of money and some service or product."

"This company paid for things, but you've no idea what?"

"Exactly. Simon Winton had the answers, but he's gone."

"Now what?"

"Now? Not sure, but I want to see that entitled, bastard pay for what I know he's behind. Just can't find the proof." Collette looked hard at Lindsay. "Has Karl learned anything new?"

"Oh, I don't know."

Collette reached for the phone on her desk. "I need to call him, okay?"

Lindsay watched as Collette scrolled through her cell's phone listings. Before she dialed, she looked at Lindsay for approval.

"Sure."

Dieter answered on the second ring. Collette listened.

"Oh, okay, thanks, great, bye."

Lindsay's quizzical look brought Collette's answer.

"They just got a search warrant for Simon's apartment and Thompson's too."

For the second time that morning Collette smiled.

Darko had met Thompson in the elevator where they first connected. It was to be their usual meeting place. Public. But private once the elevator was emptied of other riders. His assignment was to find out all he could about Collette Riccardi. He was given the name of her company and her deceased husband without further clarification. Darko liked this assignment. It allowed him to use all the experience gained as a police officer in Croatia. The Internet gave him a start. He paid the few dollars to search her name and background connecting her with family, previous addresses and a stepfather who had a criminal record of spousal and family abuse. The college she attended and her previous employment was easier since she was on a website linking possible business possibilities. Her photo was on this site. He printed it. It would help him follow and report her whereabouts to Thompson at all times.

Darko arrived at Collette's office building by taxi on the busy NYC main street. He never got accustomed to the extremely busy streets of his new home city. Taxi cabs were his usual mode of transportation. He didn't like the high fares and the need to tip drivers. Back home, he was the respected, if not merely feared, police officer. In this new world he was no one; a foreigner in a world of foreigners. He entered the building and went to its directory of companies. Crawford & Bigelow was listed. He walked to the bank of elevators and took one going up. The crowded car stopped several times until it reached his destination.

Crawford & Bigelow's doors were to the right behind a large glass wall separating the reception desk and a pretty blonde. He tried the locked doors. The receptionist's voice came over a speaker at the door.

"Can I help you, sir?"

He was surprised at the security. Darko had learned that if he affected a meek persona and added a heavier accent, he'd be trusted by almost anyone.

In a thick accent he began, "Ah, I…hello, can you hear me?"

"Yes. How can I help you?"

"Okay. Yes. Thanks to you very much." He stood smiling and nodding his head respectfully.

"Sir is there something you want?"

"Oh, yes, I want to speak with a person about money."

"Money? Sorry, sir, we cannot give money…"

"Ah, no, not money. How you say, financial matters. Yes, financial matters."

He stood proudly presenting a grateful immigrant pose. A buzzer sounded, and he quickly opened the glass door. Darko quick-stepped to the desk and stuck out his hand. The blonde respond only by giving him a steely look.

"My name is Vladimir, I am here in your country to start a new life, to start a new business. I seek help with the financial matters." His eyes scanned the offices behind and beyond the receptionist seeking Collette's face which he had memorized.

"Sir, we are not a bank."

"No, I don't need money. I have good money. Yes, not to borrow. I seek help in financial matters. I was told your company can help."

While she was answering, Collette and Lindsay walked toward the door.

"Thanks for stopping by."

"What do you say we have a girl's night in later? Stay at home, chat, maybe drink some wine?" Lindsay asked.

Collette smiled and hugged Lindsay. "Perfect."

Lindsay left.

Darko had stopped listening to the blonde receptionist as soon as Collette entered the area.

"Do you want to make an appointment with a financial advisor?" the blonde asked.

"Yes, of course. Maybe a pretty one like that woman, but she's a secretary probably."

The blonde was peeved. "No, she is not a secretary, and she is not available to meet you."

"Sorry, sorry, I mean no disrespect to her." Darko had all he needed. "Okay, I apologize. Thank you." He turned to leave as the blonde receptionist shook her head disapprovingly and answered the phone that chirped.

Darko left but didn't take the elevator. Instead, he walked around the floor surveilling the other large company, a law firm, also locked behind closed doors. He took the elevator down and left the building once he completed the surveillance of the area.

Dieter and McClure headed the team that entered Thompson's building. He flashed his badge.

"Call Bertram Thompson."

"But, I don't..." the concierge muttered.

"Now, call him now."

Dieter followed by the other officers strode to the elevators and waited.

The concierge after a brief phone call signaled the thumbs up to Dieter and they all entered the elevator.

Thompson was waiting for them when the elevator arrived.

"Detective, is this really necessary?"

Dieter took out the warrant to search all the premises.

"Yes," was his curt reply. "We'll start here and work our way down to Simon Winton's apartment."

"Here? Why here?"

"The warrant allows a full search of the complete premises."

Dieter waved the police investigators to begin. They dispersed throughout the apartment carrying satchels for evidence retrieval. Thompson feigned both surprise and irritation.

The irritation became real when Dieter declared, "Stay here, sir."

"Stay here?"

"Yes, that's right, stay here."

Thompson fumed.

Dieter mixed with the others as they went through all the floors of the multi-level apartment.

When he returned, Thompson asked, no longer hiding his mounting belligerency. "Detective, why are you searching my premises when Simon is the one under investigation?"

"Because he could have hidden something here that would incriminate him and others."

"Others? Are you insinuating that I might be involved in what he did?"

"Just checking all possibilities. That's my job."

Dieter liked taunting Thompson. He also knew that Thompson was playing the role of the aggrieved citizen. One for which he had no right.

Dieter spoke to an investigator and then to Thompson.

"We need to get into Winton's apartment now."

Dieter walked toward the elevator, turned and looked at Thompson.

"We'll need to get into the apartment," he repeated.

He waited for Thompson's reply.

Thompson slowly walked past Dieter and the investigators to the elevator. They all followed and entered with Thompson. The small elevator was populated with four investigators, McClure, Dieter and Thompson all cramped for the short ride down.

Thompson exited first, followed by the team of police who scattered to the rooms leaving Thompson with Dieter's orders to, "Stay here, sir."

Twenty minutes later a technician presented a woman's hair in a plastic bag.

"McClure, I guess he brought women here."

"Not likely with all the gay paraphernalia we found hidden in the bedroom."

Dieter turned to Thompson, "Is that true?"

"I have no idea," he lied. "If he was, so what?"

"Then it's likely that the hair belonged to the kidnap victim. It'll corroborate her story that she was kidnapped right here in your place."

"My place? This was his, not mine."

"You own it, don't you?"

"Well, yes, of course, I own it."

"Then it's your place."

McClure chimed in for added effect to Dieter, "You think the media will say it that way?"

Dieter added, "Likely. You know the media likes a good story."

"That's enough!" Thompson stood with controlled anger.

McClure and Dieter turned away and went to speak with the technicians who had gathered several bags of evidence.

"He doesn't seem happy," McClure snickered.

Chapter
44

Dieter spoke with the lead forensics technician before they left Thompson's building.

"Get me all you've got from the samples found. ASAP."

"Sure thing, Detective."

"Where to Karl?" McClure asked.

"Let's try the garage."

Once again, Dieter approached the concierge who gave him a wary look.

"I need to see Thompson's car. Which parking area is he in?"

The concierge heaved a troubled sigh, but let his finger run along a book which listed the names for each parking number.

"One, his parking space is number one," he said.

"Figures, McClure chuckled."

They re-entered the elevator and descended to the garage. The building held only the wealthiest of New York's residents and their cars were a testament to that wealth. Every major European luxury brand was represented along with high-end Teslas for the few who believed in elegant sustainability.

Thompson's dark blue Bentley was indeed parked in the number one spot. It was also closest to the elevator. The slightly tinted windows did not hide the caramel-colored leather interior nor its opulence. No vanity plate number here. The car alone was vanity enough. McClure wrote down the plate number. Both men walked around the car in the well-lit area. Dieter stopped and looked at McClure.

"See that?"

McClure looked. "No, what?"

"Dust covering the whole car. Lots of dust."

"I guess he doesn't use it much."

The parking attendant for the building approached.

"Can I help you guys?"

Dieter flashed his badge and the attendant held up his hands in mock surrender.

"Open it."

"What? Open it? I'll get fired for that."

"You'll get arrested if you don't. Your choice."

The attendant jogged back to his post and returned with the smart key. He clicked the doors unlocked but held onto the key.

Dieter and McClure entered the car from opposite sides. McClure ran a hand across the leather.

"Nice."

Dieter wrote down the odometer number. Five thousand eighty-eight miles.

"Barely driven," he told McClure.

"New?"

Dieter chuckled, "No idea."

Both men entered the back seats after inspecting the glove box and side compartments. Spotless and empty.

Dieter exited the car and spoke to the attendant who was waiting, "Pop the trunk."

The man pressed the key's trunk release causing it to open slowly. Its interior was pristine and noted by both men.

"Not like my trunk," McClure said. "Mine has softball gear, my weight training belt and all kinds of junk."

Dieter took out a pocket flashlight and sprayed its light slowly around the trunk. There was no sign of anything ever having been in there.

"How often does this car get out?" Dieter asked the attendant.

"Never saw it leave this spot during my shift."

"Okay, close her up."

Dieter and McClure walked back to the elevator. In the ride to the main floor, Dieter mused. "If he doesn't use it that means he takes other means of getting around. Let's find out what that is and see if we can track his travels around town. My guess is he doesn't take everyman's taxi ride. Probably a private car service."

"Will do."

Dieter's cell phone rang. It was Captain Grover.

"Yes, Captain. Just finished up here at Thompson's place."

"I know. My phone was on fire with calls from Downtown, and Adam Walther, Thompson's attorney. It seems you pissed him off. You said you were going to tread lightly. Right?"

"Yes, I did say that, and I did tread lightly. Must be hiding something. Right?"

"More importantly, did you find anything at Thompson's or the other guy's place, Winton?"

"The techs are putting together all they bagged and found, but nothing obvious at this time."

"The folks Downtown want this to end. Either get something hard on him or let it go, they said."

"Captain, this is an open investigation that has three people murdered, a kidnapping and probably much more. We can't walk away. You got to support us."

There was a moment of silence which ended with an audible sigh, "I know and that's what I did. They didn't like it, but I said we must finish the investigation regardless whose toes get stepped on. Listen, Karl, I'm glad to be here in this division. There are good folks here and important work to be done, so keep that in mind. Okay?"

"Are you being threatened?"

"Threatening me? Not at all, they're reminding me of the future and how certain possibilities can fade quickly from outside pressure. That's all."

Dieter felt a moment of guilt from Grover's comments. "Thanks for your support. There's much more to these murders than is clear right now. All we need is a connection in the evidence chain. I'm going to get it."

Bertram controlled his rising anger long enough to return to his apartment. Once he exited the elevator he exploded. He cursed Simon, Collette, Andrew and the Turkish buyer for their complicity in his present situation. If they had not brought trouble to his door, he'd be content with the ancient antiquities that he bought. Their grandeur was for him alone, not for the common crowds. He took out his wallet and found the one remaining coin in his possession. The face on the coin was his favorite king who once ruled vast worlds centuries ago. Thompson walked to his desk and took out a magnifying glass. He passed the magnifier over the coin and steadied his hand to see the regal face. This king represented all that Thompson could not have in a world surrounded by common thinking people. Their rules were for the masses, not for him. Their rules, however, held sway over his life at times. He rejected their rules and their limited thinking. That Detective's arrogance was infuriating. "Stay here."

He called Darko who answered on the first ring.

"What did you find?" Thompson asked.

"I found Collette Riccardi at her offices. Now, I am getting background on her. I can send you a report in a few hours."

"No. Meet me at the usual place. Bring paper only."

"I will call you when the report is complete."

Thompson hung up the phone.

Chapter
45

Collette left the office after barely eating lunch at her desk. She wondered why Captain Grover, Dieter's supervisor, wanted to talk with her. It cluttered her mind unnecessarily.

She walked to the street corner and hailed a taxi and so did Darko. He told the driver that he needed to catch up with his wife in the taxi ahead. The driver didn't believe the lie, but he had a paid fare, so he followed the taxi that Darko had pointed out. Both driver and Darko were surprised when Collette's taxi stopped in front of a police station. Darko watched her enter after a chivalrous officer held the door open allowing him to ogle the pretty women. His partner laughed at him and shook his head as they walked to a police car.

"We're here," the driver said.

"Yeah, but that was not my wife. Sorry for the mistake." He read the meter and begrudgingly paid the driver adding a modest tip. The taxi drove off the instant Darko's feet hit the street.

Darko called Thompson.

"She went into a police station."

"Stay there until she leaves."

"Okay."

Darko looked around the street populated by uniformed police and black and white police cars. Where could he perch himself without being noticed? Butch's Coffee Shop was across the street and a few stores down the block. He entered, bought coffee and commandeered a window high top seat that faced the street. The crowded shop served coffee and pastries to officers going on duty and those finishing their shift. An hour passed slowly, but Darko had often spent long hours staking out homes, offices and dreary sites back in Croatia. He was well schooled in the process.

Collette exited escorted by an officer who walked her to a black and white. They entered and left the busy street.

Darko dumped his empty coffee cup and exited. He saw the car reach the corner and turn left heading back uptown.

"She left," was all Darko said before Thompson ended the call. Darko shrugged and walked to the corner where he hailed a taxi.

Agents Tim Carnahan and Flora Ventura entered the television studio where they flashed credentials and asked to speak with Robert Collins. Young female staffers scurrying to meet deadlines checked out Carnahan's good looks and tall stature. Agent Ventura received similar looks from male staffers for her model-like appearance. Each pretended not to notice. While waiting, agent Ventura sidled next to her partner, "It's happening again."

Carnahan didn't have time to respond to her joke, "Agents, I'm Robert Collins. You want to see me?"

Ventura answered, "Is there somewhere we can talk?"

"Sure," he walked them to a small glassed-in conference room.

Collins knew the subject of their questions before they began.

"This is about the murders in Turkey, right?"

"Yes and no. It's more about the sale of stolen antiquities. We are from the FBI's division investigating sale of these items here in the United States."

"I see. How can I help?"

"Your television piece spoke about an American, here in New York who purchased stolen antiquities from the Turkish man who was killed," Carnahan said.

"As well as the man who sold them."

"Yes, we know. But, we are after the man in New York. Do you have a name?"

Collins sat back and shook his head, "No, but my staff is researching anyone who buys art or artifacts from that area."

Ventura leaned forward, "The sale of these antiquities and other art brings in lots of money for the terrorists. It helps fund their attacks around the world. Ancient sites are plundered, some destroyed completely, while vast amounts of ancient coins, statues and more are sent from disreputable art dealers with full knowledge or total ignorance where the money goes. It's an arduous task to track the import of these items. We'd very much like to stop the sale to wealthy collectors here in the States."

Collins stood and walked around his chair. "I agree completely." He turned to face the two agents, "But, I spoke with this man Abu Mustafa. I saw his body covered and wheeled out of a hotel room in Gaziantep that I reserved for him. He had plans to move out of the country. I was going to try and get him to England and...away from ISIS."

"You are not responsible for his murder. You were doing your job, reporting all he told you. Helping to fight ISIS."

"Fight ISIS? I was just telling a story of a man tricked into working for ISIS. A simple, certainly naïve man, who was murdered."

Carnahan rose, "And helping to support ISIS by selling the stolen antiquities. The terrorist groups in the Middle East have long been involved in international crime. They've worked with drug cartels in Colombia bringing in millions, in some case billions, to support their attacks on innocent people. If your guy, Abu Mustafa, was involved with this activity, he was not a victim. The people who died from the hands of ISIS attacks were the victims. He was a criminal."

Collins struggled with his next words, the agents waited.

"I still see the body wrapped and hauled out on a gurney from that hotel room. He was scared."

Agent Ventura shot upright from her chair, "Robert, imagine the children who saw their parents murdered. Imagine the parents who held the dead bodies of their children whose limbs were blown away. Imagine that instead of someone complicit in the murder of innocent people."

A silence fell among the three. Ventura held her thoughts in check. Carnahan grew impatient.

"Robert, we need your help finding the New York buyer and shutting down the sales in our country." He paused, "All we need to know is whether you are in."

"Of course, I'm in. I'll do anything to help, but I have no more information than what is in my report and my files about this matter."

"We'll take your files and dig around too. Maybe we can uncover more than you have with international police support." She turned to Carnahan, "We'll start with the Turkish broker, Emre Arslan, whose car was bombed. Our New York buyer was not his only customer."

"No, probably not the only one." Collins felt the same rise in interest that a new blockbuster story evoked. "What can I do?"

"For now, we need all your files. We'll see what comes next," peppered with head nodding approval.

Twenty minutes later, after the files were duplicated for the FBI agents, they left Collins with an idea for future stories detailing the ways ISIS and other terrorist groups made money to pay for their terrorism. He sat down with a research assistant and explained his need for more information about the terrorist groups, who they were, how they existed and whether they were zealots supporting a cause or opportunistic gangs of thieves and murderers seeking to gain vast sums of money and power over innocent people.

"Verify the amount of money gained by these groups. Come up with a solid estimate, at least. A dollar amount will declare the need to stop Americans from buying these stolen antiquities."

"And make the story important?" the fresh-faced researcher asked.

Collins chuckled, "Yes, money is always at the bottom of a good story."

"Even a murder."

"Especially a murder." Collins didn't like his answer. It came too quickly and too dismissive of myriad reasons for what people do to each other.

"What about the buyers? Why do they buy if it's against the law? Aren't they already rich?"

"Probably."

"So, what do they gain by taking a chance of committing a crime? Isn't it risky?"

Collins hadn't thought this through completely. The objects bought could not be displayed for the public heralding the good taste or class of the purchaser. They couldn't be displayed in art galleries or museums with their family name adorning the exhibits.

"Not sure." For the first time, Collins looked at the young researcher with a sense of value. Why, indeed, would a wealthy New Yorker buy from a Turkish man murdered in a car bombing with such a public display? Why buy from a man who eventually is slaughtered in a hotel room? What motivates the New York buyer?

Chapter
46

Liz Fortunato waited thirty minutes for Cliff Edwards to show at Crosby's Bar and Grille. When she thought he wasn't going to show she left the bar stool and walked toward the doors. Cliff entered hurriedly and saw her.

"Liz, sorry, got caught up in the labs. Can you stay?"

Liz wanted to know what he had to say about the crash of the sports car and she liked his intelligence and good nature.

"Sure, sure, I figured you were working on something."

"Yes, I was but I'd like a beer now."

They walked back to the bar and sat. He ordered a Long Island craft beer, Liz demurred, "Nothing more for me, thanks."

"I thought you'd want to know the results of the report on the car."

"The car?"

"Yes, we did a thorough analysis of the damages to the car. The rear bumper was damaged in an unusual way for a car sliding off the road."

"I don't understand."

"There should be no damage to the rear bumper since it went down the side of the road front end first and then exploded." He looked at Liz for understanding and approval of his good work.

"So, what are you saying?"

"We believe the car was forced off the road by another vehicle. The damage was high on the car's rear and severe indicating a truck or large SUV hit the car repeatedly."

"Someone pushed the car off the road?"

"Looks that way."

Liz's face beamed with excitement. She leaned toward Cliff and kissed him on the check.

"Thank you, thank you."

"Remember, you can't tell where you got this from."

"No worries, this won't get me in trouble with the station."

"Maybe not, but it might get me in trouble with the lab. Promise to keep me out of this. Okay?"

"Absolutely."

"Okay. You hungry?"

She wasn't but said, "A little."

They ordered burgers and fries and he ate hungrily while she nibbled checking her watch for the time of the next news airing.

Clifford's supervisor had called Detective Dieter with the same information thirty minutes earlier. After the call, Dieter entered the Captain's office.

"Just got a call from the Suffolk County police department, they said Simon Winton's sports car was pushed off the road. No accident."

Captain Grover, "Somebody's covering their butt."

"Looks that way. Thompson."

"Yeah, but what is he hiding and why go so far to have his own employee killed?"

"Simon Winton must have had something on him."

"Lots of somethings to kill him, you think?"

Liz Fortunato's heart was beating rapidly as she approached Edie Baron's office. Edie looked up from her desk and waved Liz in.

"What's up, Liz?"

"Uhm, my source, at Suffolk PD believes the car that exploded off road was most likely pushed from behind deliberately."

"Really? Your source?" She smiled.

"Yes…"

"How solid is this…source?"

"He works in forensics…"

"He?"

Liz smiled, "Yes, he is an acquaintance."

"Can you be sure about him?"

"Oh, yes, very."

"The car was registered to a New York City resident. Right?"

"Yes, why?"

"Let's nail it down, air it locally and pass it on to the network in the City. They may even want to report from the scene of the crash."

"I can bring them there."

"Maybe you can do the reporting from the scene."

Liz smiled broadly, "Yes."

Chapter
47

Dieter looked across the table at Lindsay in Victor's restaurant. They had, as usual, been taken to a table set just for Dieter.

They had finished a delicious meal, not on the menu, prepared under Victor's wife's watchful eye. Lindsay wanted to have an evening out with Dieter since their time had been abbreviated due to the never-ending problems with Collette's case.

"Karl, I'm feeling disappointed with myself for tonight."

"Why? We had a great meal in a place that frankly caters to us."

"Not the meal, nor the place. I love Victor's restaurant. Glad you took me here that first time. It's me. I'm disappointed with me and my feelings."

"Tell me about it," Dieter said with a smirk as he mimicked what he thought a shrink does.

Lindsay playfully tossed a crumb from a piece of uneaten bread at him. Dieter's reflexive action caught the crumb and he gobbled it down.

"Thanks." He leaned in toward Lindsay, serious now, "You okay?"

"Yes, sure, maybe. Hard to say. I want to get back to us."

She looked at Dieter for understanding. He sat back and thought about what she had said. It had been a long time since they shared carefree moments. He remembered how she described the breakup of her marriage because she and her husband led busy lives that separated them.

"What are you thinking?"

Lindsay shrugged, cocked her head to one side then the other trying to clarify her thoughts.

"I feel empathy for Collette and all the horror she has faced. I probably was sympathetic at first. Now, her life has overtaken mine...ours. That is selfish."

"Not really, you've helped her every day since she arrived. You've housed her, cared for her, probably even had talks that were more like therapy sessions."

"At first, yes. Now, I want this to end. I want the people caught who killed Andrew." Her eyes moistened. "I want whoever is behind all this to be punished. It's complicated my thinking beyond anything I've experienced. It's draining my strength."

"Well, Doctor Lindsay Riccardi, you've just had a breakthrough. I'm proud of you."

She tossed another crumb at him with far more energy and a bit of anger.

"You're human, just like the rest of us," he spread his arms wide to indicate the restaurant. "Don't beat yourself up for that. Hell, we're all in the same boat at times. You know that better than any of us." He smiled and sat back with a self-mocking smug look on his face. "No one gets out of life alive."

She grabbed several pieces of bread and tossed them, one at a time, at him as he ducked to the left and right dodging the onslaught.

Victor came over and asked, "Would you like more bread?"

Dieter said, "No."

Lindsay said, "Yes."

The trio of friends laughed.

"Maybe some more wine?" to Lindsay.

"Thanks, Victor, I think I've had enough already."

Victor looked at Dieter questioningly.

"Yes, Victor, after the attack of the bread I do need another drink."

Victor left the table amid a moment of silence between them. Dieter swirled the bits of remaining ice in his glass, then drank, chomping on the ice. Lindsay looked around the restaurant. Couples sat eating. Young couples flirted. Older, married couples ate quietly. Some tables held four or six friends who chatted amicably, laughing. They all had lives outside this restaurant. Some good, some bad, some terrible. But, they were living in the moment sharing the special time with friends and loved ones. Lindsay looked at Dieter as Victor arrived with his drink.

"Victor, I'm sorry but we have to leave."

Dieter looked puzzled.

"No problem, of course, I'll nurse the drink myself," Victor said and left for the check.

"Why did you say that? Where do you have to go? We're having a good time...I think."

"Let's go to your place. We haven't been alone since she..."

Dieter rose and walked to Victor where he paid the bill. They left holding hands.

Later, the first time they made love was filled with passion and energy. The second time was slow, loving and pleasing to each other. Afterward, Lindsay slept with her head on his shoulder and one leg over his. For the first time in a very long while, Dieter slept peacefully.

Before the sun crested the nearby buildings, before Dieter and Lindsay's eyes opened to each other, Collette sat shaking in her bed. She had awakened from a dream about Andrew. He was sinking in the waters outside Cruz Bay, St. John, US Virgin Island. His eyes bulged imploring her to grab his hand as he sank only inches from her outstretched arms. No matter how hard she tried she was immobile and couldn't reach him. Water flowed around her, but it had no effect on her breathing. He gulped for air and choked as he sank away from her. Terror reigned on his face and in her heart. She awoke screaming when he vanished from view. Her heart was pounding, her eyes were tear filled and her hands were reaching out into the darkened room.

Collette's breathing was rapid and shallow. She pushed the covers from her body and rose on unsteady legs. Her first stop was the bathroom to wash away the vision that stalked her. The cold water was of no help. She went to Lindsay's bedroom and listened at the door for any sound. Nothing. She knocked timidly at first, then she knocked harder and eventually called out, "Lindsay."

She opened the door when there was no answer. The bed was made, unused. Lindsay was not home. Her anxiety increased twofold. Collette went to the darkened living room. No sign of Lindsay having been home. She rushed to her bedroom, took her phone and dialed Lindsay's cell number.

Dieter heard the cell phone first and sat upright. Lindsay moved and blinked awake.

"It's my phone."

Lindsay jumped from the bed and followed the chirping sound of her phone. She located her pocketbook on the dresser and rummaged in it until she found the phone. Collette's number came up and she answered it.

"Lindsay, oh my god, are you all right?"

"Yes, fine. Are you all right."

Collette felt a sudden wave of guilt. "I'm sorry, I just...was worried...is all."

"Where are you? Are you okay?"

"Yes. At your apartment. I'm sorry, I had a dream...never mind."

Collette hung up. She tossed the phone onto the bed and wept.

"Who was it?" Dieter was now standing next to Lindsay.

"Collette." Lindsay held the phone deliberating whether she should call Collette back. She turned to Dieter and went into his arms. They stood together as Lindsay fought the guilt that ran over her.

"Should I call her back?" Dieter asked.

"No," a little too quickly. "She'll feel worse if she hears from you. She knows we're together. I think she's had a panic attack."

"Okay, so what do you suggest?"

"Nothing right now. She's riddled with guilt and anxiety."

"Guilt? For what? She didn't do anything."

"Her call, during a panic attack, has rekindled reality. It interrupted us from our time and she knows that now. I'm sure she feels guilty for that."

"I see. Both of you are feeling guilty."

Lindsay looked at Dieter, reached up and put her hands around his neck, stepped close on tiptoes and kissed him with open-mouthed passion.

They separated, and Dieter said, "Doctor, control yourself."

She punched him in the chest.

"Maybe that's a healthier response for both of you?"

"What do you mean?"

"Anger. Replace your guilt and hers with good, old-fashioned anger."

"Healthier?" She thought for a moment. "And more productive than guilt which can be debilitating." Lindsay became serious again. She held Dieter close and he responded. To the darkened room she uttered, "You know Detective Dieter, I think I'm falling for you."

Chapter
48

Detective McClure read the final report on TB Inc. and was intrigued by a small passage connecting it to another company in Turkey that offered consulting services regarding the sale of ancient antiquities. Arslan Consulting was headed by Emre Arslan, an antique dealer with questionable business practices.

"What has this got to do with our murder case?" Captain Grover asked, exasperated with the twists and turns of the murder investigation. "What do we know about the Turkish guy...Arslan?"

McClure searched on his phone. When he was finished Dieter looked questioning at McClure as they sat in Grover's office waiting for an update. McClure, "He was murdered, blown up in a car bombing...his car."

"In the States?" Captain Grover asked.

Dieter responded, "No, Turkey. Simon Winton was directly connected to TB Incorporated, although I think he was the fall guy for Thompson."

"This Winton guy, same guy whose car was run off the road and exploded in the Hamptons?" Grover asked.

"Yes. The guy who kidnapped Collette Riccardi..."

Grover interrupted, "Andrew Ricarrdi's new wife...on their honeymoon?"

McClure and Dieter answered, "Yes, Captain." They exchanged a quick look at each other.

Captain Grover stood, "So, we have three possibly connected murders here and abroad, one kidnapping and all participants of the kidnapping are dead." He turned to McClure and Dieter. "Is that about it?"

"Maybe. The head is still on this monster even though some of its arms are cut off." Dieter stood too.

"Thompson? The head? And do we have any direct link to Thompson for any of this?"

"Not direct but cozy. Winton used this account to do business with Arslan Consulting. He sends them money from TB Inc. and in a week's time or so, he deposited in his personal account an amount about one hundred and fifteen percent of the last payment."

"You're saying he was getting money from a source that was about fifteen percent more than his last business transaction?"

"Exactly." McClure chimed in. "Then that money was taken out of the account."

"And what happened to it?"

"Winton's personal banking would show a deposit of exactly the amount taken from TB Inc."

"Winton was skimming money from the TB Inc. account." Grover mused. "How much money are you talking about?"

"Over two years, several million into TB Inc. and then Winton skimmed his cut," McClure said.

"Fifteen percent of several million. That's more than he could make as Thompson's lackey."

"Do we have a direct line to Thompson for the money deposited in TB Incorporated?"

Both Detectives shrugged.

"All right, then let's nail down that connection and get this guy." He looked sharply at Dieter.

Liz Fortunato's stomach ached. It always ached before a final exam when she was in college. Today, it ached because she'd be on the national television network reporting from the site of the car crash that may lead to a bigger story for the local affiliate. She scrolled through her phone, checking notes and bullet points. Her cameraman, Bill Evans, had set up his lights and had the feed ready to connect when signaled. He looked at Liz who projected nervousness. Bill had spent many years on network television until he decided to cut back his lifestyle and spend time with his ailing wife. They'd moved to Long Island's East end where he took the job as a cameraman alongside newbie Liz.

"It's going to be just like any other live report. You'll be fine."

She smiled at Bill, "Thanks, I know, once we get rolling I'll be fine. It's the moments before."

"Athlete's call it pregame jitters. No problem once we're rolling." He looked at his watch. "Coming up in two minutes."

The producer sounded in her headgear to get ready.

Liz took several deep breaths and in a little more than two minutes she was live.

Collette Riccardi sat in Lindsay's apartment watching the news oblivious of its content until Liz's report came on. She focused on the report reliving the terrible moments of her kidnapping. Once the report ended the New York City anchor elaborated on the story and the possible connection, as he called it, to a kidnapping of a New York City resident. When Collette's photo-filled a corner of the screen, she gasped and stood with clenched fists.

"They had my picture on television for everyone to see. Everyone!" she yelled at the heavens and into Lindsay's ears.

"How'd they get your picture?"

"I don't know." She thought for a moment trying to empty her mind of the competing violent images. "Business networking digital sites I guess."

Lindsay thought about her professional pictures on several psychological association's websites.

"Yes, you're right. We've surrendered our privacy to the digital world." Lindsay surveyed Collette whose body language evoked defeat. She stood slumped, beaten and without energy.

"I know. There's no place to…I don't know…be safe anymore."

Safety had been lost the moment Andrew was murdered. All life was turned upside down. And now, her personal privacy was stolen, spread out to the world for judgment, pity and perhaps ridicule. Social media posts would draw pity posts and post ridiculing her for being so foolish to have been kidnapped. Her fault by some, her approval by others. Much more than she wanted or needed. Collette didn't know what she needed to suppress her increasing level of frustration at each turn of events. She had become the center of it all. She didn't truly know why, but rising anger was once again aimed at Thompson. His employee, his house, a vague connection to him from a shell company always brought her back to Thompson. Now, as she stood before Lindsay, the rising anger reappeared and pushed aside the frustration.

"I want to kill him," she muttered with animal fury. Her eyes were aglow with hatred and ferocity. Lindsay saw it.

"Collette…."

Collette was not in the room with Lindsay any longer. She was standing over Thompson's body relishing his death.

"Collette, what are you thinking?"

Lindsay witnessed the change in Collette's posture; the slumping body became erect, her demeanor purposeful. She moved closer to Collette and took her hand. Collette pulled away abruptly. It frightened Lindsay. But, Lindsay persisted. She moved in very close to Collette's face.

"Listen to me." Collette's eyes did not move from the distant place. "Collette! Listen to me." She took Collette's arms and held them tightly.

Collette blinked away the images and returned to Lindsay.

"I need you to stay with me right now. Can you do that?"

Collette shrugged. "Okay. I'm here. What is it?"

"Sit down, please." She pointed to the couch. Collette sat.

"I'm sitting."

Lindsay had seen adolescents stuck in petulance mode. Now, she witnessed Collette's fight with the moment and the churning emotions.

"My picture was on television for all to see. Everyone will know what happened to me. The news will tell every detail of my capture. People like you will discuss how I felt under confinement." Collette stared at Lindsay with pleading eyes.

"You need to get control now. Do you understand?"

Collette's face displayed confusion. "Control? I have no control! Not for anything anymore."

"Yes, you do. What is it that you don't want?"

"All this that happened to … my life."

"True, now what is it that you do want? That's the road ahead to take. You see?"

"No, I don't see! I can't see anything but Thompson's dead body at my feet."

Lindsay stood to regroup. "You do know that is not possible? Right? Another murder is not the answer? It won't lessen the pain that you feel. Revenge never does, it's fleeting. Reality lives on…always."

Collette rose from the couch and stepped around in a circle until she faced Lindsay again.

"What do I do? Give up? Lay down and wait to die?"

"No. That is not an option. You persist by returning to your life, let it fill you up again. It will take time. Small steps forward. Karl will get to the bottom of this…I promise."

With eyes ablaze, "And if he doesn't?"

"He will," mustering all the conviction she had left. Her cell phone rang with Dieter's special ring.

"It's Karl now."

276

Lindsay turned and walked a few steps away from Collette.

"Hi. I was just talking with Collette. She's hoping for some news…"

"There may be a connection to Thompson and stolen antiquities from overseas," Dieter said.

"I don't understand."

"We're trying to sort it out here. Can she come in?"

"To the police station?"

"Yes, we have a lot to show her. Maybe it'll help lead to an end to all this."

"Now?"

"Yes."

"Okay, I'll tell her."

When Lindsay ended the cell phone call, Collette moved to her quickly. "Tell her what?"

"Karl needs your help."

The afternoon traffic frustrated Collette as she sat next to Lindsay in the taxi cab ride to the police station. The driver honked at pedestrians who were on cell phones in the street only steps from the corners while he tried to turn onto a cross street. He muttered something unintelligible, then he scanned the rear-view mirror to see if his passengers heard. The two passengers sat stoically awaiting the ride's end.

Neither women nor the driver noticed the rental car which followed two cars behind ever since they entered the taxi in front of Lindsay's apartment. Darko had followed Collette to the apartment building as part of his surveillance for Thompson. He recorded her whereabouts the several times she left the building as was his custom. He was surprised, however, when the taxi stopped near the police station. He watched as they hurriedly entered the building and entered. He wrote the time and place of Collette's arrival in a notebook he had used when a police officer in Croatia. It took several minutes, enough time for an NYPD officer to walk to Darko's car, and tap on the window.

Darko reacted by putting his notebook between the seats; a motion that caught the officer's attention. Darko rolled down his window to the now suspicious officer. He smiled at the officer's dour face.

"Can I see your identification sir?"

"My identification?" He had done this many times in Croatia to people in expensive cars or suspiciously parked cars with motors running. Often it would lead to an arrest or violence against the civilian. He knew the possibilities, so he decided to tread lightly. "May I ask why officer?"

When the officer heard the heavily Croatian accented response he asked Darko to, "Step out of the car sir."

Darko frowned openly which exacerbated the officer's response.

"Let me see your hands. Step out of the car now."

Darko held his hands in the view of the officer who watched Darko's exit with a hand on his weapon. Once Darko had exited, the officer put his hands on Darko's shoulder and turned him around. "Put both hands on the car sir."

Darko held his growing anger in check but turned toward the officer. "Officer, I am a police officer from Croatia. My identification is in my wallet. May I get it for you?"

"I'll get it." The officer reached into the rear pocket for the wallet and retrieved it. The passport was also in the same pocket. He opened it but held one hand on Darko's back. After carefully reading the identification which included his visa, passport and an unofficial police identification card.

"This doesn't prove you are a police officer sir."

"I was an officer. I now live in this country."

The officer ignored his response, "Don't move." He leaned into the car and took the notebook.

Darko was annoyed. "That's mine officer."

The officer flipped through some pages but could not understand the written Croatian language.

"It's only my personal notes...nothing important to anyone but me." He smiled benignly, offering a conciliatory pose.

"Sir let's go into the police station, I'd like to check this out with my people."

Darko took a few seconds too long to move. The officer grabbed his arm to move him along. Darko's patience reached its peak. He swung around releasing his arm to step away from the officer. Two officers rushed to his side and pushed his face down on the street.

"What are you doing? I've done nothing!" Darko yelled loud enough to gain the attention of other officers exiting the building. A group of officers surrounded him, hands on their weapons while Darko was handcuffed and pulled to his feet.

The arresting officer nodded thanks to his fellow officers and pushed Darko, again, toward the building holding onto his arm. This time, Darko did not resist.

Chapter
49

Lindsay and Collette met Dieter when they entered the detectives' squad room. The detectives looked at each woman with smiles of approval, especially when Lindsay involuntarily leaned in for a kiss on the cheek. One detective waved a thumbs up to Dieter's back then returned to his paperwork.

Collette was drawn and jittery. She looked around the squad room at a world which she never wanted to enter again nor be part of for any reason. This place that was filled with an air of crime and deceit surrounded her. For a brief moment, she wanted to escape, to hide again and retreat to safety.

"Collette, thanks for coming in. My Captain would like to speak with you. Okay?"

Dieter looked at Lindsay for support.

"I can go with you," Lindsay said.

"He wants to speak with her…"

Captain Grover saw them enter and was striding toward them when Dieter looked up.

"Here he comes."

The woman turned to see the tall man approach.

"Thanks for coming in. I'm Captain Grover," to the two women. He looked to Dieter for an introduction.

"Captain, this is Collette Riccardi," nodding toward her. "And this is Doctor Lindsay Riccardi."

Grover smiled at both women. To Collette, he said, "Missus Riccardi, I'd like to speak with you in my office?" He turned and pointed.

Collette hesitated a moment, looked at Lindsay and followed the Captain to his office. Lindsay and Dieter watched Grover and Collette enter.

"How is she?" Dieter asked. "She looks…anxious."

"She is very anxious and angry and overwhelmed."

Police Officer Atkins took Darko into the police station and sat him down facing the intake desk.

"Stay here." He commanded to Darko.

Darko scanned the area that was populated by police entering and exiting. Some came in with handcuffed prisoners. One officer told an obviously inebriated man to, "Stay put, don't even think of moving."

Atkins walked to the sergeant's desk with Darko's notebook in hand.

The sergeant saw him and looked up from a pile of papers. "What you got there Atkins?"

He held up the notebook. "This guy," pointing to Darko, "was sitting in his car outside the station taking notes."

"Notes? About what?"

"You take a look."

The sergeant flipped through some pages then looked at Atkins. "What am I supposed to do with this. It's some foreign language." He looked over to Darko. "Who is he?"

Atkins handed over Darko's papers.

"Croatian, a cop over there, what's he doing taking notes out here?"

"No idea, but he was very fishy when I asked him to move his car. He tried to hide this notebook. I figured something's not right."

Two officers came in with a handcuffed man who was resisting, causing a commotion, and taking the sergeant's attention from Atkins. "Gimme a minute for this." He said to Atkins.

Captain Grover surveyed Collette as she sat in a chair facing him. He leaned forward, hands in a contemplative steeple, "I'm sorry for your loss."

Collette forced a thank you smile.

"You've been through a lot I hear."

"Yes, and now everyone knows about me and…" tears welled in her eyes.

Captain Grover reached into a desk drawer and took out a small package of tissues which he pushed across the desk to Collette. She took one and held it in her trembling fingers.

"The picture on the news?"

"Yes, why do they do that? I mean, put the picture of the victim on television…. I don't understand. It's hurtful."

Captain Grover felt the need to appease her feelings, but he wanted to get to the issues at hand. "I guess it's part of the information the public gets. I'm sorry."

He waited a very long moment, then leaned forward, "I have questions about what happened to you and the men who took you. But, first I'd like to know about their employer, Bertram Thompson."

Collette nearly exploded out of her seat. "That bastard! It's all his fault…I know it."

Captain Grover was surprised by the sudden transformation in Collette's behavior. But, he was glad to see it. It validated the questions he and Dieter had about Thompson. "How is it his fault?"

Collette's face screwed up in an admixture of anger and utter confusion. Serious now, she leaned into the desk toward Captain Grover, "I don't know for sure, but I know he is involved in everything that happened to me, to the kidnappers, and to Andrew."

"Tell me what you mean."

For the next twenty minutes, Collette explained the events and how Thompson was always just outside the boundaries of involvement.

Lindsay looked toward the Captain's door.

"They've been in there a long time." She looked at her wristwatch. Dieter did also.

Just then, the door opened, Collette and Captain Grover exited. He stopped and put out his hand which she took and gave him a brief hug. Captain Grover entered the office. Collette walked with a newly found sense of purpose to Lindsay and Dieter.

"Thanks for meeting with my Captain."

"He's a good man," was the surprising comment from Collette. To Lindsay, "Can we go back now?"

Lindsay looked at Dieter.

"Sure, I'll get an officer to take you back."

"Karl, I think we'll take a cab, Collette's had enough notoriety."

"Yes, I'd rather not be dropped at the building in a police car," Collette said.

"Okay, sure, I understand. I'll call you later."

The women left the squad room and took the stairs down to the hustle and bustle of the main floor. They passed the seated Darko who recognized Collette just as Atkins summoned him to the sergeant's desk. He rose, and Collette caught a brief look at the stranger who seemed to be staring at her.

Collette seemed more in control in the taxi cab drive back to Lindsay's apartment building. Lindsay noticed.

"You said Captain Grover was a good man...."

Collette looked at Lindsay with calm eyes. "Yes, he listened to me. Didn't judge me. And he said that Detective Dieter will get to the bottom of all this. He likes him."

Lindsay knew that her Karl would do as he promised.

"He said, he'd do everything to help Detective Dieter get the man responsible."

Lindsay took Collette's hand which she accepted this time.

"Why are you taking notes outside a police station?" the sergeant asked in a voice that was so cold icicles could form on his lips.

Darko had no response at the ready. His indecision caused further concern to the sergeant.

"And why is it in your country's language? What are you hiding? Geez, the only thing I can read is a name...Thompson, just once, but very clear. Who is Thompson?"

Darko had never been on this side of questioning when he was a policeman in Croatia. He didn't like the feeling. He didn't like the meaty sergeant's arrogance.

"I asked you a question. Who is Thompson?"

Finally, Darko's mind clicked into place. "It's a company here in New York City. A friend back in Croatia told me it's a good place to get furniture for my new apartment."

"Bullshit! Try another."

"No, no, I don't lie. It is a good place to get inexpensive furniture."

"Where is it?"

Darko's face contorted into confusion.

"Where is it? Did you go there? Buy furniture?"

Darko returned to the immigrant who knew nothing status.

"Oh, I cannot remember. It was in a different part of the city from here."

The sergeant lost all patience. "Atkins find a place for this guy until we can get a translator for this notebook. I don't like his answers."

Captain Grover stood with Dieter pouring a cup of coffee in the break room.

"She's been through a lot," Captain Grover mused.

"Yes, she is. Underneath it, she is one tough lady."

"I think it might be time to speak with the District Attorney's Office. Get some guidance."

Dieter knew this was not normal procedure, but he agreed aware that his Captain had connections he didn't. Furthermore, he began to understand the motives, and his aspirations to move up the command ladder.

"Are you thinking about increasing the pressure on Thompson?"

Captain Grover eyed Dieter with a feigned countenance defined by innocence. "Good idea. Once again you show your keen mind that I'd like to keep around."

He strode away leaving Dieter to wonder when the Captain will ever stop lobbying him to stay on the job, and whether he should.

Officer Ivan Gonzalez approached the sergeant's desk after being told he was needed.

"What can I do for you, Sergeant?"

"I might need you to translate something for me. You speak Croatian, right?"

Ivan chuckled, "Yes, speak it, write it too. My Mom is from Croatia. My Dad is from Cuba. I was named after my grandfather Ivan. The only similarity is the C at the beginning of each country's name," he chuckled.

The sergeant handed over Darko's notebook. Ivan quickly read the first line. "Yes, this is Croatian writing."

"Yeah, well it's all Greek to me. What does it say?"

Ivan read a few lines, turned the page and looked up at his sergeant.

"It looks like this guy is following someone. It lists places and times where she, a woman entered a building."

"What's her name?"

"Only uses the letter for C in English."

"What's the name Thompson have to do with this. He said it is a furniture store. Is it?"

Ivan laughed. "No, it's a man's name. The guy he's snooping for...I think."

"What a minute. This guy is following a woman named C something for a guy named Thompson?"

"Yeah, that's it."

"And he was parked out front?"

"Yeah, why?"

"Two women came in just before you brought him in here. They went up to see Detective Dieter."

"How do you know?'

"They asked for Detective Dieter. Ivan, take this up to the detective and see if it makes any sense to him."

Chapter
50

Dieter walked quickly to Captain Grover's office once he was finished talking with officer Ivan. With the door open, Dieter walked in and said, "I think we have the bastard."

Captain Grover swiped his hand across his face to regroup from the reports he was reading.

"Okay, tell me."

Dieter explained the information from Officer Ivan and the name Thompson on the Croatian cop's notebook.

"Two things. Get his ass up here and get an officer over to the women. See if they're all right."

Dieter responded quickly, "McClure is already on his way and a local officer was dispatched before McClure gets there...just in case."

Captain Grover picked up his phone, punched in numbers, "Sergeant, send that Croatian cop up here with Officer Atkins and Officer Ivan Gonzalez."

Darko hated to be seated surrounded by NYPD officers in Captain Grover's office. The money he receives from Thompson lessened the worrisome situation. His disdain for these officers was held in check. Instead, he offered up the confused immigrant persona as a shield from the truth.

"Who are you tailing for Thompson? Collette Riccardi? She's the C in your notes? Right?" Captain Grover demanded.

Darko looked around with as much innocence as he could call forward.

"Tailing? I don't understand." To prove his ignorance, he searched the eyes of all who surrounded him imploring their support.

"You were following Collette Riccardi for Bertram Thompson. Isn't that true? Why?"

Darko continued the charade, "I don't know this Cosette lady you speak of."

"Collette, not Cosette. Stop playing dumb Mister Horvath."

Smiling now, "Please Captain, call me Darko."

"You said you were a police officer in Croatia. We're checking that now. If you were, then you understand my questions, so stop playing dumb."

Darko smiled, "Okay Captain," he looked around at the assembled, "officers. I was a police officer. Yes, I have been on the other side of this before, many times."

Captain Grover rose to his full height behind his desk, "Why are you following this woman?"

"I don't know."

"You don't know!" Captain Grover exploded.

"No, I was hired to follow her…keep an eye on her as you would say. Maybe a lover's situation. I don't know. He only said to report on her moves around the city."

"He? Thompson?"

Darko decided it was time to protect himself. "Yes, Mister Thompson, a very wealthy man. This was not uncommon in Croatia. The wealthy could pay for many things. It's normal."

"No, Darko, it's intrusive and maybe against the law."

Captain Grover spoke directly to Dieter, "Take this man for an interview with Officer Gonzalez, make sure we understand all he says."

Dieter grabbed Darko's arm and added an extra tight squeeze to escort him from the office.

Captain Grover's next phone call was to Judge Jeffrey Schuster. "Jeff, it's James, I have a request today."

Judge Schuster laughed, "What makes this day different from any other day? What can I do for you?"

Captain Grover explained the circumstances to his long-time friend and card-playing buddy. Judge Schuster responded with the possible retaliation that both might get from the likes of super-rich Thompson.

"True, Jeff, but the results of a conviction of a man like this might be beneficial to each of us." A serious tone of silence entered into the friendly conversation.

"Okay James, but if he beats this we're going to pay a price...you know that."

"Then I'll have to see that we have all the facts in place to make sure the prosecution has a strong case."

"You do that. Is the card game on for Thursday night? I need to get back some of my lost funds."

"Jeff, we play nickel and dime poker."

"I know, but it's the principle that counts. I'm a judge...I have to be right, don't I?"

They ended their conversation with the usual comradery that has held them together for fifteen years.

Dieter's call to leave a police officer at Lindsay's apartment allowed JB McClure to relish the trip to Thompson's building. He never liked the entitled billionaire nor his manner of dealing with the police as though they were his employees. McClure's car was joined by a black and white with two officers assigned to accompany McClure. The cars parked in front of the building in a no parking area and entered as a trio.

The man at the desk hollered to them as they entered the elevator, "Officers, where are you going?" No one responded.

Thompson's face showed his annoyance to the trio. His face burst into anger when McClure commanded, "We need you to come to the station with us."

"I will not."

McClure signaled to the two officers who moved quickly to Thompson. He froze, then regained his composure.

"You'll be very sorry for this."

"Just doing my job," McClure said smugly.

Thompson sat in the rear of the black and white. The man at the building's front desk and one other tenant saw him being put into the police car. They quickly shared the incident with other gossipers in the building.

At first, Thompson showed his anger to the two officers. But, when they didn't react, he sat in the back of the car quietly planning his response to this new circumstance. Lastly, he began to wonder what they may have uncovered causing the ride to the police station for questions.

The officers walked him into the building like any other perp. They brought him upstairs to the detectives' questioning room timed at Darko's exit in handcuffs. The two men stared momentarily at each other. Darko with a drop of fear and Thompson with overflowing rage. They sat him in the now empty room and left. Dieter and Captain Grover watched him through a one-way glass from an adjoining room. Thompson knew the mirror in front of him was a way for the police to see him. He stared at it with unbridled hostility.

"Let him stew a little," Captain Grover said.

"You know the first thing he's going to say?"

"I want my lawyer?"

"Oh yes."

They enjoyed a good laugh.

Dieter waited almost ten minutes before he entered the room. Before the door was closed Thompson demanded to see his lawyer.

"Absolutely, but first I want to share some things with you. Is that all right?" The game began. Dieter was well versed in the game, Thompson was not.

"Share? What have you got to share?" I've done nothing wrong."

Dieter sat facing Thompson and waited a moment. Thompson's hands fidgeted with each other. Dieter noticed.

"Do you know a man named Darko Stevnich Horatio Horvat?" The fidgety hands turned into clenched fists.

"No, I do not."

"That's a surprise."

"Surprise?"

"Yes, he says he's working for you."

Thompson sought to gain control of his mind and the situation.

"I want my lawyer." He sat back with arms folded across his chest. He stared into the mirror to show whoever was watching that he meant business.

Dieter rose, "He said you hired him to follow a woman."

Thompson didn't respond.

"You know the name Collette Riccardi I'm sure."

No response.

"She was kidnapped and held at your home in Montauk by your other employee, Simon Winton. Remember him? He was killed in an auto accident."

Thompson's eyes fluttered.

"You know the woman I'm talking about...the one whose husband was murdered in St. John?"

Finally, when no response came.

"Okay, you have the right to an attorney." He turned to the mirror with a smirk and left Thompson to boil alone.

Dieter returned to the viewing room.

"You have his attorney's number?"

291

Dieter reached into his sports coat pocket and pulled out a card, "Right here."

Captain Grover took the card. "I'll give the lawyer a call in a little while." He looked into the glass at Thompson. "Let's give him time to think about things. After all," he joked "we're a busy police station."

Before he called Thompson's attorney he called the District Attorney's Office to bring them up to date on the ongoing investigation and potentially high-profile prosecution.

Assistant District Attorney Gerome Donofrio took the call from Captain Grover.

"Captain Grover, this is ADA Donofrio, how can I help you?"

Captain Grover didn't know ADA Donofrio. The cases he was connected to while in the narcotics division went to ADA Sylvia Cruz a no-nonsense prosecutor. She'd prove to be dogged with the likes of Thompson.

"Listen, I've worked with ADA Cruz before. Nothing against you, but is she around?"

Donofrio's desk was piled high with cases so he was not insulted. "She's out of the office for a while."

"Oh, for how long?"

"She's visiting her sick mother in Colombia."

"Okay, here's what I need."

Captain Grover briefly detailed the investigation to date. The new information piqued Donofrio's interest. He glanced at the pile of folders on his desk glad to put them aside for such a case.

"Let me talk to my boss. I can get over to you in about forty-five minutes. Okay?"

Captain Grover told Donofrio the precinct and station house where Darko and Thompson were held.

"Thompson already lawyered up, so step on it."

Donofrio arrived within thirty minutes to Captain Grover's office.

292

"Captain, I'm ADA Donofrio."

It took twenty minutes to explain the very convoluted case and its various connections. Donofrio recorded the information as well as taking notes on how to proceed.

A young detective knocked at Captain Grover's opened door.

"Captain, that guy, Thompson has been asking for his attorney. He's getting pretty pissed off. What should I tell him?"

Donofrio looked at Captain Grover for his response.

"Tell him we are making every effort to reach his attorney."

The young detective nodded and left.

Donofrio smiled and asked, "Is that true?"

"Every effort? Sure, it's true." He stared down Donofrio's smile until it faded away. He added, "This guy is entitled to everything he can dream up. His attorney should just appear out of nowhere. We should never have brought him in for questioning, even though he hired a man to follow a woman who has been through hell and back."

"Do we know why he hired that Croatian cop? It could be very important."

"My question is more important. Can we hold him on something until we can put all this together? I have a strong feeling he's behind everything?"

Donofrio uncrossed his leg and stood. "There are lots of people who are being scrutinized by private investigators. Jealous husbands, jealous wives, businessmen who suspect a partner is embezzling money."

"But he's not a cop or a PI in this country."

"Okay, I'll make sure we get through to his attorney. Can you hang around?" Donofrio smiled knowingly again.

"Yes, Captain. I'd like to talk with the Croatian cop."

They left the office and went to Dieter's desk. After the introduction to Dieter, Donofrio accompanied him to where Darko was held.

Donofrio entered the room with Dieter. Darko rose immediately deciding that deference was better than belligerence. He stood showing the immigrant pose once more to the newcomer in a suit.

"Please, sit down sir. I am assistant District Attorney Donofrio. I'm here to learn about you."

Darko sat. "Me? I am a simple man, new to your country, who had a job for a wealthy man."

"I see. Let's begin from the beginning." All business. "Why did you come to my country?"

Dieter smiled and looked at the young ADA with approval.

"Why did I come to your country? Same as many people. Freedom. My country is not so like yours. We don't have the same opportunities you have."

"True, but you were a member of the police. I'd imagine you had plenty of opportunities to succeed."

"Well, not so many and so good as here."

Donofrio opened his attaché case and took out a folder. He opened it and read from it detailing Darko's police record, and expulsion from the police in Croatia.

"Is it fair to say that you had no more opportunities at home, so you came here seeking…special opportunities. One that Thompson gave you?"

Dieter leaned into the table between the trio. "We don't like crooked cops here. It hurts all of us."

"The detective is right mister Horvath. I'm sure you agree…now. So, please put on your police hat and help us," he challenged.

Chapter
51

Attorney Adam Walther was escorted to Thompson as he sat boiling in an empty room save for a table and chairs. He entered and stared down the detective who lingered too long at the door before he closed it with force.

"Where the hell were you?" Thompson barked.

Adam Walther had been on this side of Thompson's anger before. Like the other times, he ignored it and stayed on the issue at hand. He took a chair and set it next to Thompson facing away from the mirrored wall. Thompson turned his chair around so that both backs were facing the mirror. Walther leaned in and whispered into Thompson's ear.

"What did you say to them?"

"Nothing. I'm not an idiot."

"Why are you here?"

Thompson explained all that occurred from the time police came to his apartment to their attempt to interview him at the police station.

"You hired someone to follow Collette Riccardi? The woman who was kidnapped and held at your Long Island house? By a man who worked for you? Damn, Bertram, that is not good."

Thompson spoke angrily, spittle spraying from his lips.

"I was looking out for her. I wanted to protect her," he lied.

Adam Walther knew Bertram Thompson for more than twenty years. He never heard him speak this way before. The anger was real, he knew, but he also knew it wasn't because he wanted to protect the woman. His anger rose from the lack of control he had at the moment. Frustration leads to aggression he remembered from college psychology class.

"Okay, okay, then that's what we say. You hired this guy to watch out for her. Right?"

"He was asked to follow her and report to me."

"So, you could then protect her, right?"

"Exactly."

The attorney turned toward the mirror as did Thompson. In a minute the door opened allowing Donofrio and Dieter to enter.

Walther spoke first. "My client has a statement to make and then we're leaving."

Both men stood facing the officers of the court.

Thompson spoke, "Yes, I hired that man because I was looking out for her. So much happened to her surrounding me, my house, my employee. I was fearful for her. I wanted to protect her."

He puffed out his chest for emphasis.

Donofrio looked at Dieter and both men broke out in fake laughter.

"Is that the best you two could come up with?" Donofrio challenged.

"Listen, sir, we are here at the request of the police to help with a case. We are not staying to be ridiculed by the likes of you," Walther responded. "We're leaving."

"Not so fast," Dieter moved toward Thompson.

Walther stepped between the men, "Charge him or let him go, now."

Dieter looked at Donofrio who shrugged. Walther saw it and took Thompson's arm and left the room, but not before Thompson glared at both men angrily.

****

The three people most involved in Collette's case sat around the dining table in Lindsay's apartment. The balloon filled with expectation that began the dinner for Lindsay and Collette soon deflated and fell to earth.

"That horrible man said he was protecting me?" Incredulity defined her.

Dieter answered, "Yes, that's what he said after speaking with his attorney."

Lindsay interceded, "What did the ADA think?"

Dieter sipped some wine, wiped his lips with the cloth napkin.

"He thinks Thompson is not telling the truth. He thinks there is another reason the Croatian cop was hired. We're trying to find out, but everything seems to stop at Thompson's door."

"Then break down the door," Collette exploded.

Lindsay turned to Collette who sat to her left at the roundtable, "Karl will get him. Thompson will go to prison and you will get a breather from him."

Collette flashed a withering look at Lindsay but cut it short. Her head hung lower shaking from side to side in disbelief.

"He has power, money to buy favors from judges, attorneys, even the police…"

"What are you saying?" Lindsay asked.

Collette looked at Dieter, "Not you, I don't mean you. Not your Captain, but…"

No further response from Collette. She sat fighting back anger.

Dieter asked quietly, "But what?"

"I wish he was dead."

Dan Withers was about to retire from the warehouse which held thousands of items from Thompson's companies. He had spent twenty-five years as a fireman and the last ten as warehouse boss. He always wondered what was so important in the specially sealed boxes sent at odd hours to the warehouse for "safe keeping". On his last full shift, he decided to find out. He'd open the sealed boxes, check them out and then reseal.

The first box held several tiny statues of strange exotic characters. Bits and pieces were missing from very old, maybe ancient statues, he thought. That first box triggered his curiosity. He was not a history buff, but he thought these may be important since they were stored, maybe hidden, here at his job. The next box was smaller holding coins from ancient foreign eras. Each separately wrapped. Raised aristocratic faces with bits broken off still showed the power of men who reigned long ago.

Dan Withers wondered why these artifacts were boxed and sent far away from their home in New York City. Why not show these off to everyone? They must be worth a fortune. He re-boxed the contents after taking several photos with his cell phone and fighting off the urge to take one coin for himself. Might be interesting to see where these came from in my retirement, he thought. *Got to fill my days doing something.*

Chapter
52

Thompson returned to his home engulfed in a degree of anger he'd never felt before. No subordinate had ever spoken to him the way those people at the precinct did. No person ever ridiculed him with such a lack of impunity before. And it took away all focus from his life. If only he had his coins to console him, to bring clarity for the men rightfully in power over all others. He took out the one remaining coin in his possession and held it feeling the power of its predecessor; an ancient king who ruled peasants, like the peasants who disrespected him today.

The ancient men could do as they wished because they were the law of the land. He knew this, but he was governed by the laws that others legislated. What right did they have to legislate to me? In business, he was able to replace those laws that bind in place of a higher law, the law of profit.

As he sat at his desk without the sun warming his back, he was transported back to the room where he was held and questioned like some peon from ancient Spanish servitude. He felt the cold chair on his buttocks, the crushing walls around him demanding he stay and wait for his captors to arrive.

He knew he could muster the power to beat them and ascend above the fray and regain his rightful position. Money and power were his weapons which he'd use freely.

Adam Walther answered the phone when Thompson called.

"What can I do for you?"

"Let's have dinner."

Thompson decided that a public place allowed for more privacy than a phone call. They were to have dinner at an elegantly appointed, Michelin rated restaurant that catered to the most prominent New Yorkers. Even if he were to be seen with his attorney, it would be no surprise.

Dan Withers showed his wife the photos he took of the stored items at work.

While they cleared away the dinner dishes, he asked her, "What do you think of this stuff?"

She wiped her hands across an apron and took the phone for a closer look.

"Give me my glasses," she said after squinting. The eyeglasses which needed to be updated helped slightly.

"Let's put these on the computer. It'll be easier to see."

They finished the cleanup and sat down at the monitor attached to the desktop computer that he'd bought her for their last anniversary. She'd learned how to transfer the photos from their daughter Dawn when she was in college.

"These statues look very old," she observed.

"You think?"

She punched him lovingly in his arm. "Seriously, they look ancient, like from centuries ago. Right?"

"I thought so too. How do we find out about these?"

She typed on the keyboard and placed a photo into search mode. Several sites displayed. They clicked on the first and leaned in to read the explanation of the duplicate of the photo they searched.

They looked at each other with confusion.

"What's he doing with this statue? It's from Iraq centuries ago."

"No idea," he said. "We just get this stuff and store it for him, like all the other stuff for the company."

They searched each photo and found similar results for each. Ancient artifacts from Iraq. One site had a link to an FBI site which detailed stolen artifacts from Iraq.

"There's an FBI site for stolen Iraqi antiquities?" she asked Dan.

"Looks like it."

"What should we do?"

"Nothing. We do nothing. I want to get my severance from this company. It's not huge, but it'll add to my pension and social security when it's time. You know we're going to need every penny we get."

She nodded a silent agreement.

"Come on," he said and took her hand to walk into the living room and the television. He switched it on to watch their favorite game show in silence. Their eyes saw the television screen, but their minds were on the statues.

Robert Collins' broadcast reports of stolen antiquities and the death of an Iraqi and his buyer in Turkey brought little more than a ho-hum response from the viewers. Local and national news headed the interest with little concern for overseas issues, especially those that were from centuries ago.

"How are we going to make Robert's story relevant to today?" Executive Producer, Sam Solomon asked.

Editors and broadcast producers sat around a large table, some munching on bagels and cream cheese for their morning energy boost while others sipped coffee.

"Isn't that the purpose of any story? Give the people what they need. We give the daily weather and traffic reports first thing in the morning," John Robbins commented.

"You know we could stop the traffic reports in the City…it's always crowded," Caroline Benson laughed.

Some chuckled, some nodded approval between bagel bites, but Sam Solomon didn't

"The underlying issue is the sale of these antiquities here in New York to a probably super wealthy guy," Sam said.

"Guy?" Caroline challenged.

"Person...a super wealthy person." He stared her down and she laughed.

"This is a story that has to be told. The FBI is involved. Murders have been committed and money went to a Middle Eastern terrorist group. And history is being erased." Sam explained. They all knew that the ancient antiquities were being stolen or destroyed by the terrorists in Iraq. Temples were razed, and all their contents sold or destroyed.

The morning moment of joviality had ended. The group sat forward, cell phones and digital devices at the ready.

"Do you know how many millionaires there are in town?" Joanne Silvano asked.

The group chorused several answers gained from their devices.

"Exactly. A hell of a lot," Silvano responded.

"So, how are we going to find the one...*person* who bought these and caused the murders of two men in Turkey?" she asked

"You think he's at the bottom of those murders?" Calvin Ott asked.

A pensive moment was shared.

"No. Makes no sense," said Sam Solomon. "This person is a collector. He would not cut off the source of his collections."

"Unless he felt threatened," Caroline interjected.

All eyes went to Robert Collins who sat listening to the group.

"I don't think the murders came from the buyer. My source believed they were from the seller in Iraq. He was fearful for his life from the man he worked for, not from the broker who was murdered and not from the New York buyer that he never knew."

"Your source was right," Caroline said.

"We have to find the buyer, make the connection to Robert's story and out him to the FBI, and the public," Solomon said. "That's our next step...that's our relevant story. We need to learn who the collectors are from the millionaire group."

"You mean billionaires," Caroline added.

"Yes, the super wealthy. Research the collectors...what they collect...where their purchases come from. Investigate the black and gray market for all items bought and sold."

The meeting ended, the group dispersed, and Caroline walked behind Sam Solomon and pinched his butt laughing. He didn't laugh, but he wanted to.

"What are you up to today, Robert?" Solomon asked Collins.

"I'm going to talk to the FBI's Art Program Manager. She's back in town. She heads the investigation into all we've discussed."

"Keep digging."

He held up an imaginary bag. "Got all my shovels right here."

The small compact offices that housed the several agents working in the Arts Program was plain and unadorned. He'd imagined an artsy place with famous prints of expensive paintings on the walls. He was wrong.

"Robert Collins?"

"Miriam Cantrell? Thanks for seeing me."

"Well, you said you had information for me. Am I right?"

"You are."

"Okay, let's talk."

She turned and walked to an office equally plain except for the requisite family pictures of kids and her husband joyfully at play.

In a little more than an hour, they had finished discussing the deaths in Turkey and the possible connection to a New Yorker who has bought stolen antiquities. Miriam Cantrell had been building a list of the very wealthy in New York City who might be buyers of stolen art. However, she neglected to share that information with Collins. She was gathering information but not giving any out. Her department knew that ISIS was a major factor in raising money for their terrorist activities. Iraqi locals who found or dug up ancient antiquities were paid a small fee from ISIS that would bring in far more money than the fee paid. It was good business to use the locals as pawns under the guise that they were doing the work for the people against the infidels. For those who didn't accept the ISIS propaganda, it was a way of making some money and perhaps assuring one's safety.

Even though he believed the information that Miriam Cantrell gave him was limited, Collins knew he was on the right track. She didn't dismiss his comments about a buyer in their City and his gut told him she may have been on this trail.

He was determined to keep digging as he was advised but he needed more background on the scale of the stolen ancient antiquities, their value, and their origins. A minor in world history in college, which he was later told would prove to be worthless in the real digital world, might gain value for this story.

Once he was caught up with the ancient world he'd speak to several of the city's super wealthy and massage their egos to get a line on who might be interested in such items.

Collins enjoyed the quest for information as much as he relished reaching the end game.

When he left the building, his pace quickened to the nearest corner where he hailed a taxi back to the television station.

Chapter
53

Adam Walther was five minutes late meeting Bertram Thompson for dinner and his client didn't like it. When Walther arrived, Thompson didn't bother to look up. He did, however, look at his watch and then at Walther.

"Hello Bert, thanks for the invitation."

"Don't thank me, you're paying."

Walther knew he was being punished for being late, but he also knew he'd add the price of dinner to his billing.

A waiter came to the table and asked if they'd like a drink before dinner.

"No, we're not drinking," Thompson said.

Walther looked at the waiter gaining his attention, "I'll have a Macallan neat, thank you."

Thompson didn't respond.

"Since I'm buying. Now, what can I do for you?"

"I want this all to go away. I want the police, and the DA's office to back off...because I didn't do anything. Was not involved in anything that happened to that woman."

The waiter returned and placed the Macallan in front of Walther.

He asked Thompson, "Are you sure you don't want anything, sir?"

Thompson glared at the waiter and looked back at Walther. The waiter left them alone.

Walther sipped before he began, "Listen, Bert, if there is nothing to connect you then there's no reason for concern."

"If! There is nothing."

Walther moved through Thompson's anger.

"I can slow down the investigation. I can probably stop the DA's office from bothering you. We both have friends downtown."

He took another sip, "However, we have to play this very cool. Like a victim, not an angry one. Remember you said you hired the Croatian guy to protect her. From what you've told me she is a victim, but we need to get you out of the spotlight."

Thompson spun around and waved the waiter to the table. The waiter hurriedly moved to Thompson.

"I'll have what he's having." His attention went back to Walther. "How do we do that? Get me out of the spotlight?"

"Let's review some possibilities...see what you like best. We'll chat quietly," he looked around at the other dinner patrons, "just a quiet meal...two people talking. Okay?"

Thompson looked at the other tables. Some noticed him, perhaps recognizing his photo from the news.

"Let's order."

Walther offered a faux laugh, several decibels too loud to set a jovial tone for the onlookers. The few who were looking returned attention to their dinner partners and their own worlds.

The dinner with Walther had resolved some of the possibilities that could arise from the police and DA snooping around, but Thompson knew that at the core of the issue he was vulnerable and that would never be acceptable. It was not possible for him to give up control. While Walther initiated the steps for their plan he'd engineer his own.

****

That night the District Attorney's phone rang. He didn't answer the first three times it rang. He knew the phone number and the caller but didn't want to have his evening disturbed. The third call was followed by a vague voicemail. No specific information regarding any case, but the DA knew the case and the circumstances and the flak that would fall from the sky should he answer the call and deal with the pressure it would bring. DA John J. Malone worked with Walther many years before they both gained success in their chosen careers. Malone took the high road he often said to Walther who became an attorney to the wealthy and powerful. Two paths that rarely crossed were about to and Malone knew why. He didn't want to deal with Walther on this one because it would bring forth past moments that he'd rather have buried for all time. Donofrio had updated him on the interview with Thompson and Walther and Thompson's obvious animus at being challenged by Dieter and Donofrio.

Malone decided to take the higher, safer road and not answer the call. No phone records attached to him. If Walther wanted to see me, he thought, let him come to the office in the light of day. Even so, he felt the pressure rising and it angered him.

"The phone rang a bunch of times. Work?" Malone's wife asked.

"Probably, but it will have to wait until tomorrow." He smiled reassuringly.

"Really? Not like you. But, I like it. Hope this is a new you." She kissed him on the cheek.

Collette met Naomi Davis, a CPA at the accounting firm against her better judgment. She liked Naomi because she was smart and a friend when others judged Collette for her relationship with Andrew. Naomi never judged. However, Collette was not ready for a girl's night out and wine. Naomi talked her into an early night, and she agreed.

"You look great," Naomi said when she met Collette at *The Winery and Eats* near their office.

Collette smiled, Naomi never said anything bad about another person. She relaxed thinking that maybe getting out will be a stress release.

"Thank you…you look great in that suit."

Naomi waved her off, "Oh this old thing." She giggled, and the tone was set for their time together.

They sat at a high-top table in the center of a bustling after happy hour crowd that had nursed several glasses of wine.

"It's been a long time since we got out," Naomi said. "Just girls. Girls? We haven't been girls forever."

For a very brief moment, Collette allowed her angst to subside.

"You're right. Those days were fun." But the recent past showed on her face.

"Times, they are a-changin'," Naomi sang and looked at Collette.

"Oh, my have times changed."

Naomi waited for Collette to continue or not. They both sipped their wine. Collette looked around at the happy crowd of seemingly carefree people enjoying life's bill of fare. A meal she could no longer enjoy.

"It's like a never-ending nightmare. A bad movie that only gets worse. When I started at the firm, I wanted to do a good job. You know?"

"You did a job."

"I didn't have any goals other than to do good work. But, then…" she saw deeply into her psyche. "Andrew came into my view. At first, I paid him no mind at all. He was married." She looked away from Naomi.

"He was a good boss and very smart."

Collette's eyes misted briefly. She smiled, "He was so smart. It was like all the financial information was stored on his personal hard drive. All he had to do was hit a key and the data would …"

"Yes, I saw that many times in meetings with clients."

They relived moments together about work and about Andrew. Naomi raised her glass in a toast.

"To Andrew."

Collette raised hers too, "To my Andrew."

They clinked glasses and drank.

"Good evening ladies," a suited, heavily into his second bottle of wine, younger man approached.

They looked at him then at each other and burst into laughter. He laughed too, but he wasn't sure why and nodded moving on.

"That was cute." They shared a moment of silence. "It's time for my question."

"Question?"

"How are you doing?"

The wine was beginning to work its magic.

"Oh, that question...let's see...." She sipped again. "Well, I guess if all that is happening now with the police and the DA's Office doesn't get derailed, I'm okay. Yes, okay is my goal."

Another sip.

"Why would it get derailed? My Dad was a cop and my uncle Charlie worked in the DA's office. They were good honest guys. You're going to be more than okay."

Naomi suffered an internal wince at what she just said. Her motive was good, to help her friend stay positive, but she often saw the frustration that her father felt with cases being derailed. She would sometimes eavesdrop on discussions with uncle Charlie and her Dad, after Sunday dinners, when both men shared their work frustrations.

"Thanks, Naomi." She released a self-deprecating laugh and remembered Lindsay told her that Karl promised to make it right.

Chapter
54

Adam Walther talked his way past the host of people who asked what he wanted with the DA. He held up the container showing two cups of coffee and a small bag from the local coffee shop. He walked rapidly to John Malone's office where the door was ajar. Walther pushed the door open and stood in the doorway holding up the coffee and bag.

"You ordered coffee, sir?"

Malone looked up, hiding his disdain for the interference and what would follow. "Ah, remember the Greek proverb, beware of Greeks bearing gifts."

Walther disregarded the comment. "One old friend, who happened to be nearby brought his old friend's favorite coffee, black with three sugars...and a cinnamon bun. What's the harm?"

"Besides the sugar? Been off that much for years."

Malone rose and pointed to a coffee table that fronted two easy chairs. Both men sat. Walther pushed the coffee toward Malone and took out the bun with napkins. For a minute each man prepared their drink and food.

Malone sat back, crossed his leg and asked, "So what do I owe this grand feast today?"

"You know it's been a while since we broke bread…so to speak. Just wanted to reconnect with a buddy, a former colleague. That's all."

"I see. I missed your call last night." Malone searched Walther's eyes.

"Yes, I called. Wanted to ask how life was treating you. How is life treating you?"

"And so, you came here, now, to ask me personally how my life is going?"

Walther burst into another faux laugh. "Johnny, you were never good at subtleties. Yes, I have a reason to be here, to speak with you. But, I'd rather catch up on old times."

"Old times?"

Walther sat forward showing exuberance. "Remember that time we got wasted," he turned to look at the opened door. "That was one hell of a night. Those were the days. We had good jobs, a future path, lots of ladies and booze. Not always a good combination. Am I right?" Walther stared knowingly at Malone.

Years earlier they had gone out to celebrate a case they had won working together as newbie ADA's. Malone's memory of that night never faded nor did the women they met and bedded. Two young recently graduated college girls, a few years younger than the two colleagues, had joined them and spent the night together. The girl who spent the previous night with Walther called the next day crying. Her friend had killed herself by hanging in their apartment.

"What should I do?" she cried. "She was engaged to be married. Last night ruined her."

Malone jumped up from the chair sending shots of rage at Walther.

"What do you want?"

"Me? No, I don't want anything. I've got your back…as I did then. Remember?" Malone didn't answer. "John, do you remember that I had your back on that day. I shielded you. Took you out of the spotlight. Remember?"

He too rose and wiped some crumbs from his slacks.

"Yes."

"I don't want anything. Not me. Thompson does want something. He hopes this unfair interference in his life will end. He has nothing to do with anything the young ADA said to him."

Walther bent to the table and retrieved a napkin to wipe his hands. He tossed the napkin back on the table.

"Just stopped by to catch up and go over old times...you look well." Walther looked at his watch. "Got to go. Nice seeing you."

He stuck out his hand which Malone ignored.

"I'll see myself out." He left walking leisurely out of the DA's offices.

Malone moved to his opened door and watched Walther walk through his office as though he owned it. He stopped at the desk of a pretty young new ADA. She smiled up at him from her desk. He laughed a little too loud as usual for effect then he gave her his business card. She actually rose and shook his hand. When Walther was about to disappear from view he turned suddenly and looked at Malone standing in his doorway and smiled.

"Putz!"

Malone turned and entered his office closing the door behind him. The very thinly veiled threat about that night and the girl's death, if it were made public, would ruin his chances at any future movement in the city's government or beyond. It might even cause him to lose his job. Walther had often wondered what caused her to hang herself. Was she emotionally disturbed before they met? Was it me? He had dismissed that idea before, but now it revisited him. Did I do or say something to trigger her action? Eventually, after too much thought, he decided he had no choice.

He returned to his desk and dialed Donofrio's phone extension.

"Good morning John."

"Gerry, bring the Thompson file to my office for a review."

"Sure."

The call ended but Donofrio was not truly sure why he was asked to review the case which they had only done yesterday. Nevertheless, he complied, retrieving the file and his personal notes he reported to Malone's office.

"Close the door, Gerry," Malone said.

Gerome Donofrio's emotions returned to Principal Father Gagliardi's office in high school where he was called only once for a minor school infraction. He didn't like the feeling then nor did he like it now.

"Here it is John. Is everything all right?"

"Yes, yes, just doing my due diligence." He reached out his hand for the file folder. After several minutes he closed the folder and looked at Donofrio. "Okay, this is not going to go anywhere, and I need you on several other cases." He pushed a pile of new and old cases toward Donofrio. "I'll finish up on this one," holding onto Thompson's file.

"But I believe this guy is hiding evidence. He was nervous at the interview. Did I do something wrong, John?"

In a fatherly tone, "No, no you were fine. You always do a good job and that's why I have my eye on you for the future."

His big smile put a period on the statement.

"Okay then," Donofrio rose.

"Good work Gerry," he eyed the stack of folders which Donofrio took and left.

Malone sat back in his chair, resting his head against its back. His mind went to Walther's visit and the angst it brought up along with a drop of bile.

"Putz!" he shouted to the empty office.

Chapter
55

Collette left Naomi and their girl's night out together feeling somehow better than she believed possible. The heaviness that was ever present lightened in the taxi ride back to Lindsay's apartment. For the first time since she arrived from St. John and stayed with Lindsay, she had a need to see her apartment. To see her world. Collette asked the taxi driver to go to her apartment when only a few city blocks away from Lindsay's. The driver acquiesced and quickly rerouted his course and took her home.

She gave him a very substantial tip and exited the taxi. For a long moment, she stood before her building remembering the times she'd come home from work feeling tired, or excited or happy to go out and meet Andrew later for dinner. Oddly, she thought, these memories buoyed her spirit. This was her world...her home where she claimed independence for all she had accomplished. It was modest compared to Lindsay's doorman building, but it was her world and she was happy to see it again. She entered the building and climbed the stairs. The downstairs blind neighbor heard the familiar footsteps pad around the apartment and knew Collette had returned.

Collette's bedroom was as she left it that frightful time she ran from it. The professional photo of Andrew taken by the firm was on her bedside nightstand where she put it. She sat on the bed and held the picture frame reviewing each feature on his face. Soon she lay back on the bed, fully clothed and held the frame against her chest. Perhaps it was the wine or the comfort of the room that sent her off into sleep…she slept deeply.

The cell phone in her pocketbook rang at one thirty in the morning. Collette heard it but missed the call by the time she was alert enough to answer. In a moment a voicemail notice arrived. She listened to the message from Lindsay asking where she was and if she was all right. Lindsay's voice seemed nervous.

"Hi, Lindsay it's Collette."

"Are you okay?"

"Yes, sorry, I missed the call." She looked around the room lit only by the small lamp on the nightstand. "I'm home. Sorry, I fell asleep. I should have called."

Silence for a moment from Lindsay. "Okay, no worries, just…" she searched for the words.

"I'm fine. I'm going to stay here tonight. I'll pick up my things tomorrow. Okay?"

"Yes, sure, okay. Do you plan to move back into your place?"

"It's time…I think it's going to be okay from now on. Do you agree?"

Lindsay evaluated a response. She hoped that Collette could get back to her world and she wanted to get back to being with Karl too.

"As long as you're ready…."

"I'm ready. I need to…."

Collette rose early the next morning as the sun crested the buildings nearby. She made the barefoot trek to the kitchen where her coffee pot waited to be filled. The coffee can held her favorite blend. Soon the comforting smell of coffee filled her apartment. Routine would be her benefactor. A long hot shower followed energizing her body as did the familiar smell of the soap and shampoo which she bought on a weekend getaway with Andrew. Her spirit for life increased above the sadness that lived beneath.

Clean underwear, clean clothes, and the hot coffee sharpened her mind. She'd go to the office soon. Back to work, back to life if not only baby steps. For many years Collette had fought off the label of victim from the abuse by her stepfather. That feeling of helplessness was long ago defeated until it came rushing back after Andrew's death. Now she had support from Lindsay of all people. She leaned on her and Lindsay was there for her. Detective Dieter promised that he'd solve all the issues surrounding the case. There seemed nothing more for her to do except focus on herself; to get stronger, to return to Collette before Andrew.

The downstairs neighbor heard the shower running, the clip-clop of shoes above and then the door closing as Collette made her way down the stairs.

When Collette arrived at the office, she experienced the familiarity of another welcoming place. The comfort surrounded her, and she felt secure.

Naomi popped her head in the doorway.

A broad smile greeted Collette, "Morning. How'd you survive last night?"

"Just fine thank you," she joked. "You?"

Collette didn't feel the need to explain more.

"Lunch later? Oh, no, sorry, I have an appointment with a new client."

Alex Francisco came by as Naomi left. He walked into Collette's office.

"Hey, what are you doing here?"

"I work here, remember," she said.

He smiled, "Yes you do. I've got a bunch of work for you...if you're ready."

"Bring it on."

Collette busied herself with new cases and folders of older clients in the catch-up phase for the remainder of the morning. Her eyes and mind clicked along the columns of data like the old days.

"What the hell are you talking about?" Captain Grover shouted into the telephone to DA Malone.

"There's been too much time and money on this case with nothing solid to show for it except this dead guy Simon Winton. So, I'm putting it on the back burner."

"Where it will simmer and die out?"

"Easy Captain, my office is piled high with cases that we can convict, that's our job. This is a run around in circles case. I've read all the evidence, but nothing directly connects this guy Thompson to any of it. In fact, he might be the victim of fraud by his dead employee."

Grover sat boiling. He'd gotten involved with this case and with the victim, Collette. He liked her and wanted to help.

"Someone got to you." Not a question.

"Be very careful Grover. You've been there a short while, and that can change quickly."

"Are you threatening me?"

"No, just being real. You should be real too."

Malone hung up. Grover slammed down the landline phone and left his office. Dieter and McClure were at their desks.

"You two come back with me."

Back in his office, he told the two detectives about the DA's phone call. Grover called for a step by step review of all events and people involved with the case.

"Make a connection damn it. Is it possible Winton is at the bottom of all this?"

"No. He was run off the road. Killed. I think he's involved but not the prime mover here. I think it's Thompson," Dieter said.

"Winton did kidnap Collette Riccardi."

"He was covering his ass because he was swindling Thompson who maybe didn't know about it."

"Or maybe he did and that's why Winton is dead."

"Captain, this circle keeps going around and around but it just doesn't ring true. I want to keep looking."

"Quietly, keep the DA's office out of it until we lock something down about Thompson."

Dieter and McClure left Grover's office to review their files.

"JB let's try a new road. See what you can find out about his personal life, interests and such. Anything at all. What he likes to do. Hobbies."

"Hobbies?" McClure asked, "Really?"

"I know I'm reaching but what the hell."

"Will do."

Robert Collins had finished the editing of his background story on stolen ancient antiquities from Iraq. His discussion with Miriam Cantrell, although not very informative, gave him the opportunity to mention the FBI Arts Program and its work to uncover art theft that leads to ISIS. He'd highlight that portion of their work indicating the vast sums of money ISIS gained from the worldwide sales. ISIS also had worked with Colombian cartels to raise more money from the sale of drugs.

"Rob, this is amazing stuff," Kenny Strudmire declared as he edited the footage for the evening teaser. "I didn't know the FBI had this division."

"Well, now everyone will. Show me the lede again."

Kenny played the lede which named Miriam Cantrell, head of the FBI Art Program, as the primary tease. He gave Kenny the thumbs up. Both men went through the video several more times tweaking a bit until each was satisfied.

"It's a go?" Kenny asked.

"Nice work Ken," Collins said tapping the younger man on the back.

Chapter
56

Collette stopped at Lindsay's apartment after work to get her clothes. Lindsay saw a better Collette than had been apparent since they met. More relaxed and prettier. She could understand what Andrew had initially seen in Collette. She was younger, more vibrant and a drop more vulnerable.

Lindsay sat on the bed in the spare room that Collette used while she gathered her clothes and toiletries into a small suitcase. Collette stopped and looked at Lindsay with grateful eyes.

"How can I ever thank you for all you've done for me...of all people?"

"No need to thank me." She thought for a moment. "We have a connection...such as it is...with a man we both loved."

Lindsay rose, "I could use a drink? You too?"

"Absolutely."

They walked to the kitchen where Lindsay opened a bottle of Chardonnay and placed two white wine glasses at the kitchen table's center. She uncorked the bottle and poured each a half glass. Both women held the glass firmly in two hands as though this was to be an auspicious moment.

Dieter's special tone sounded on Lindsay's cell phone.

"Hi, Karl. Collette and I are having a drink."

Dieter stopped her from continuing. "The case has bee stalled by the DA's office. Things may take a little more time to resolve. Can I see you tonight?"

Lindsay flashed a look at Collette, "Sure that would be nice. Why don't you come here for dinner?"

"All three of us is not what I had hoped."

"It will be the way you want it to be," speaking elliptically.

"Just us?"

"Yes, that's right, from now on."

"Great, see you about eight?"

"Perfect."

Lindsay ended the call. Collette raised her glass to Lindsay who picked up the wine glass and they clinked.

Once the wine was sipped and the chat reached its end Collette decided it was time to leave. She moved to Lindsay and gave her a hug.

"It's, time to go."

Lindsay felt selfishly relieved when Collette moved out. She looked forward to an evening with her Karl. A respite from a world gone mad she thought.

Collette felt a minor victory over sadness.

Thompson's level of power and control regained strength each day since the interview with Dieter and Donofrio. Walther called and said he had quashed the investigation. It was only a matter of time until he would be reunited with his trophies boxed in the Pennsylvania company storage. Someday he'd find another source to purchase more ancient artifacts.

Lindsay prepared a dinner of pasta with shrimp, clams, and scallops. She made garlic bread and a green garden salad topped off with a bottle of red wine. Dieter was impressed and delighted.

He held her tightly in his arms as she rested her head on his chest. They stood for a long while enjoying the shared comfort.

"Karl," she looked up into his eyes, "you think we'll ever get back to us again?"

"Soon. You know I'm thinking about retiring after this case is over. What do you think?"

"Yes, I know? What will you do?"

"Now you sound like my Captain. Not sure, but I never had choices before."

"What do you mean?"

"I can move on to something else, or nothing else…you know to sit on the couch, watch television and drink beer and grow a big belly."

Lindsay pulled away and lightly punched him in his midsection.

"Sit down, let's eat and fill your belly."

After dinner, Lindsay asked, "Why has the case been stalled?"

"Not sure."

"Guess."

"Well, my guess is that the DA had pressure put on him and he reacted."

"Pressure? Who can do that?"

"Someone powerful, rich maybe…."

"Thompson?"

"Probably."

"That's just not fair…."

"We both know that fair has nothing to do with politics."

"What do you do?"

"I keep on investigating."

Dan Withers stayed up to watch the late news while his wife slept soundly. It was his routine each night before he joined her in bed. This night the local Pennsylvania affiliate of a major network began with the Robert Collins story detailing the sale of ancient artifacts stolen and sold by ISIS. A sample photo was displayed of a Roman coin, not unlike the ones in the storage unit he'd recently found. Dan switched on his cell phone and reviewed the photos. They seemed similar, maybe the same era and place of origin to the photos on the television. He couldn't be sure if they were the same. Sleep was elusive to Dan all through the night. His wife awoke once and asked, "Are you okay?"

"Yes, just thinking."

"What about?"

"Tomorrow. What I'm going to do tomorrow."

She believed he had thoughts about retirement and what to do each day. His mind was elsewhere. She patted his chest and rested her head on his shoulder and slept. His eyes scanned the ceiling for an answer.

Dan finally fell off to sleep just before the sun rose. His wife let him sleep believing he needed it. She busied herself with the kitchen chores left undone the night before. Pancakes, juice, and coffee would be the order of the day's menu. She'd start him off with his favorite blueberry pancakes and sausage.

When he didn't come down for breakfast she returned to the bedroom to find him looking at his cell phone. Puzzled, she asked, "What are you looking at?"

"Those pictures." He stared at them.

"The ones you took at the company storage units?"

"Yes, makes no sense."

"How do you mean?"

He told her about the television report which caused a serious change in her demeanor. "Terrorists are profiting from these things?"

"Maybe? If they are the same things I saw on television. I don't know."

"I think we need to find out." She declared with a mounting distaste for the artifacts.

"How?"

"We call the FBI, that's how."

"Oh, come on. They have serious work to do besides this."

"Really? More serious than stopping the sale of these things for terrorists' profits so they can kill innocent people?"

Dan put the phone down and looked at his wife who rarely was upset by outer world things. She liked to stay centered in her world where it was safe and free of complexities.

They skipped the morning breakfast of Dan's favorite pancakes and drove to Lancaster Pennsylvania from their hometown of York for the thirty-five-minute ride. The statue of an American Eagle with its wings spread stood beneath the Federal Building United States Court House sign on 228 Walnut Street. They parked the car and walked hand in hand into the building. Dan's cell phone had been fully charged to allow its use.

Miriam Cantrell received a call from a Pennsylvania FBI agent a few minutes after the Withers left the office. He sent the photos to her.

"Where were these items found?"

"At a warehouse near York...owned by Thompson Industries. The man who brought these photos in said the owner lives in New York City."

"Yes, he does."

"You know about him?"

"Getting to know him. Can you get those items? I'll send some people to pick them up from you."

"I'll do the paperwork and make it right. The judges are in our building. Will let you know when they're in my possession."

By eight that evening, the boxes holding the ancient antiquities were delivered to Miriam Cantrell's office in Manhattan. She stayed late waiting for her staff to return from the trip to Lancaster. Careful research indicated that these were part of looted artifacts from Iraqi sites. Thompson's conviction was probable.

Chapter
57

Attorney Walther happily represented Thompson on the case brought against him for the illegal purchases he made. The billing would be very high.

"My client, your Honor, was new to the world of acquiring these items and did not fully appreciate the complexities of the acquisitions process. We admit he made regrettable mistakes. Mister Thompson relied on dealers and shippers who did not understand the correct way to document and ship these items. He was not hiding the purchases. No fault of his own. He should have exercised more oversight and carefully questioned how the acquisitions were purchased and handled. Those steps were left to a former employee now deceased. My client has cooperated with the government throughout its investigation, and with the announcement of today's settlement agreement, is pleased the matter has been resolved."

When Collette received the news about Thompson's case she was livid.

"Thompson paid a multi-million-dollar settlement, the objects were confiscated and he was absolved of major federal charges?" She complained incredulously. "What about Andrew's murder and the men who kidnapped me? He did that. I know it!"

Dieter, who had delivered the news, had no answer.

"Karl is that all there is to this?" Lindsay asked.

"We can't make a definite connection to show that Thompson was behind all the events. His lawyer implied that Winton was murdered by the terrorist with whom he dealt."

"That's crazy. Winton spoke to me about Thompson. He was afraid of Thompson."

Collette slapped her hips repeatedly in frustration and anger while glaring at Dieter.

"You promised me you would get him. You did, you promised me he would pay for Andrew." Collette crumbled into a chair in Lindsay's apartment.

Lindsay looked at Dieter who did not react to Collette's state of mind.

"Is there nothing more to be done? No more investigation?" Lindsay beseeched Dieter.

Dieter held her eyes, "No. Everything we have is circumstantial. Nothing conclusively connects him. In fact, it all seems to revolve around Winton."

"Do you believe that?" she asked.

"No, not entirely anyway."

Collette's anger reawakened, "What does that mean? Not entirely? Are you saying I lied about Winton?"

"No, no I'm not saying you lied. But Winton did kidnap you, not Thompson. Am I right? He did it to protect himself."

Collette's heart raced at breakneck speed. It's over she thought. Nothing will bring Andrew back. No one will pay for his murder. Thompson will go free. She raced to the door with Lindsay following but she was out immediately.

"What was that?" Dieter asked.

"Fear, anger, resolve."

"Resolve to do what?"

"I hope nothing."

Collette made one stop before heading back to her apartment. She held the unusual purchase in her hand rolling it around against her palm eventually placing it in her purse.

An hour later with full intentions in place she arrived at Thompson's apartment building. The concierge asked if he could help.

"Yes, I'm here to speak with Bertram Thompson," she flashed her business card. "I'm from his accounting firm."

The concierge called and spoke with Thompson. He asked to speak with her.

"What do you want?"

"I need to speak with you about the events...you know."

"No, I have nothing to say to you."

"But, I need to...apologize for my behavior in person. Please, I have to get this off my chest. I've been through a lot. This will help me, please." She feigned a whimper.

"Two minutes and that's it."

Thompson wanted to see her grovel at his feet. His ego needed to see her in defeat and to be declared the winner. All else was righted by the attorney. Now, he could win over the victim that he destroyed.

The elevator doors opened to find Thompson standing erect before her. Shaking hands were dug into the light jacket that Collette wore. He looked pleased to see her which caused surprise. She exited the elevator and approached him.

"I guess you've finally come to your senses. You know I had nothing to do with what harmed you. It was all Winton. You've caused me a lot of harm and wasted time."

Collette's anger exploded at his words. Her right hand quickly released the keychain pepper spray hidden in her jacket. The first shot at six feet hit him squarely in the face. He screamed and fell backward, stumbling with hands over his eyes and face. The second shot at only three feet forced the pepper spray down his agape mouth and throat. He coughed violently and fell to his knees. She unleashed a soccer style kick from days long ago at his head which snapped it back and sent him flat on his back. He lay writhing in pain from the attack. Memories of the attacks on her from her stepfather returned as she watched Thompson. The childhood fantasy she had was alive and being played out on Thompson. With hands in the air, she jumped around him declaring victory to an unseen audience.

Collette left him on the floor in pain and took the elevator down. She pulled her blouse open exposing her bra and unzipped her jeans partially after messing her hair.

"Help, he tried to rape me. He's crazy. Call the police."

She ran from the building while the concierge called up to Thompson's apartment. When there was no answer, he called 911.

Collette returned to Lindsay's apartment disheveled and distraught.

"What happened?"

"He tried to rape me."

"Who?"

"Thompson. I want him arrested. Help me."

"Where were you?"

"At his apartment."

"Why?"

"I wanted to get closure. I just wanted to know for sure that he was not involved in Andrew's death."

"What did he say?"

"He denied everything. Then he offered me a drink and when I refused, he attacked me."

"How?"

"He came at me, pulled my blouse, tried to undo my jeans."

"Oh my god!"

"Then I pepper sprayed him and ran."

Lindsay had interviewed several rape victims who did not match Collette's behavior. Perhaps she was different because it was an attempted rape, she thought.

"Did you contact the police?"

"No, I yelled at the concierge to call them."

"Did he?"

"I don't know. Can I wash my hands and face, please?"

"Yes, of course."

While Collette went to the bathroom, Lindsay called Dieter to tell him what had happened.

"Stay with her, I'll be right there."

Later that night after another round of questions by police and after witnessing Thompson being brought in handcuffed, she took a long shower and tried to wash off all the day's events. The shame she might have felt if she believed he was innocent was not present. Moments of joy visited her as the water cascaded over her body...and she knew she could begin the road back. Whether Thompson was convicted of anything no longer interested her. She had seen him down where she put him. Her personal revenge was satisfied. The vision of him cowering on the floor in pain would be held in her mind's gallery forever. That night she slept soundly and revisited her last hours with Andrew.

Chapter
58

"Billionaire Bertram Thompson has had a really bad week. After being fined three point five million dollars for buying stolen ancient Iraqi antiquities, a crime because the money goes to ISIS, he was charged with rape by the female kidnap victim held at his Montauk mansion," television news anchor Todd Adams declared.

Collette sipped her coffee at home before the morning news, not at all concerned that, once again, they put her picture up, this time with a disheveled photo of Thompson the night he was arrested. She'd add that picture to the mounting gallery.

Detective Dieter answered his cell phone, "Dieter here."

"Detective, my name is Spencer Arnold, Junior. My late father called you some time ago. I am finalizing much of his work. Sorry, it took so long to get back to you."

Dieter raced through his mind. "What's this about?"

"My Dad was Valerie Hudson's attorney. I'd like to speak with you regarding her estate."

"Why me?"

"Because you and Lindsay Riccardi are sole beneficiaries of her very substantial estate. When can you come to my office?"

www.ingramcontent.com/pod-product-compliance
Lightning Source LLC
Chambersburg PA
CBHW050552260626
47157CB00002B/528